I0722305

PRAISE FOR THE NOVELS OF
KATIE MacALISTER

Memoirs of a Dragon Hunter
"Bursting with the author's trademark zany humor and spicy romance . . . this quick tale will delight paranormal romance fans."—*Publishers Weekly*

Sparks Fly
"Balanced by a well-organized plot and MacAlister's trademark humor."—*Publishers Weekly*

It's All Greek to Me
"A fun and sexy read."—The Season for Romance
"A wonderful lighthearted romantic romp as a kick-butt American Amazon and a hunky Greek find love. Filled with humor, fans will laugh with the zaniness of Harry meets Yacky."—*Midwest Book Review*

Much Ado About Vampires
"A humorous take on the dark and demonic."—*USA Today*
"Once again this author has done a wonderful job. I was sucked into the world of Dark Ones right from the start and was taken on a fantastic ride. This book is full of witty dialogue and great romance, making it one that should not be missed."—Fresh Fiction

The Unbearable Lightness of Dragons
"Had me laughing out loud. . . . This book is full of humor and romance, keeping the reader entertained all the way through . . . a wondrous story full of magic. . . . I cannot wait to see what happens next in the lives of the dragons."—Fresh Fiction

ALSO BY KATIE MACALISTER

DARK ONES SERIES
A Girl's Guide to Vampires
Sex and the Single Vampire
Sex, Lies, and Vampires
Even Vampires Get the Blues
Bring Out Your Dead (Novella)
The Last of the Red-Hot Vampires
Crouching Vampire, Hidden Fang
Unleashed (Novella)
In the Company of Vampires
Confessions of a Vampire's Girlfriend
Much Ado About Vampires
A Tale of Two Vampires
The Undead in My Bed (Novella)
The Vampire Always Rises
Enthralled
Desperately Seeking Vampire

DRAGON SEPT SERIES
You Slay Me
Fire Me Up
Light My Fire
Holy Smokes
Death's Excellent Vacation
(short story)
Playing WIth Fire
Up In Smoke
Me and My Shadow
Love in the Time of Dragons
The Unbearable Lightness of Dragons
Sparks Fly
Dragon Fall
Dragon Storm
Dragon Soul
Dragon Unbound
Dragonblight
A Confederacy of Dragons
You Sleigh Me

DRAGON HUNTER SERIES
Memoirs of a Dragon Huner
Day of the Dragon

BORN PROPHECY SERIES
Fireborn
Starborn
Shadowborn

TIME THIEF SERIES
Time Thief
Time Crossed (short story)
The Art of Stealing Time

MATCHMAKER IN WONDERLAND SERIES
The Importance of Being Alice
A Midsummer Night's Romp
Daring in a Blue Dress
Perils of Paulie

PAPAIOANNOU SERIES
It's All Greek to Me
Ever Fallen in Love
A Tale of Two Cousins
Acropolis Now

CONTEMPORARY SINGLE TITLES
Improper English
Bird of Paradise (Novella)
Men in Kilts
The Corset Diaries
A Hard Day's Knight
Blow Me Down
You Auto-Complete Me

NOBLE HISTORICAL SERIES
Noble Intentions
Noble Destiny
The Trouble With Harry
The Truth About Leo

PARANORMAL SINGLE TITLES
Ain't Myth-Behaving

MYSTERIES
Ghost of a Chance
The Stars That We Steal From the
Night Sky

STEAMPUNK ROMANCE
Steamed
Company of Thieves

CONFEDERACY OF DRAGONS

A Blue Dragon Novel

Katie MacAlister

FAT CAT BOOKS

Copyright © Katie MacAlister 2022
All rights reserved

Without limiting the rights under copyright reserved above, no part of this publication may be reproduced, stored in or introduced into a retrieval system, or transmitted, in any form, or by any means (electronic, mechanical, photocopying, recording, or otherwise), without the prior written permission of both the copyright owner and the above publisher of this book.

This is a work of fiction. Names, characters, places, and incidents either are the product of the author's imagination or are used fictitiously, and any resemblance to actual persons, living or dead, business establishments, events, or locales is entirely coincidental.

The scanning, uploading, and distribution of this book via the Internet or via any other means without the permission of the publisher is illegal and punishable by law. Please purchase only authorized electronic editions, and do not participate in or encourage electronic piracy of copyrighted materials. Your support of the author's rights is appreciated.

Cover by Croco Designs
Formatting by Racing Pigeon Productions

C.R. Rowenson helped me figure out just why Bastian was having issues, and for his help and illumination, I'm very grateful.

CHARITY DOE
NOTES TO MYSELF ABOUT WHO IS WHO IN THE DRAGONKIN

Aisling Grey: mate to the green wyvern, Drake. She's also a Guardian, and has a demon in dog form named Jim.

Aoife: mate of Kostya. Nice, but shy. Unless you zing her mate, then she goes into scary dragon mode.

Baltic: wyvern of the light dragons. I could say a lot about Baltic, but since I'm now his stepmom, it's probably better if I keep those thoughts to myself. I like him even though he makes his father crazy, but in a weird kind of way, I think that's good for both of them.

Bastian Blu: wyvern of the blue dragons. He has sad eyes. I want to ask him why, but that's probably overstepping some bounds or other.

Bee Dakar: Constantine's mate. She's fairly quiet and watchful.

Constantine Norka: wyvern of the indigo sept. I gather it's super small, and he has some sort of history with Baltic and Ysolde, but I haven't figured all that out. He is very funny, and has a disembodied head named Gary, who is oddly charming.

Drake Vireo: wyvern of the green dragons. Intimidating. Reminds me of a panther.

Deus (Amadeus) somebody-or-other: kinda pushy ouroboros leader of the Chaos Tribe. Not my fave person in the world.

Gabriel Tauhou: wyvern of the silver dragons. Supersweet, and has a gorgeous Australian accent.

Kostya Fekete: wyvern of the black dragons, and Drake's brother. Prone to dramatic speeches. Lots of hand waving.

May Northcott: Gabriel's mate. Aisling told me she's a doppelganger, but I have no idea what that means. She has a twin who raised a ruckus sometime back, evidently.

Rowan Dakar: used to be mortal, now a dragon and wyvern of the red sept. There's a big involved story about his past, too, but I haven't sorted it all out yet.

Sophea Long: Rowan's mate. Ysolde said she was mated to another red dragon wyvern, but he died, and Sophea … inherited, I guess … Rowan. They're both sweet and very much in love, so I'm glad they found each other.

Ysolde: Baltic's mate. She has quite the history with him and the First Dragon, who has a special fondness for her. I think it's because she isn't the least bit in awe of him. The FD, not Baltic. Although come to think of it, she's not overly impressed by Baltic, either. I like her.

ONE
THE MORTAL

14 July 1901

The woman caught Bastian's eye the moment he saw her. She was dressed in gauzy white, a material that floated around her in diaphanous layers as she strolled down the street, hints of her strawberry blonde hair visible under the large hat that shadowed her face. She held a parasol, but it was furled, allowing Bastian to appreciate her lively expression.

"Bastian? We will be late if we stay out here much longer, and you know how angry Pierozzo gets if we aren't on time for sept meetings." Rey, Bastian's oldest friend, nudged his shoulder before starting up the stone steps that led into the building owned by the blue dragons.

Bastian remained standing with one foot on the lowest step, his gaze still on the woman across the street. She was in the company of two other women, one older and dressed soberly in black, clearly a chaperone, but he could tell there was something special about the blonde. Her aura was golden and warm, lighting up everything around her. Without thinking, he unshielded his mind in order to gently probe hers, wondering who she was.

He met with instant resistance, but not before the woman, who was laughing with a dark-haired young woman, stopped in midsentence and glanced around the busy street, her eyes finding his after a few seconds.

For the count of three, their gazes locked, and he felt as warm as if he were standing in a shower of dragon fire.

"Is something wrong?" Rey marched back down the stairs to nudge him again, but his unwavering gaze caused her to glance across the street. "What is it you are—oh, a woman? Really, Bastian, are you so deprived of female company that you must ogle women on the street? I thought I taught you better than that."

Laughter was rich in Rey's voice, the laughter of a woman who was happily mated.

"There's something special about this one," Bastian told her, and with reluctance took his gaze from the woman, feeling for a moment as if the sun had gone behind a cloud.

"You can find her later. Right now we must go or Pierozzo will have words to say to both of us."

He allowed Rey to pull him up the stairs where her mate waited impatiently, his mind still reaching out for that of the woman with the shining aura.

Bastian found the woman the following day after having pulled in three of his friends—Rey excepted, since she refused to be a party to what she called a hunt—to scour the streets of Firenze. One of the friends, Luca, found the three women entering a museum, and rushed to tell Bastian.

He managed to arrive when they were a mere block away, obviously on their way back to their hotel after having viewed the museum's offerings.

"Signora," he said, bowing low first to the chaperone, then to her two charges. "Signorine. I am Bastiano di Giardino. You are new to Firenze, yes?"

"Yes," the woman with the shining aura said, her hazel eyes lit with laughter. Now that he was close to her, he could see she had a heart-shaped face and the pale skin of the English. He basked in the warmth of her gaze while her smile deepened. "How clever of you to know that. I'm Alex."

"Alexandra, really," murmured the chaperone, casting Bastian a wary glance. "One does not respond to strangers introducing themselves in the middle of the street."

"But he's not a stranger, Mrs. Erwan," the woman named Alexandra said, her eyes dancing with obvious mischief.

"Oh?" She glanced again at Bastian, who gave her his best smile. "You've met, then? Properly met?"

"I wouldn't think of speaking to a stranger," Alexandra said, her lips twitching a little as she gestured toward the third woman. "But I don't think Mr. di Giardino has met Mary. Mary is my cousin, and this is her former governess, Mrs. Erwan."

"Bastian, please," he replied, bowing over the dark-haired woman's hand when she offered it. "You will permit me to escort you back to your hotel? I have lived for many years in Firenze, and would be happy to point out sights of interest."

"How very thoughtful," Alexandra said, and, with another look brimming with amusement, took her friend's arm and strolled forward.

That was the start. He did not fool himself that Alexandra was a mate, but she was unusually prescient, and if she had training, he had a feeling she would make a gifted oracle. Instead, he wooed her and spent five years with her before she died of consumption, leaving Bastian with a heart made heavy with grief, and a two-year-old daughter named for her mother.

He rocked Alessandra to sleep each night for a week following the death, her tears wetting his face and neck as he tried to provide comfort where he himself found none. He slept fitfully, his dreams haunted by Alex, by his guilt in not being able to save her when she grew ill.

The dreams seemed to gain in intensity as the weeks passed. Alessandra was more resilient than he, and found solace in friends and sept members who came by each day. Two months later, Alessandra was back to romping in the garden, laughing and singing and talking to the flowers, and leaves, and little beetles she found crawling in the loam.

"Alessandra has forgotten her mother," he told Rey, watching his daughter at play. "I find myself torn between being relieved that she is not suffering, and dismayed that she could so easily forget."

"Sandra is but two years, my friend," Rey told him, her hand resting on his arm. "And Alex had been sick for much of the last year. I know it pains you—as well as your own grief—but, Bastian, Alex was mortal. You knew that someday she would grow old and die. At least her daughter will be spared such a fate."

"She is most definitely a blue dragon," Bastian admitted, even giving a short, pained bark of laughter when Alessandra pulled her pinafore and dress over her head, and proceeded to run around the garden clad in nothing but her shift, drawers, and stockings.

"And you?" Rey tipped her head to the side as she studied Bastian's face. She touched a spot on his cheek, near his mouth. "You have lines that were not there a year ago. You grieve. That is right and proper. But do not make yourself ill. Pierozzo will not grant you the position of heir if you are pining for the loss of a mortal who was not your mate."

"She was not my mate, no, but I could do no less than grieve her passing," he argued, feeling that Rey did not understand since she had never engaged in relationships with mortals. "Just because she was not a mate does not mean I did not value her."

"No, of course not. I know how much she meant to you, and you to her. I apologize if I seem uncaring. It's just that mortals … well, I have said enough on that score. I will respect your desire to honor Alex as you choose." Rey hesitated before she asked, "Are you still having the dreams?"

"Yes," he said, turning away and returning to the relative darkness of the house.

Rey's forehead furrowed as she followed him. "I do not profess to understand why you are unable to sleep without dreams of Alex, but perhaps …" She bit her lip before saying quickly, "Perhaps you should do as she wants."

"Alexandra is dead. Her appearance in my dreams is simply a manifestation of my grief," Bastian said flatly, avoiding the knowledge that he was lying to himself. At that realization he mentally *tsk*ed, and was obligated to add, "It is, perhaps, something beyond my grief that causes her former chaperone to visit me in my dreams, but that is surely guilt that I could not stop Alexandra from falling to her own mortality."

"I'm not so sure," Rey said slowly, her gaze now on the door open to the garden. "Perhaps … perhaps this woman wants something from you."

"They are dreams, Rey, nothing more," he said firmly, scribbling a note to be given to Alessandra's nanny. He gave himself a mental shake, telling himself he needed to heed Rey's advice and focus on his petition to be named heir to Pierozzo Blu. Although his nephew Fiat had mentioned giving him a run for the position, Bastian knew Pierozzo viewed him with favor. He would not let down his wyvern, or his sept.

"Perhaps," Rey repeated as he left the room to change for a meeting with Pierozzo. "Or perhaps it's a sign."

The woman came to him that night, after he was finally able to drift into a restless sleep.

"You have tried very hard to avoid me," Mrs. Erwan's voice came from behind him.

Bastian spun around, surprised to find himself once again on the street outside the museum in Firenze where he had first spoken to Alexandra. "Why do you haunt me? Is it not enough that I must live with Alexandra's ghost?"

"Her spirit does not remain bound to the mortal plane," Mrs. Erwan said in what Bastian thought of as a cold, proper English voice, but there was a hint of gentleness nonetheless. "She has moved on to her choice of afterlife, so if you are being haunted, it is not Alexandra who is responsible."

"Then why are you here? Why do you come repeatedly to my dreams?" Bastian asked, brushing aside the woman's comment. "My mind must be much troubled to keep manifesting you, for I can think of no reason for it to do so."

For a moment, amusement flashed across the woman's face, but almost before he could register it, her expression had returned to its normal dour state. "You have hidden from yourself for long enough, Bastiano di Giardino. It is time that you face the truth."

"Face what truth?" He straightened his shoulders and looked down on the woman, drawing about him the natural dignity that all dragons possessed when dealing with mortals.

The woman reached up and brushed a thumb across his forehead. He jerked back, both in surprise at the unexpected gesture and with the heat that seemed to sear deep into his brain. "You are a dream walker, a dream warrior, and yet you have refused that calling for too long. Now it is time that you face your true self. Embrace that which you were always intended to be. Protect those who cannot protect themselves. Guide your kin who do not see a path. Follow your heart."

Bastian rubbed at his forehead, confused and disoriented for a few seconds. "Guide my kin? Do you mean become Pierozzo's heir? I have already petitioned—" He stopped, realizing that the dreamscape had shifted, leaving him standing alone in a forest. Ahead of him through some trees, a light glittered, and he heard voices.

He stumbled forward, almost falling over a downed log, mentally shaking his head at the disturbed dream his mind was producing. Three shadows moved against the trees, the moon overhead casting a ghostly light that filtered through gently rustling branches.

"Fine. I guess we're going to go with outright idiocy instead of self-preservation today. Hello, Xavier. As usual, it's horrific to see you," a woman said in English. There were two others with her—one man who stood slightly ahead of the woman, with his back to Bastian, and a third man who stood in shadow—but it was the woman who drew his gaze.

Where Alexandra had exuded a glittering golden light, this woman was surrounded by a gray mist, one that wove around her with long, smoky tendrils. He could see only the back of the woman, but she had chocolate-brown curls tipped blond, and was clad in tight-fitting men's trousers that left little to the imagination when it came to her ass and legs.

If he hadn't been deep in mourning for Alexandra, he would have appreciated those trousers, but he put that thought aside. Someday, perhaps, he would find women such as this one catching his attention, but he was not ready yet. His heart might not have been bound to a mate, but it had been touched by Alexandra nonetheless.

"A dream walker," the shadowed man said. "I have not heard of another dragon who was such."

"Dream walker?" Bastian spoke the word aloud before he realized it. He backed away from the three people, shaking his head. "Dragons can't walk in dreams. It is impossible, beyond our natures. Only the First Dragon can—" He stopped, touching the spot on his forehead, struck with a thought so amazing, he was almost unable to process it.

"Dream warrior," he heard Mrs. Erwan say again, her voice carried on the wind. He spun around, trying to find her, trying to protest that he was not worthy of such a boon as the First Dragon had evidently decided to bestow upon him, but there was nothing surrounding him but shadows and tall firs. Even the three people he'd overheard were gone. All that was left was wind and shadows and a mild sense of panic.

He lifted his hand, aware of the pressure of a palm-sized object digging into his flesh. He spread wide his fingers and stared at the narrow blue crystal.

"You do me a great honor, dragon sire," he said softly, his fingers closing back around the crystal. It elongated in a blue-white light the shape of a sword, heavy in his hand despite its appearance.

He knew he should be grateful that he had been sought for such an honor, that any other dragon would be thrilled to be so singled out.

And yet, he had a horrible presentiment that rather than a boon, the First Dragon had instead laid a curse upon him.

He just hoped he'd survive it.

TWO
THE END

December 1922

"Do you think to defeat me?" The mage's mocking laughter filled Bastian's mind. "You haven't the strength. Begone, dragon, and let those who know how to wield the magic they possess claim the rewards of victory."

"Victory," Bastian snarled. He was on his knees, panting, his heart pounding so hard it almost blocked out the mage's words. He looked up, trying desperately to catch his breath, struggling to his feet even as he lifted his hand. For one horrible moment, he thought his exhausted muscles were going to refuse to act, but at last his arm rose, his fingers clutched tightly about the narrow blue crystal given to him by the First Dragon. "You are not the victor here, Ge Hong. You are merely a dream walker, a tormentor of mortals."

"Whereas you are what? A *savior* of mortals?" The mage's voice cut through him like a razor. Even though they were in a dreamscape, Bastian could taste the acid of the mage's words.

He spat out a ball of mingled fire and blood, hoping the former would purge his mouth of the bitterness. "I am as you see me."

"Dragons do not dream walk," Ge Hong said, moving around him, his sword held easily.

"I am no mere dragon," Bastian replied, pulling on the last of his strength to square his shoulders, flexing his fingers to urge the crystal into the form of a sword made up of blue-and-white light, arcane power sparking down its length. "I have just been made wyvern of the blue sept. And I am a dream warrior, so named by the First Dragon himself."

"You are deranged if you think I believe in the fables of dream warriors. Such beings do not exist. There are only dream walkers, of which I am the best. I say again, begone, lest I teach you the humility you so obviously lack."

As the last word left his lips, Ge Hong attacked, forcing Bastian backward until he was pressed against an impossibly tall bookcase. To his right cowered a mortal man, gaunt and balding, with haunted eyes, his mouth working as he spoke silently to himself. He presented a piteous figure, but Bastian had only sympathy for him. He parried Ge Hong's light sword, but only just, his arm burning and trembling with weakness.

Pain slashed across his shoulder, and his sword dropped to the ground, reverting back to its crystalline dormant state.

"*Peste!*" Bastian swore, clutching his shoulder briefly before lunging at the crystal when Ge Hong turned his attention on the man cowering on the floor. He triggered the sword, now in his left hand, his right arm hanging limply at his side, blood dripping from the tips of his fingers. Although Bastian wasn't truly ambidextrous, he had been trained to use a sword in both hands. He thrust hard at Ge Hong, catching the mage's blade and spinning him backward. "Why do you torment this man? What is he to you?"

"A tool, of course." Ge Hong took a step back, a slow smile spreading over his face as he took in Bastian's weakened state. "What else use would I have for a mortal? You claim to be a dream walker, but you are ignorant of our abilities?"

"Dream walkers can enter the dreams of others," Bastian said, desperately attempting to gather his energy. It hurt to breathe, every limb aching with exhaustion and pain. "They can influence, but not command. They cannot make the host commit actions against their will."

"Which shows just how ignorant you are. Why would I waste time entering dreams of mortals if I could not force them to my desires? Mortals are so pliable when they sleep—but you know this. Or you would if you were a true dream walker."

Bastian fought hard to stand up straight, but his shoulder screamed in pain. He wanted badly to shift into dragon form, knowing it would give him strength, as well as heal the wound Ge Hong had dealt him, but such things were impossible in the dreamscape. His breath came in even shorter gasps now, black blotches starting to leach across his vision. The fight to keep Ge Hong from tormenting the mortal was more intense than any other he'd experienced, but the idea of failure was not to be thought of.

"I am a dragon," Bastian snarled through teeth gritted against the pain and effort of raising his left arm, the sword glittering in the candlelight that filled the mortal's dream. He lunged forward, pulling hard on the power of the First Dragon, with each sentence slashing and stabbing at Ge Hong. "A wyvern. A dream warrior. I will protect those who can't protect themselves, and I will not allow you to torment this man any longer."

Ge Hong gave a cry and fell backward just as Bastian was filled with a brilliant light, one that left him feeling as if he was standing in the center of a lightning storm. Energy didn't just give him strength; it coursed through his veins, charged each atom of his being, quickly overwhelming him, spilling out around him. Panic gripped him hard as he struggled to contain the power, to leash it and control it, but it was too much.

He heard the mage scream, but he was blinded by the white-blue power, the rushing sound of it as it flowed around and through him drowning out even that high wail of the mortal man.

"Noo!" Bastian's throat burned with the word as it was torn from him, but he couldn't hear it over the torrent surrounding him. Frantically and desperately he tried to shape the power, to use it to save the man he'd fought so hard to protect, but it was beyond his control, heedless to his desires, simply flowing out of him, consuming everything in its path.

The blackness eating his vision swallowed him, as well, pulling him into its depths with long, inky fingers that clamped around him no matter how hard he fought.

I have failed, was his last thought as he went under the still, thick blackness. *Failed myself … and the First Dragon.*

* * *

"Where are they?" Two days after the worst night of his life, Bastian pushed open the door that led to the central hall of a small villa. Although he still bore the physical scars of his battle with the mage Ge Hong in the form of a shoulder that hadn't quite healed, it was the emotional scars that seared deep into his being, the rage, guilt, and doubts inside of him manifesting behind him as fiery footprints. "Where are the kin who have betrayed me?"

Luca, the second of his elite guard, rushed forward, his face flushed. "In the salon. As you suspected, Fiat is there. He has spoken to them. Convinced them."

"Then I will simply unconvince them." Bastian ignored the emotions that fought inside of him, leashing his anger, telling himself he had to focus on the here and now before he could deal with the repercussions of failing the First Dragon. "I am wyvern, not Fiat. It is me they must listen to. Did you prepare the documents?"

"Yes, but, Bastian—"

Luca's words were lost when Bastian burst into a small west-facing salon. The afternoon light filled the room with a golden warmth that made his soul want to sing, but it couldn't battle the fury wrapped around him with stinging barbs.

He had been betrayed by his own kin.

No one has betrayed you more than you, yourself, a cruel part of his mind pointed out. *What will the First Dragon think when he finds out you failed to save even one small mortal?*

Pain lashed him, tearing off little bits of his soul. He would give anything he had in his lair to have kept the mortal alive, but he had not known—the First Dragon had not told him—to kill a dream walker was to doom the host to the same fate.

Desperate though he was to decry his actions because he was unlearned, he couldn't deny the truth: by killing Ge Hong, it was Bastian who was to blame for the loss of the mortal's life.

The First Dragon must never learn of his shame.

"Bastian?" Luca appeared at his shoulder, giving him an unreadable look as they stood in the entrance of the room.

With an effort, Bastian pushed away the guilt and pain burned into him by the tragedy of two nights past, and focused on the trial that faced him.

"So. The foul rumors were true." He stopped in front of a large round table inlaid with precious woods from around the world, and met the gaze of each of the three dragons who leaped to their feet, their expressions ranging from guilty to pugnacious.

Only Fiat, the son of his beloved sister, stood looking out of the window, clearly distancing himself.

"I have been wyvern for less than a week, but already you test me?" He stared at all the three dragons before him, sick at heart with what must be done, but knowing he could not show weakness.

Certainly not the sort of weakness he'd shown two nights before.

"Zuan Amante, I have known you since birth," Bastian said, ignoring the cruel voice in his mind. "You betray me now?"

The blue dragon's gaze dropped, his fingers working on the fine material of his suit jacket, but he said nothing.

Bastian shifted his gaze to the second dragon. "Arlotto Cava. You have long been a friend, a valued confidant. And yet here you stand."

Arlotto's gaze was as fiery as Bastian's soul. He opened his mouth to speak, but a noise from Fiat had him casting a glance at the latter, then snapping his teeth shut, his jaw tensing.

Bastian turned to the last man. "Nascimbene Dell'Anno. You saved my father's life on more than one instance, but you have thrown away your honor."

"We have done what was necessary," the older man said, his voice slow and heavy. "You left us no choice, Bastian. Fiat has told us of your wild claims. He has warned of the madness that runs in your family, the same madness that caused your sister to take her own life. And now you show those same signs. Fiat says you are not fit to be wyvern, and we agree."

"Not fit?" Bastian's rage spilled out, again manifesting itself into dragon fire. It ringed Nascimbene, licking up his legs. "In what way am I not fit?"

"There are concerns about what you said regarding abilities that are not normal. Not natural to blue dragons. To *any* dragons—" Nascimbene started to say, but Arlotto thrust himself forward, his pale blue eyes narrowed into slits.

"You say you can walk in dreams, other people's dreams, that you can influence and affect them." Arlotto spat the words, seemingly edged with steel. "We are dragons, not gods. We can touch the waking minds of mortals, but not possess them in sleep as you claim you can. If that is not delusion and madness, then what is?"

"It is not madness, because it is true." Bastian took a deep breath, guilt and doubt eating away at him. He had to keep control of his emotions and bury them deep in his soul. Rigid control was the only way he could withstand this attack. "The First Dragon himself—"

"The First Dragon has not been sighted in centuries," Arlotto said, his voice reflecting his sneer. "Pierozzo was wrong to name you heir over Fiat. You are too unlearned, too unstable. Fiat was heir for half a century. *He* has been trained. You have not."

"I challenged for the position of heir and won. Fiat himself ceded the position to me," Bastian argued, then clamped his lips closed. Regardless of the malcontent Arlotto, he was wyvern, and it was beneath him to squabble. "As it is, Fiat was welcomed as a member of my guard. That you would listen to him over your wyvern, that you would conspire against the sept, turn against your own kin, tells me much about the lies Fiat is spreading. And yet you believed him. You plotted and planned and schemed to depose me. Can you deny it? Can any of you deny your betrayal?"

"There is nothing to deny," Fiat said, strolling forward to face Bastian, his expression carefully neutral. Bastian had never seen the similarity in their appearances that others claimed could have made them twins, for they were as different as day was from night.

"You think I won't punish you for your treachery simply because of our relationship?" Bastian asked, and reached out blindly for the decree that he'd ordered Luca to draw up. "You are wrong, Fiat. Very wrong. Sfiatatoio del Fuoco, I strip from you kinship of the blue dragons, and cast you from—"

"No," Fiat said, moving forward to stand before him. "No, you will not remove me or any kin from the sept."

Bastian's brows pulled together as he realized about what Luca had wanted to warn him. Pain mingled with anger, threatening once again to boil out of him. "You threaten me? Your wyvern?"

"Not wyvern," Fiat corrected, a smile flirting with his lips. "Prisoner. A triumvirate has been called, and stripped from you the position that you stole from me."

"Stole!" The word rolled around the room like thunder. Bastian's fingers twitched for the light sword, which unfortunately was locked away in a secret cache. "There was no stealing involved. I challenged you for the role of heir and won. You ceded."

"I gave Pierozzo what he wanted, because you were much favored in his eyes," Fiat said, his lips curling, his eyes glittering with a cold light. "And in his bed."

Bastian's rage set the room ablaze. "You bring shame to the blue dragons by implying nepotism on Pierozzo's part. My relationship had nothing to do with being made heir. I was so named before he even turned his attentions to me."

"And I have been named wyvern by the triumvirate," Fiat snapped. "The sept tires of the deranged wanderings of your mind. You are unfit to lead, and have been removed as wyvern due to the madness that has claimed you. You will be confined—"

"Madness!" Bastian snarled the word, dragon fire building inside him until the pressure was too great to bear. "I am not mad. I am a dream walker, a dream warrior, blessed by the First Dragon himself!"

"—confined here, to this villa, where you can do no harm to any members of the sept." Fiat breathed heavily through his nose, a few wisps of smoke curling out of one nostril. "Dream warriors do not exist, and certainly not in the dragonkin. For you to invoke the First Dragon's name in your madness proves how troubled your mind is."

Bastian fought the desperate sense of everything slipping through his fingers. It was as if, once again, he was merely a vessel for powers that he had no ability to harness. His guts twisted with anguish and something very like fear.

No! his mind shrieked. *True wyverns do not feel fear. Do not show weakness! You must be a leader, a strong leader.* With an effort that seemed almost superhuman, Bastian clamped down hard on his emotions, saying in a voice that he hoped sounded calm, "I have neither the time nor patience to argue with you. I am as I have stated, and I will not discuss the matter further."

"There is no such thing as a dream warrior," Fiat screamed, slamming a fist down onto the table. The faces of the other dragons looked first shocked, then wary as Fiat continued, storming around the table and waving his hands with wild, choppy gestures. "Do you not think that we, masters of the mind, would know if such a thing was possible? There has never been such a thing as a dream warrior. It is fiction, nothing more, and the fact that you refuse to admit the truth drives home the point of just how insane you are."

"I will not allow this," Bastian said, his voice low and ugly even as he battled to contain his fire. Pain pricked his palms as his fisted fingers changed into the green-tipped claws of blue dragons. "I am wyvern. I am—"

"A delusional old man who is a danger to himself and others," Fiat shouted, and at a snap of his fingers, the room was filled with blue dragons, men and women whom Bastian had trusted. The copper taste of betrayal lashed him even as Luca leaped to his side, shifting into dragon form in an obvious attempt to protect him.

It was too late. Bastian had time only to shift before a sting burned the back of his neck, followed by a growing warmth down his spine that warned that one of his dragons, one of his beloved kin, had injected him with a drug.

"You think this will end," he said, trying to reach Fiat, needing to see into the soul of his nephew. The words came out slow and thick, as if he were speaking through molasses. "But it will not. I … will not. I …"

Darkness swallowed him, sucking him down into an abyss that the tormented part of his mind welcomed, for with the darkness came calm. And peace. And relief from the torment of the rage and guilt and shame.

Until he dreamed.

THREE
THE DREAM

Present Day

"You can't hide, Phyllida. I know you. I know your scent, your taste, the feeling of your body against mine. You will never be able to escape me, for I have taken you into my essence. You are a part of me."

"I'm dreaming," I told a goldfish that stared at me with wide, watchful eyes. He sat in a squat round bowl next to the window. For some reason, his unwavering gaze made me uncomfortable. I looked out of the window at the vast expanse of buildings—from the ground, which looked impossibly far away, up to clouds that encircled the tops of the skyscrapers. "I'm dreaming that I'm in a very big city. Hong Kong? Shanghai? I don't recognize this place, but at least I'm anonymous here. No one can find me with millions of people around me."

"I will find you."

I shivered at the voice that seemed to come from nowhere and everywhere, rubbing my arms at the sudden chill that made goose bumps ripple down my flesh. "No one can find me," I repeated.

"You think because you have hidden from me for almost ten years that I cannot draw you to me should I wish it?" The deep male voice, tinged with an Eastern European accent that I used to find incredibly sexy, was filled with genuine amusement. "It is almost, but not quite, time. But when everything is in place, when the sacrifices are ready to be made, then you will learn your true place in this world you love so much."

"I am alone," I told the goldfish. It didn't even blink, just floated in its bowl, its fins gently waving in the water while it continued to stare at me. "Do goldfish blink? Maybe you don't blink. Maybe I'm holding it against you even though it's not really your fault, although you could look somewhere else for a bit."

"You try so hard to pretend, and yet, the fact that you are here now reassures me that our connection is as strong as ever. And soon it will be stronger, for the time is almost upon us. Be ready, Phyllida, for I am almost there."

"Fish," I murmured to myself, leaning against the floor-to-ceiling window, the glass cool against my cheek. I closed my eyes, my palms resting against it, straining to hear the sounds of the city beyond the barrier of the glass … and my dream. "Think about fish. Do they or do they not have eyelids? Don't think about anything else. Fish eyelids are of the primary importance until you wake up."

"Shall I tell you what I'll do when I find you? It's always amusing to feel that delicious spike of fear that never fails to manifest when I tell you my plans. Or should I save that pleasure for when we are face-to-face, so I can watch your lovely eyes darken with despair?"

"And hands!" I almost yelled, pushing back from the window, suddenly feeling too exposed, as if Xavier could pinpoint me in the millions of inhabitants of whatever city my mind had chosen for a hiding place. "Why don't goldfish have hands? Hands would have been so awesome, evolutionally speaking. Fish hands could have made a life-and-death difference in how they turned out."

"What?" Annoyance rolled through me as if it was a wave. For a moment, I froze, the sensation of Xavier's emotions so unexpected, I wasn't sure how to react to it. "When? Then we will have to be there, as well. Make it happen."

I stood for a moment with my mouth hanging open when I realized that Xavier wasn't speaking to me. The words—and emotion—were intended for someone else. Someone who must be physically near him. What madness was this? Since when had he the ability to do more than torment me in my dreams?

Before I could do more than rub my arms again, Xavier's presence withdrew from my mind.

But not before he spoke one word that left my teeth chattering with fear.

"Soon."

"You can stop dreaming now. Xavier has gone off to torment someone else," I told myself, glancing over at the goldfish. "Maybe I'm not dreaming. Maybe you're the one dreaming, and I'm just a part of it. Is me yelling at you about not having hands a dream, or a nightmare?"

"Perhaps it's both?"

I spun around at the voice, clutching my throat with horror before I could register that it belonged to a woman, not Xavier. "What—who—how—"

"Why, where, and when?" the woman asked, give me a ghost of a smile. She looked middle-aged, with dark hair that had a big white Cruella de Vil streak, and wore clothing that looked like it came straight out of the 1920s.

"That covers all the interrogatives, I think," I said, wary to the tips of my toenails. "Er … who are you? Did Xavier send you?"

"Why would he do that? He seems to have no trouble finding you when you sleep," she said, strolling over next to me, placing one hand on the glass as she gazed out of the window. "Ah. Hong Kong. It has been some time since I was last here. I see it has grown."

"If you're not with Xavier, then you must be … what, just a random dream walker?" I asked, backing away. "I have to say that I feel a little violated by that. I didn't ask you to come here. I know you people can march into any dream you like, but it's only polite to ask, first."

The woman scanned the skyline, then pressed her forehead against the window to peer down at the street. "So many people in such a small location. All busy with their lives, individuals, and yet moving in a dance of unity, bound to each other by their mortality, their loves, their desires." She stepped back, and tipped her head slightly as she looked me over. "All but you. You are not part of their dance."

"No," I said, suddenly wanting to cry. "I'm not."

She watched me for a few more seconds, then smiled.

I felt like I was bathed in sunlight, the golden glow reaching the deepest atoms of my soul. The light was so bright it blinded me, but at the same time, it made me want to throw my hands to the sky and sing with the sheer glory of it. I was filled with jubilation, with happiness, and for a few seconds, felt I was a part of humanity.

And then the light faded and I found myself in a sunny room, some sort of a florist's shop, behind a desk, my hands working to arrange a spray of eucalyptus. A shadow fell over the bouquet, causing me to look up, my breath hitching at the sight of the man who entered.

"Good morning. I seek flowers for—" He stopped speaking, his eyebrows rising a smidgen while I tried hard not to gawk. He was blond, with short hair that had a thick wave to it that I was willing to bet was curly if he didn't comb it out. He was taller than me, probably a bit over six foot, but wiry, as if he was an athlete. And his voice—oh, his voice. He spoke in Italian, his voice a lovely rich baritone, reminding me of brandy.

"Hi," I said before I realized it.

His eyebrows rose a little higher before settling down to normal, his lips curling in a smile. That just drew my attention to his mouth, and the blunted square of his chin, and the slight indentations in his cheeks that made a shiver ripple down my back and arms. "Hello. You are English?"

"American. You're Italian."

"I am," he said, a spark shining in his clear blue eyes that made me feel very warm and feminine.

"That's nice. I haven't met many Italians other than my roommate in college. She taught me to speak a little of the language. What are you doing here?"

"This is Italy. Many Italians live here," he said gravely, although now his eyes were positively dancing with humor.

"No, it can't be," I said, shaking my head. "I'm in the US. I can't be in Italy."

He stepped back and swept a hand toward the open doorway, through which sunlight spread in a glowing pool on the tiled floor of the florist shop. "See for yourself."

"All right, but I warn you, I know where I am. I have reasons for not being out of—oh." I released the fragrant eucalyptus and moved around the counter as I spoke, very aware of his nearness as I passed him to look out of the open doorway.

Outside was a bustling street full of people, and a line of shops in either direction.

The shop names were in Italian.

The people were speaking Italian.

I shook my head, unable to believe what I was seeing. "No, this can't be—oh, wait." I reentered the shop, relief filling me. "This isn't real. It's a dream. I was in a dream before, so this is just another part of it."

At the word "dream," the smile on the handsome man's face faded. "A dream? Why would he send me here?" He studied me for a few seconds, his eyes now serious. "Are you in trouble?"

"No," I answered, honest, but only to a certain extent. I certainly wasn't going to go into my life story with this handsome figment of my imagination.

What if he's not a figment? my brain asked.

I gave a mental eye roll at that. In all the long years of my life, Xavier was the only one who had ever been able to enter my dreams. The woman in Hong Kong was clearly a manifestation of some protective part of my id, trying to give me solace in a time of stress. "You didn't … Xavier didn't send you?" I asked, suddenly worried.

"I do not know of anyone by that name," he answered, his eyes as pure as a summer afternoon sky. "Is he your lover?"

"Lord, no!" I was unable to keep from giving a little shudder, trying to decide if the Italian was telling the truth. Since he had none of the miasma of dread that always accompanied Xavier and his cohorts, I decided he was being honest, although I had a suspicion a big part of that feeling was due to the fact that my body was more than willing to accept the sexy, sexy man my brain was offering.

"What's your name?" I asked, feeling that if my brain had gone to all the trouble to summon up a man for what I very much hoped would be a smutty dream, then I might as well appreciate it.

"Bastian." He gave a little bow, the kind people made in historical dramas, but much nicer. "And you?"

"Phyllida. You said that you were here for some flowers?" I bustled around the counter, picking up stray flowers and greenery. If my brain wanted to play, then I'd play. Goddess knew it had been forever since I had flirted with a man, even if he was the imagining of my romance-starved mind. "A bouquet for your wife? Girlfriend? Boyfriend? Or did you hear about my expertise with eucalyptus, and wanted to see for yourself the wicked things I could do with it against your naked flesh?"

His eyebrows rose for a second at my blatant words, but then the smile returned to both his lips and eyes, and he gave me another bow. "I am here because I was sent here, although I will admit that the purpose of my visit is as yet clouded. I will, however, be happy to learn of your ways with eucalyptus. You would prefer me to disrobe here, or do you have a bedroom nearby?"

"You get right to the point," I said, laughing.

"I was simply taking my lead from you." His smile faded a little until just the edges of his lips curled. "I must warn you that I can't help you, *cara*. Not in the manner you need."

"Why? Are you dysfunctional down there?" I asked, glancing at his fly. Since his pants were fairly tight, I had no trouble identifying a bulge. "Oh, I'm sorry—how do you prefer to identify? I don't want to make an assumption that isn't comfortable to you."

"Dysfunctional ... ah." The few lines appearing between his eyebrows smoothed out. "I am male, and do not have trouble with my ... parts, if that's what you are asking. The help I was referring to was the reason you summoned me."

"I don't think that I did," I said, a bit confused. Was my mind playing tricks with me? Or had Xavier finally driven me around the bend? I pushed aside the fear and worry and loneliness, and smiled instead. "And I don't need any help."

"Indeed." He studied me for a handful of seconds, then relaxed. "Then it would appear we have been fated to meet thusly. You are alone here?"

"I am. It's just me and my naughty eucalyptus." I decided that the encounter, while singularly odd, wasn't one I was willing to dismiss. "Would you be shocked if I suggested we go look for a private room? There must be one around here somewhere. I mean, there usually is in shops, right?"

I turned first to the right, but there was nothing but a refrigerated display case filled with flowers. To the left, however, was a curtained doorway. I took a handful of long eucalyptus fronds and, casting a look that I hoped was pure come-hither, went thither.

"I've never done this before, you know," I told him as I entered another sun-filled room, this one an obvious living room, with French doors that opened onto a small, tranquil garden filled with butterflies, drowsy bees, and flowers that waved gently in the breeze.

It looked like something out of a glossy magazine, and for a moment, I felt like crying.

I'd never be able to have that perfect little garden, or the shop in Italy, or even the delicious man who moved up to stand beside me and gaze out at the small square of emerald lawn.

Life is what it is, I told myself, and turned back into the room, my heart unexpectedly sad. "If fantasy is all I can have, then I'll have to grab it by the balls and enjoy the hell out of it."

"I can think of many fantasies involving my balls and your hands … and other parts … but please be gentle with how you grab. Such body parts tend to be grateful for considerate touches rather than rampant enthusiasm. Ah. That divan looks promising. Would you like me to lock your shop door so that we won't be disturbed while you are educating me as to the erotic ways of eucalyptus?"

"Sure," I said, pushing down my ever-present despair, and willing the dream to be everything I needed it to be. "I've never been one for voyeurism, not that I think that would happen, because I'm in control of this dream."

Bastian went out to the shop proper. I glanced around the room, noting a long, wide daybed with wrought iron back, two chairs around a small wood-burning stove, and a tall glass-fronted bookcase.

I contemplated the daybed, decided what the hell, and by the time Bastian returned from locking the shop up, I was lying in what I hoped was a seductive pose on the daybed, clad only in a gauzy navy-and-silver scarf I found draped over the back of one of the chairs.

"Ah," he said, his eyes lighting again with a flash of interest. "I see we think alike."

He moved toward me, his clothing melting off him as he approached, until he sat next to me naked, aroused, and so handsome it momentarily stripped me of thought.

Except one: my libido was doing an exceptionally good job with my dream lover. I would have to think of some way to reward it.

"I like a man who arouses easily," I told him, running a finger down his bicep. He had nice arms, suitably muscled without going into the territory of buff Hollywood actor. "And I like your hands. You have long, square-tip fingers. That means you like order."

"You read hands?" he asked, looking down at his fingers.

"Kind of. I did an online course in palmistry a while ago. Let me see yours." I took his hand and turned it over to examine the palm, more than a little aware of the heat that resulted in my fingers on his. "You're very good about keeping appointments and almost always arrive exactly on time. You like to have structure and regularity in your life, and dislike rude people. You like art and sculpture, and are very good with math."

"Ah, now, there you are wrong," he said, curling his fingers around mine before bringing my hand to his mouth to kiss my knuckles. "Everything but the math is correct; I never have had a head for figures. And what of you, my temptress? What does your hand show?"

He uncurled my fingers, pressing his mouth to my palm.

My breath hitched in my throat.

"Right now it's screaming that it wants to touch every inch of you, and have you reciprocate. Bastian?"

"Hmm?" He had finished kissing my hand, and was moving his way up my arm. My eyes widened at the trail of fire that followed his mouth, but I reminded myself that anything was possible in a dreamscape.

"I don't know why I feel like I have to say this, because after all, you are only in my head, but regardless, I should tell you that I normally don't do this."

"Read palms, or engage in sexual acts?" He stopped kissing my shoulder, leaning over me so that I fell back on the daybed, my scanty covering slipping off my breasts. "You are a virgin? I have not been with such before, but if you will tell me what you are comfortable with, I believe we will cope well."

"No, not a virgin. I just don't—you know—" I freed a hand that had been pinned under him, and waved it in a vague gesture before deciding that so long as it was free, I might as well use it, and stroked it down his chest. "I don't normally see a man and jump him two minutes later. Not even in my dreams."

"Ah, but dreams are where you can indulge in your wildest fantasies without fear, are they not?" he murmured, turning his attention to my chest. I arched beneath him as he caressed my now highly needy breasts, first with his hands, then with his mouth. A moan slipped out of me as I stroked my hands down him, reveling in the warm, silky flesh. I wanted badly to be able to reach his penis so I could do some caressing of my own, but he shifted slightly, moving his lower half just out of my range.

"Not fair, I want to touch," I said, moaning again when he rubbed his cheek against the underside of my breast.

"All's fair in dream sex," he said, and then glanced up with a wicked look in his eyes. "And as long as we're indulging in fantasy, I think we should try this."

"Try whaaaaaaa—" My voice rose an octave when he shifted again and sent his fingers questing in a highly erogenous part of my body at the same time he breathed fire on my sensitized breasts. "You're a … that was … oh goddess, do that thing with your thumb again. Glarg. Once more." I gasped at the sensation of his fingers dancing in my intimate flesh, that pleasure mingling with the heat as the fire burning on my breasts slowly sank into my skin, making my blood steam with want and need and desire.

"I am a dragon, yes. And you, my temptress, are too delicious to resist. Tell me you want this."

"Seriously?" I paused in the act of moaning and writhing beneath him just long enough to say, "If I wanted this any more, I'd burst into flames."

"I can make that happen," he said, his eyes shimmering topaz with passion. He moved my knees aside to accommodate him, placing himself where he would be guaranteed a welcome. My inner muscles tightened in anticipation even as I dragged my nails gently up his arms, my legs moving restlessly with the need to be filled.

His head dipped down to mine, capturing my sigh of pleasure as the tip of him pushed inside me, my body as tense and tight as a bowstring. I arched up to meet him, the feeling of him being gripped by a hundred intimate muscles almost too much for me.

"My brain ... dear goddess, is there an end to you? My brain is going to get a raise, or whatever you do for brains that give you erotic dreams so good they make you ... nrng! Bastian!

He'd risen up on his knees, sliding his hands under my hips in a way that elevated my pelvis, the new angle allowing him to reach parts of me that left me shaking on the edge of an orgasm. "I thought you might like that. Now if we adjust you so ..." He pulled my legs up so they were over his shoulders, my hips tipped up to greet him, my body and mind aflame with need and lust and desire, building in a bonfire of pleasure so great, I had a feeling I might just cry from the glory of it all.

And then my alarm went off.

I opened my eyes to stare up at my ceiling, my phone chirping its wake-up alarm next to my head. My body was positively screaming with the need for fulfillment.

"Argh!" I yelled, grabbing the phone and throwing it across the room before collapsing back on my bed, aroused, unfulfilled, and so sexually frustrated I could spit.

FOUR
THE SÁRKÁNY: DAY ONE

"You look like hell," Rey told Bastian when he emerged from his bedroom for coffee and fruit. She was seated at the table, a bowl filled with yogurt and berries propped on her big belly, her gaze far too piercing for his liking.

"I'm not surprised. I feel like something that crawled out of Abaddon. Has there been any word on Alessandra?"

"You know I would tell you the second anyone heard from her," Rey said in gentle chastisement.

"Yes, but I'm still trying to decide if she's actually missing, or just out of contact." Bastian thought over the recent sept report that had his own daughter marked as being unreachable. "Since no one has heard from her for some time, I will go on the assumption that she has been captured or detained."

"Why would anyone do that?" Rey asked, looking skeptical. "Not that I'm saying she's not a valuable person in her own right—you know how fond of her I am. We all are. But why would someone go to the trouble of kidnapping a dragon?"

"She is a diviner," Bastian said, tapping absently on the table. "Someone must have taken her for that reason."

"Possibly." Rey didn't look convinced. "Regardless, every member of the sept has been told to keep a lookout for her, so if she's spotted, we'll know."

He made no answer to that, the worry making his belly ache.

"Not to change the subject, but I don't suppose you went … traveling … during the night?"

Rey was the only one who knew he'd dream walked two days before. He looked away from her, accepting the coffee that Luca brought to him. "Would it matter if I did? I am, as you see, still sane."

"Bastian, I have never thought you dream walking was a bad thing. In fact, just the opposite. The First Dragon gave you that gift for a reason." Rey's gaze, as usual, saw far too much.

His glanced past her to the opened doors, the brisk morning breeze making the long white curtains ripple. "That might be true if I was not as I am." He didn't want to have to point out again how he'd failed the First Dragon. The memory of his debut as a dream warrior was all too fresh in his head despite the passage of time. "Another dragon—"

"Another dragon wouldn't have been picked by the dragon sire to be his warrior. You have. Yes, you had a horrible experience with that mage and the mortal, but, Bastian, you are not to blame. Not for that, nor for what Fiat did."

"I went mad. I lost control. I destroyed an innocent life." The pain within him was deep, so deep, and yet it still had the ability to make him suck in his breath at its sharpness. "I will not risk that again. Not even for—"

"For whom?" Rey watched him, a slow smile curling her lips. "Is it a woman you visited in your dreams?"

"Her dream, not mine," he was quick to point out, then held up a hand when she would have continued. "No, do not say it. I will not dream walk again. I can't put the blue dragons at risk. Now, have you everything you need?"

She looked like she wanted to argue, but impending motherhood evidently gave her a bit more patience than she had been known for in the past. Instead, she hoisted herself to her feet, saying, "I do, yes. I wish I could go with you to the *sárkány*, but Cole would have a fit if I flew. You'll just have to cope with an inferior guard until I have this baby."

She gave Luca a punch on the arm as she passed, laughing at the grimace he gave her in return.

Bastian was relieved to be away from uncomfortable subjects, and yet, he found more than once that his mind drifted to thoughts of Phyllida. What was it about her that had so caught his attention? She wasn't a dragon, but she wasn't mortal. She didn't raise the slightest objection to the fire he'd breathed on her, but at the same time, he had a feeling she was inexperienced, not a virgin, but unused to the natural ebb and flow of foreplay.

And yet, there was more to his interest than just sex. There was an air of need around her, sadness, which called to the protector that he had buried deep inside him. It was as if she had been waiting for him to rescue her—

"Bastian?"

He blinked, aware that Luca was standing before him, clearly waiting for an answer to a question he hadn't heard. "What? My apologies, I was thinking about something."

Luca's lips twitched. "So Rey has told me. I hope she was worth missing my discussion of who we should bring with us to Paris."

Bastian sighed the sigh of the martyred. "No doubt she told you I am smitten with a woman. It is not true."

"No? But Rey said that you had met someone. ..."

"That is not important now, and make a note in my diary to have strong words with Rey as soon as she is done having this babe."

"And to replace her at the *sárkány*?" Luca prompted, following when Bastian took a bowl of berries and went out to the verandah.

"We will have Gio," Bastian said, dismissing thoughts of the intriguing Phyllida from his mind. He had to focus on the sept, and the happenings in the weyr. That was of prime importance, and where his duty lay.

His dragons came before all else.

Four hours later, he paused in a doorway, noting the gathered individuals.

"Hey, Bastian, long time no see. How they hangin'?" A dog's muzzle poked into Bastian's crotch in an invasive snuffle before quickly removing itself. "Gender and identity check is good to go. Everyone's inside, waiting for you. Just an FYI—there's lots of hand-waving and profanities and really abominable threats of gruesome physical damage flying around, so if you've got delicate sensibilities, you may wanna stay away from the mates and stick to the wyverns. Heh heh heh."

Bastian took a deep, calming breath, and reminded himself that it would be in poor taste to light his host's personal demon on fire.

No matter how provocative it could be.

Gio, who had just been named one of his elite guards that morning, took a step back at the sight of the demon, causing Bastian to mentally damn himself. He'd meant to have a talk with Gio about the *sárkány*, but he'd been busy with sept affairs and his own mental distractions until the last moment.

Luckily, Luca was there, and experienced in the etiquette of the weyr. The latter murmured softly to Gio, who moved into place behind Bastian.

"Thank you for the warning, Jim," Bastian told the demon in Newfoundland dog form, and, with a squaring of his shoulders, strode into the room with Luca and Gio in flanking positions behind him. The large ground-floor salon of Drake Vireo's Paris home was, indeed, in chaos.

For one, it was filled with wyverns, their mates, and one or two elite guards tied to each wyvern. For another, everyone seemed to be talking at once.

"—and I told Gabriel that there was no way those ouroboros dragons really want to join back in. They're sneaky, Aoife, very sneaky. And I *know* sneaky."

"That is May, the silver mate," Luca told Gio in an undertone. "She speaks to Aoife, the black sept mate."

"Bee! How nice to see you again. You and Constantine really must come by Dauva the next time you are in the area.

Don't pay any attention to Baltic's grumbles. He's pleased as punch that Constantine has finally settled down."

"Ysolde de Bouchier," Luca murmured.

Gio sucked in a bit of breath. "Mate of Baltic?"

"Yes."

"She is much favored in the eyes of the weyr," Bastian said without turning his head, keeping his voice pitched to be heard only by his men.

"—and I told Nora that I was able to take up my Guardian duties again, but she said something about the guild insisting that I take a refresher course or something insane like that to catch my skills up since I was on maternity leave. Me, need a refresher course! I'm a freakin' Guardian savant!"

"Aisling Grey, green mate." Luca's voice was barely audible.

"Ah," Gio said on an exhalation, clearly impressed. "It is she who freed Bastian from imprisonment."

"Yes," Luca answered, sending Bastian a quick glance. "She's a demon lord as well as a Guardian, so do not cross her. She's speaking to Sophea, mate of the Dragonbreaker, now the red wyvern."

"It does seem a little out of line," Sophea answered, her expression one of bewilderment. "Don't they know how powerful you are?"

"Bee Dakar is Constantine's mate," Luca continued, nodding toward Constantine, who stood talking to Gabriel Tauhou.

"Bastian's here," Jim bellowed as it wandered into the room.

"And the ... er ... demon?" Gio's voice contained a fair amount of awe that both amused and annoyed Bastian. As ever, his quirky sense of humor struggled with a need for decorum when in formal settings as a *sárkány*.

"It belongs to Aisling," Luca whispered as the demon marched over and plopped down next to where Aisling was still chatting with Sophea. "Don't set it on fire, no matter how rude it is to Bastian or the blue dragons. Aisling doesn't like us lessoning it."

The wyverns, who had been clustered at the far end of the room, all turned when Bastian greeted Aisling.

"You look charming as ever," he said, giving her a little bow, and might have risked kissing her hand, but Drake was instantly at her side, his expression as impassive as ever.

"The same can be said of you," Aisling told him, smiling brightly.

A little too brightly. A pang of wariness gripped him for a second before he moved on to greet the other mates and wyverns.

"Is something amiss with Aisling?" he asked Drake a few minutes later, when Constantine Norka, former silver dragon but now wyvern of the indigo sept, announced the *sárkány* would start if everyone would take their places.

A long-suffering martyred expression crossed Drake's face before it melted away. "Nothing other than the mates have decided that their matchmaking skills are to be honed on you."

Bastian's eyes widened as he glanced toward the women. Although their wyverns were each bringing a chair to the *sárkány* table for their respective mates, there was a decided air of conspiracy hanging over the room. *"Dio,"* Bastian swore under his breath.

"Exactly," Drake said with obvious sympathy, and added quickly, "Take my advice and either find a romantic partner or pay someone to play that role, because otherwise they are threatening to put their heads together to find you a mate. Their success in finding Charity for the First Dragon has fanned their matchmaking flames."

Instantly, the image of Phyllida came to Bastian's mind, causing a responding rush of blood to his groin.

To his left, Luca gave a choked laugh. Bastian shot him a quelling look before taking his own seat at the *sárkány* table, well aware that he was the only wyvern present who did not possess himself of a mate.

Could Phyllida be a wyvern's mate? She had not complained of his fire in their brief moment together, but that may have been due to their meeting being conducted in her dreamscape. The fact that they had connected so quickly boded well, however. There was little he could do about it now, though. He could not visit her dreams again, although that didn't mean he couldn't find her after he had dealt with the current situation.

A pang of loneliness gripped him as Constantine called the meeting to order. The mental image of Phyllida lying on the divan, her silken flesh beckoning … waiting not for him, but for the Xavier she had mentioned.

Bastian snarled under his breath, causing Luca to send him a querying glance that he shook off. He needed to focus, to concentrate on the here and now. To do otherwise was to spell doom … as he knew all too well.

"We gather today to address the application regarding an ouroboros tribe that seeks admittance to the weyr," Constantine said, standing at the head of the long table. He had a slight French accent that always confused Bastian, since he knew Constantine was born in the Balkans. "Since I have been dead the last four hundred years, I am not familiar with the protocol for such demands by an ouroboros tribe. Is there such a thing?"

"No," Drake and Kostya said simultaneously, similar frowns on their respective faces. They both sounded just like their origins, Bastian mused, with Eastern European accents that betrayed their Hungarian birthplace.

"That is not entirely accurate," said Gabriel, the fingers of one hand tapping gently at the table. Gabriel always spoke elegantly, and with his roots deep in the Australian aboriginal community, Gabriel—like Bastian—could go places where other dragons could not follow … except Gabriel's journeys did not end up in madness. "We require all septs that wish to be recognized to hold a dragon relic. Would this not also apply to a tribe? Their end goal is the same—to be a part of the weyr."

"But the septs all possess a piece of the dragon heart," Kostya protested. He shot a fulminating glare at Baltic that quickly spread to Constantine. "Almost all."

"Baltic doesn't need one," Ysolde told Kostya before her mate could respond. "He's got a Firstborn talisman."

"Which he lent to me when it was time to form both the silver dragons and my current sept," Constantine added, sending Kostya's glare right back to him. "You would know this if you paid attention."

"I always pay attention! How dare you impugn me and my sept!" Kostya snarled, leaping to his feet.

"For Pete's sake, don't get him going, or he'll lecture us all about the many and varied things the black dragons have suffered over the years," Aisling pleaded, but was stopped when Kostya continued over the top of her objection.

"The black dragons have a long and glorious past, no matter how much you tried to destroy us, Constantine of Norka! That you are here now, a member of the weyr, is only because we are willing to take the word of Ysolde that you are no longer the madman you used to be," Kostya said, his face red.

The mates, as one, sighed.

Luca gave another choked chirrup of laughter. Bastian knew just how he felt, but he was a wyvern, and wyverns, as a rule, did not laugh at other wyverns. Still, he had to clear his throat and force his lips into a steady line.

"I think you've made your point," Aoife said, tugging on Kostya's sleeve until he sat down. "Everyone has agreed to let what happened in the past stay there, so let's do the same."

"Hrmph," Kostya said on a near snort, but his mate obviously soothed him with gentle touches and a few whispered words that had him smiling at her.

"The point remains that to be a member of the weyr, an artifact must be produced—whether borrowed or not," Gabriel continued.

"Hi, sorry I'm late. You know how the Venediger is about me being in Paris," a woman said as she breezed into the room. She smiled at everyone, her appearance and voice friendly, but all the wyverns instantly stood, and a general air of heightened tension seem to settle over them.

"Charity! What a surprise," Aisling said, getting to her feet. Then she made a little face and added, "I'm so sorry, that sounded extremely rude. Naturally, we are delighted to see you. Er … is your … is the First Dragon with you?"

Bastian stood with the others and looked with curiosity at the newcomer.

"Who—" he heard Gio ask in a whisper behind him.

"First Dragon's mate," Luca answered.

Gio sucked in another astonished breath. Bastian made a mental note to make sure that Gio got exposure to denizens of the Otherworld, since he seemed fairly sheltered and unused to being around the other wyverns.

"Uh-oh. It sounds like you guys weren't expecting me," Charity said, a blush warming her cheeks. "I got the Mates Union message about the *sárkány*, and assumed—er—"

"Of course we hoped you would come," Aisling said at the same time Ysolde pronounced, "You're always welcome to join us."

Bastian, feeling that it was up to the blue dragons to show proper respect to the mate of the ancestor of all dragons who ever were and who ever would be, pulled a chair forward next to his, and gave Charity one of his best bows. "We have not formally met, but I am Bastiano di Giardino Blu, and it would be a great pleasure if you would take your seat at the *sárkány* table next to me."

"Oh, yes, please," Charity said, greeting the mates and wyverns as Bastian escorted her to the chair. "How nice to meet you. I hope I'm not interrupting? I told the First Dragon that you were having a meeting about some of the outlaw dragons, and he thought it would be good for me to be here, since I don't know anything about them. Would it be too much trouble if someone caught me up to speed on the subject? I'll take notes so I can fill in the First Dragon later on what you all say."

"We just got started, so you're not interrupting," Gabriel told her, then looked around the table. "Would someone like to explain to Charity why the *sárkány* was called?"

"Sophea and I are new here, so we are most definitely *not* it," Rowan said.

"Oh, hell, yes," Sophea said with a horrified look at her mate.

Kostya narrowed his eyes at the man. Bastian was secretly amused by that, and made another mental note to take time to chat with Rowan, and see how the newly made dragon was taking to his role.

"Baltic, would you like to do the honors?" Ysolde asked.

Baltic looked bored, as he always did at gatherings. "No," he answered, and crossed his arms.

"Drake?" Aisling asked the green wyvern.

Drake pursed his lips, but said nothing.

"Come on, you're heading up this shindig," Bee said, nudging Constantine. "You can tell her."

"And have my words repeated to the First Dragon?" Constantine looked almost as horrified as Sophea had. "I'm in enough trouble with him given … given …" He waved a hand vaguely. "Everything."

Everyone turned to look at Bastian. He cleared his throat. "I suppose I could try, although I'm not sure that I'm as well versed in the subject as I would wish to be—"

"Oh, for Pete's sake," Aisling said, getting up when a woman opened the door and peeked in, gesturing at Aisling. "You guys are such drama fiends. Ysolde, you fill in Charity while I see what it is the twins are up to that needs immediate attention. Just don't say anything good until I get back."

Aisling hurried out of the room.

Ysolde, with a pointed look at her mate that he summarily ignored—being at the moment involved in a glaring contest with Kostya—gave an exaggerated sigh and, turning to Charity, said, "I'll give you the short and sweet version. A group of ouroboros dragons—those are the outlaws you mentioned, aka dragons who either left their septs or were born outside of them—called the Chaos Tribe petitioned the weyr to join us. Their leader—er—what do they call them? It's not wyvern …"

"Master," Baltic answered, narrowing his eyes on Kostya when the other mouthed something rude in Zilant.

"That's right, so the master of the tribe, Amadeus something-or-other, he wants in the weyr. Which wouldn't in itself be a huge deal except …" She paused and glanced at Bastian, giving him a sympathetic look that he acknowledged with a slight incline of his head. "Except that a whole bunch of their tribe people are blue dragons."

"Former blue dragons," Bastian corrected.

"Right, former members," Ysolde finished, glancing at Aisling when she reappeared in the room, murmuring, "Crisis averted."

"So, these blue dragons want back in the weyr?" Charity asked, looking up from the notepad upon which she was writing. "Why did they leave if they want back in?"

"Because their wyvern Fiat was batshit crazy," Aisling said, taking her seat next to Drake.

"*Kincsem,*" he said in a martyred tone, giving her a long look.

"What?" she asked, giving him the look right back. "He was crazy as the day is long. Everyone knows that, no one more so than Bastian, so don't give me that 'you shouldn't call a wyvern batshit crazy even if we all know he was' look."

The other wyverns looked pained, but no one disputed her statement.

"This is all very soap opera, but with dragons," Charity said as she continued to write. "Who, exactly, is Fiat? I'm sure the First Dragon will know, but I'm still learning the names of everyone, so I'd appreciate an up-to-date player's card."

"Fiat was my nephew," Bastian said after no one else responded. "Many years ago he claimed the role of wyvern from me, and ran the sept until recently, when Aisling freed me from imprisonment."

Charity's eyes went round, but she dutifully made notes.

"Evidently during peak batshit-crazy time, he stole Aisling from Drake, and made her the wyvern's mate of the blue dragons," May said.

"Mayling," Gabriel said in the same tone that Drake had used on Aisling.

"I'm not saying anything that's untrue, am I?" May asked the other mates. "I wasn't around, so I don't know firsthand, but that's what Gabriel told me."

Gabriel, Bastian was amused to note, looked extremely uncomfortable and quickly diverted the conversation. "Yes, that is all true, but it is water under the bridge, so to speak."

"Dude," Jim said in a drawl, looking up from where it lay on a folded blanket. "You're just saying that because you were up to your armpits in it with Fiat. You're the one who—"

"I said it was all water under the bridge. We really should focus on the situation facing us now," Gabriel said a bit more firmly, at the same time casting a pleading look at Aisling, who giggled, but gestured at her demon.

"I wonder if the First Dragon knows about the mate swapping," Charity murmured as she turned the page in her notebook.

"Fiat did a lot of other things to damage dragonkin," Aisling said. "Including taking over the red dragons, much to their detriment, but as Gabriel says, that really doesn't have anything to do with this situation."

"So the problem lies not with allowing the group of outlaw—sorry, ouroboros—dragons into the weyr, but with the fact that they are former members of Bastian's sept?" Charity asked, pen poised over her paper.

"No," Bastian said slowly, his gaze shifting between those of Drake, Gabriel, and Baltic, the wyverns to whom he felt the closest. "The problem lies in the fact that they wish to join the weyr as a tribe, and not a sept. They wish to retain their autonomy from the laws that govern the seven septs, while at the same time claiming a place at the *sárkány* table, where they have a say in laws that affect us."

"That doesn't seem right," Charity said, shifting a little in her chair as she wrote. "They want a hand in telling you what to do, but it wouldn't apply to them? Can't you simply tell them they have to be a sept, so that the rules apply to them, too?"

"It's not quite that easy," Gabriel told her. "The weyr has a canon, part of which details recognizing its members. Nowhere in the canon, unfortunately, does it state that tribes cannot apply and be made members."

"The word shortsighted comes to mind, but I suspect that's flogging a dead behemoth, huh?" Charity asked.

Drake grimaced. "When the canon was set into place, the tribes were nothing but scattered groups of discontent dragons. It's only been the last century or so that they have banded together and formed cohesive companies."

"Companies that threaten us in more ways than simply demanding a place at the *sárkány* table," Kostya said with dark intent.

Kostya frequently spoke in such a manner, so Bastian ignored the comment, asking, "What concerns me more than the fact that they wish to join the weyr is the *why—why* are they coming to us now? Why, after a century of the tribes having formed, naming themselves and their masters, living in relative peace with the weyr, are they now wishing to be recognized?"

"Could it be something as simple as them feeling bad at leaving their families?" Charity asked.

All the wyverns shook their heads.

"Doubtful," Gabriel said. "Not many silver dragons have left the weyr, but those who left have done so of their own accord, and made it quite clear they did not wish further contact with family members."

"It's the same with the blue dragons that followed Fiat," Bastian said, a little pang of sadness gripping him at the loss of more than half his sept. "They were younger dragons, to be sure, but that they would cut themselves off from kin, and yet now apparently want to return ... no. Something doesn't smell right."

"That is an interesting point," Charity said, now doodling on her paper. "But it all comes back to the fact that this is your wading pool. If you don't want anyone else in it, you can just say no."

"The coda allows dragons to present their case for membership in the weyr assuming they provide a dragon relic," Gabriel reminded her. "Much though we would like to dismiss the request, we are bound by our own laws to give the tribes an opportunity to apply."

"It's a moot point," Kostya said, flicking a paper clip down the length of the table toward Baltic. "They can possess nothing of value, let alone a relic, so we won't have to let them into the weyr."

"Or," Charity said, still drawing on her tablet. Bastian noted she seemed to be sketching the back view of a nude man, one bearing a massive dragon tattoo that wrapped around his torso and thighs. "You could simply change the rules so that they can't get in."

The dragons, to a man, looked shocked at such a thing.

"Change the canon?" Gabriel shook his head.

"It has been in place since the Prague Synod of 1198," Drake told her.

"So?" Charity gave a one-shouldered shrug. "The First Dragon said there was a thingie coming, a … shoot, I don't remember the word. It's when the Otherworld restructures itself."

"Renaissance," Drake and Kostya said together.

"That's it," Charity said, pointing her pen at Drake. "Renaissance. A remaking, the First Dragon said."

"That is for the Otherworld," Constantine said slowly, but his gaze flickered around the table to the other wyverns. "The weyr is technically outside of it, and not bound by its laws."

"That's not quite true," Ysolde said, pursing her lips. "Since the L'au-dela acknowledges me as ambassador to the weyr, we agreed to recognize their laws. We don't have to obey them, but it makes it easier all around if we at least honor them. And in case you were wondering why we made that agreement, Charity, it was just so Dr. Kostich wouldn't stuff me in the Akasha, and continue to call Baltic fat, which we all know is patently untrue. Just look at his belly! He's been working out with Brom, and I swear he has gotten buffer."

Bastian fought back a smile when Ysolde tugged up the front of Baltic's shirt, revealing a bit of his belly.

"Oooh," Aisling said.

Drake snorted fire.

"Very nice," Charity said, a tinge of smugness to her voice. "You take after your father in that regard."

"Will you stop staring at him," Bastian heard Drake whispering furiously to Aisling.

"Jealousy becomes you," she answered, booping the end of his nose.

"My point—Baltic's nice abs aside—is that you guys could simply follow suit like the rest of the Otherworld, and remake your weyr with new laws." Charity sat back, smiling at them all.

Silence descended on the table for half a minute.

"Such a thing is unprecedented, is it not?" Gabriel asked, looking to Drake and Bastian.

"I was born in 1413," Bastian said, then glanced down the table to the green wyvern.

Drake shook his head. "I'm younger than you, so it is before my time, as well. Baltic? Constantine? You were both alive when the Prague Synod was held."

"I was there, but that memory is one that has faded, as have so many others of that time, no doubt due to my resurrection," Constantine said, regret evident as he rubbed his chin. "And Baltic was naught but a babe then."

"I was twelve, but was not allowed to attend," Baltic corrected with obvious disgust. "My mother heeded the First Dragon's desires in keeping me at home, feeling that the tensions between the red dragons and the black sept were too great to risk me attending."

Charity looked like she wanted to say something, but evidently thought better of it, and simply made occasional notes on the discussion that followed.

After twenty-five minutes, Constantine called for order and said, "Then we are agreed that we will first hear what the master of the Chaos Tribe has to say to the weyr, and then we will decide whether or not the situation warrants a new synod, and remaking of the weyr canon. Is it so agreed?"

The wyverns murmured their respective consents, and a *sárkány* was called for the following day, when Amadeus indicated he was available.

"You're welcome to stay here, with us," Aisling told Charity as the dragons arose from the table. "Jim, you may speak again, but only if you don't annoy anyone."

"Geesh," Jim said on a gasp, as if it had been holding its breath the whole time it had been silent. "I really hate when you do that. Like there's anything that I say that could annoy anyone? Hey, Balters, what are you going do to if Big Daddy and Charity give you a little brother? You won't be the golden kid anymore, and—aieee!"

Jim ran out of the room, its tail on fire.

"Ignore it," Aisling said brightly to Charity. "Naturally, I'll make sure it doesn't bother you if you want to stay the night."

"Thank you, but the First Dragon has arranged for me to be … for lack of a better phrase, *picked up* … and returned to the Beyond so that the Venediger doesn't have any grounds for squawking. But I'd like to be here tomorrow, too, if you don't mind," Charity answered, stuffing her notebook into a large bag. "Av—er—the First Dragon is going to love hearing about all this."

"I hope he's well," Aisling said politely, as she escorted Charity to the door.

"Oh yes, just busy. You know how it is with demigods, there's always something to do. Right now he's helping his sister out with a project she has going with some Valkyries. You know that she's Freya, right? The one married to Odin? It's all a bit mind-blowing, but I'm learning to let his illustrious relations roll off me, so to speak."

The mates all left the room, chatting.

Bastian watched as the wyverns followed, until just Drake and Baltic were left.

"I fear there is something behind this request by the Chaos Tribe," Bastian said slowly, wishing he could put a finger on just why he was so uneasy over Amadeus's demand. "Something we don't yet understand."

Drake's left eyebrow rose. "The blue dragons are well-known for their prescience, but could your distress be due to former members of your sept returning in some form to the weyr?"

"No," Bastian said, once again stirring through his emotions. They remained jumbled, unwilling to be separated into tidy stacks. "It goes beyond that. It feels … deeper."

Baltic sighed. "It grieves me to say that I sense the same, but I do. There is a stench about it that reeks of the old times. That is why the First Dragon has sent his mate. She is our warning."

"Of what?" Drake asked as both men watched Baltic.

Bastian may not have liked actions Baltic took in the recent past, but he had a profound respect for his uncanny ability to see what others could not. No doubt it was due to him being one of the Firstborn.

"Who knows? The First Dragon has never been one to reveal his hand, and I doubt if even Charity begging him to do so would result in that. It is merely his way of warning us that we need to be wary, and on guard." Baltic made a face. "I would get Ysolde away, but since our sons are safe at Dauva, she'd have my stones on a platter if I even hinted at such a thought. You, however …"

"Yes," Drake said slowly, pulling out his phone. "I believe you are right. I will send the children to safety in the country before the Chaos Tribe descends upon us tomorrow."

Bastian said nothing, but he thought much as he took his leave.

FIVE
THE APPLICATION

Bastian lay awake, idly watching the shadows cast on his ceiling from the moonlight that streaked in through his opened windows.

"I shouldn't," he told the shadows. "I swore I wouldn't. I am no dream warrior, and thus, I can't be a dream lover."

Thoughts of Phyllida filled his head: her laughing eyes, her freckles, the tangle of long brown curls tipped with honey blond. It had been two nights since he had walked in her dream, and although he'd lectured himself ever since, he couldn't stop thinking about her. Wanting to finish what they'd started, wanting to touch and taste and explore her. Wanting her to do the same to him.

Just wanting her.

He shook his head at the ever-shifting ceiling shadows. "No. That way madness lies. I don't know how I walked in her dream without making a conscious effort to do so, but I will not lose control again. She will have other dreams, ones without me. I will not risk her or my sept for a few moments of pleasure."

Thus nobly martyring himself, he managed to fall asleep for all of fifteen minutes.

Two hours of restless pacing later, he damned himself, and stood outside bathed in the moonlight, clad in nothing but a pair of silk sleeping shorts and an open matching silk robe, the breeze from Paris whipping the material behind him as he grasped the iron balustrade of his hotel room's balcony, clearing his mind of all thoughts but one.

"I've come to tell you that I will not see you again," he said, striding into Phyllida's dreamscape. He stopped and glanced around, listening intently. "That is English being spoken. Where are we? London?"

"Bastian?" Phyllida blinked at him, clearly overcome for a few seconds before she uncurled from where she was hidden behind a stack of cardboard boxes next to a concession stand. "Yes, it's Wembley Stadium. There's a big football game going on right now." She reached out and touched a spot on his collarbone, pressing with two fingers. "What are you doing here in my dreams again? I thought you were part of my libido that wants me to get my jollies in my dreams because my real life is so bleh, but I'm not particularly angsty right now, so what gives? And how did you get here?"

"That is of no matter. I'm here to tell you that despite your attempts to lure me with thoughts of your delicious thighs and belly and breasts that I greatly enjoyed, I will not see you again. Do not attempt to sway me. I have many pressing concerns to take care of, and I cannot allow myself to be distracted by you." He hoped that he looked firm and resolute, but had a horrible suspicion he just looked desperate.

She stared at him with no expression whatsoever for three seconds; then her lips twitched. "No, I can see that you aren't going to let yourself be distracted. Er ... why are you nearly naked?"

He looked down at himself, and at that moment his penis realized that all that stood between it and Phyllida was a thin scrap of silk, causing it to go from quiescent to fully aroused and demanding in what Bastian felt was an impossibly short amount of time. "I was sleeping," he lied. "But you kept enticing me, trying to lure me into joining you. I won't have it, do you hear me? It is unacceptable. You may think all you must do is snap your fingers and I will rush to your side, but you are mistaken."

As he spoke, he helped her out from around the stack of boxes, the warmth of her hand in his stirring his dragon fire until he wanted nothing more than to give in and claim her as his body demanded.

"I didn't snap my fingers," she protested. "I didn't even know you were real. Wait, you can't be. You're just my libido doing an extremely thorough job of finding mind sex."

"Mind sex? You think I am merely mind sex?" He inhaled, simultaneously aghast and aroused. "What is mind sex?"

She laughed, the sound of it delighting him. "It's just what it sounds like—a fantasy my brain came up with because it feels sorry for me."

"A fantasy." He thought about that for a few seconds, then nodded his head. "I will accept that I am your sexual fantasy. However, we have no future together. We can't. I am wyvern. I must remain focused and in control at all times, and I can't do so if you summon me simply because you wish to do sexual things to me. I may not be the smartest dragon in the weyr, but I have learned my lesson."

Her brows pulled together in a little frown that left him wanting to smooth the wrinkles out. He much preferred her laughing than frowning. "So you *are* a dragon. I thought you said you were, but … wait, no. That doesn't make sense. You don't make sense. I didn't summon you. If you're a dragon, then … no. It just doesn't make sense."

"I am a very sensible person. All who know me say so. Which is why I must tell you to stop tormenting me with thoughts of your delicious belly and thighs. I cannot keep coming to you. We are both at risk when I do so." Bastian gave in to the need to hold her, stroking her body and feeling her warmth against him. "Do you like it when I touch you thusly?"

His head dipped to nibble along her neck, the scent of her stirring so many feelings that he knew he should quell, but was unable to do so. One hand swept over her shirt, cupping her breast, his fingers slowly stroking the soft flesh.

"Oh, goddess, yes," she said on a moan, her back arching as she clutched his shoulders, wordlessly demanding more.

"You fill my mind," he admitted, wanting to know what hold she had on him, but at the same time reminding himself that he needed to put her out of his life. "My body aches for you."

"Yeah, all of a sudden, I'm a bit needy, myself," she said, her breath ruffling his hair as she pushed the silk robe from his shoulders, her hands stroking along his chest in a way that was guaranteed to have him hard enough to hew stone. Possibly iron if she kept teasing his nipples. "OK. I wouldn't do this if this was real, but since my brain is determined to get us to hook up, I might as well stop fighting. Um. Can we go somewhere else, though? I'm not crazy about someone running across us, even if this is just all in my mind."

"We can go wherever you desire," he murmured, removing her shirt, and immediately possessing himself of her breasts. They were soft and warm and fit perfectly in his hands. "My hotel bed is reasonably comfortable."

"I just bet it is … oh! Wow. And it's big."

He deliberately pulled them from her dreamscape and into the bedroom of the Paris hotel, pausing at her words. With his hands on her hips, he said in a near growl, "You've seen it before. You've felt it before. It's been inside you. You have nothing to worry about."

"Not your dick, you idiot," she said, laughing even as she buffeted his shoulder. "I was talking about your bed. Although, I have to say that you do look a bit more … impressive … than I remembered. Bastian?"

"Yes?" He had her close enough to the bed that he could simply toss her on it and pounce as his dragon demanded, but he had a feeling that she would have words to say to him if he gave in to his desires.

"Make love to me," she said, her fingers now twined in his hair as she pulled his head down for a kiss. He obliged her, allowing his fire to wrap around them, making the inferno inside of him grow even more intense.

"Do you want to try what we attempted before?" he asked politely, stripping her clothing off and laying her down in the center of the bed, kneeling next to her while he tried to decide which part of her was his favorite.

"No, thank you. That was frustration city because we didn't get to finish. What are you doing?"

"Trying to decide," he said, his eyes narrowed as he studied her body in repose.

"Decide what?" She propped herself up on one elbow, looking down her body, her voice filled with consternation. "Is it my pubic hair? You saw it the other day. I thought you would have noticed that I don't wax. I do try to keep it beat back to an unobjectionable level, however."

"I see nothing wrong with your woman's hair," he said, spending a little extra time admiring that part of her. "I'm merely attempting to make up my mind as to what part of you I like the best. Once I make that decision, then I can ascertain if you enjoy extra attention there, and assuming you do, all will be well."

"All is going to be very far from well if you keep looking at me as if I'm a smorgasbord and you can't decide where to start. Bastian!"

"Hmm?" He pulled his attention from her thighs, paused for a few seconds on her belly and hips, then met her gaze. "You are a feast, so it's only right I should admire you."

"Admiration is good," she said, sitting up before pushing him down onto his back. "So is looking like you are a starving wolf, and I'm a tempting pot roast, but action is even better, and I'd really like to get down to business before my alarm goes off again."

"What alarm?" he asked, his body reacting when she straddled his hips, taking his penis in both her hands.

"The stupid one that Seawright insists on setting so that she can make sure I haven't slipped out during the night. Do you like this?"

She bent to take him into her mouth, but it was too much for him. Far too much.

"Yes," he said, hoisting her upward with an audible popping sound as she released him. "But I am far too close to a climax to stand that. Instead, I will reciprocate, and then—"

"Too much talking, not enough action," she said, positioning him and sinking down with what seemed like a thousand muscles that gripped him in a way intended to drive him to the brink of what he could stand.

He thrust upward, she moved down, and together, they worked up a beautiful rhythm that so consumed him, he wasn't aware that his dragon fire had slipped his control until she leaned down to nip his lower lip.

"You're on fire."

"Only because I'm trying to keep up with the things you're doing to me. Christos, yes, do that rippling thing again."

Somehow, her muscles seemed to flex on him, making him buck wildly into her with short, hard movements.

She arched back for a few seconds, her fingernails digging into his arms, her climax causing her intimate muscles to grip him so tightly he thought he might just die of ecstasy. He gave way to his own orgasm, aware that his body was starting to shift to that of dragon form, but managed to pull back before more than his arms transformed.

Phyllida collapsed down onto his chest, her breath hot and ragged on him as he struggled to get air back into his lungs. Absently, he tamped out the fire that had literally licked up their bodies, his arms wrapped around her, holding her tight.

A surge of protective determination swelled up inside him, a familiar emotion, one he lived with as a caring wyvern, but Phyllida was not a dragon. She was not a member of his sept.

But she could well be a mate, a little voice in his head pointed out.

He shook that thought away. What happened in dreamscapes were often very different from reality. No, interesting as she was, he needed to sever their connection. She might be an enticing, intriguing woman, but he had already risked tragedy by walking twice in her dreams.

He couldn't risk a third time.

He wouldn't risk a third time.

***

"I am master of the Chaos Tribe, and before you all, I claim a place in the weyr as so governed by the Canon of 1189."

Bastian sat at the far end of the table and silently considered the man who strode into Drake's salon.

In order to keep balance in the weyr, it was the custom to rotate through the wyverns as hosts for each *sárkány*, and it just happened to fall to Bastian to run the proceedings with the Chaos Tribe.

A tribe that contained more than seventy former members of his sept.

Amadeus, Bastian noted, had the arrogance natural to all wyverns, but there was a roughness to him, an air of calculated cruelty, that was not normal in the weyr.

"Well?" Amadeus demanded, his dark gray eyes all but spitting ire at the assembled group. "How say you?"

"Amadeus of the Chaos Tribe—" Bastian said, the other wyverns leaving it to him to open the *sárkány* proper, but before he could continue, he was interrupted.

"Deus."

His brows pulled together for a few seconds. "Pardon?"

"Deus." Amadeus made a sharp gesture. "Amadeus is the name I was given by the tribe I was born into. I am now master of the Chaos Tribe, and I go by the name Deus."

"Very well. Deus." Bastian allowed a slight edge into his voice. "You will do well to remember to whom you speak. We are not members of your tribe to whom you can scatter orders. We are wyverns."

Deus scowled. "I know who you are, do not fear. I have too many of your blue dragons happily living amongst my tribe to be in ignorance of the one who drove them to me."

Charity sat to Bastian's left, just as she had done the day before. Bastian heard her suck in her breath—along with Gio, behind him—at the barbed comment. She wrote a word on her notebook and casually slid it an inch or two toward him.

Asshat.

Bastian, ever aware of his more than a little quirky sense of humor, had to thin his lips to keep from smiling. "The makeup of your tribe is of no concern to the weyr," was all he allowed himself to say regarding the blue dragons. "You have asked to present your case for membership, and we are willing to hear it, but do not interpret our manners as weakness. Each wyvern is allowed a voice at the *sárkány* table, and that courtesy has been extended to you today. Do not make us rescind it because of boorish behavior."

"Oh, well done," Charity said under her breath, drawing a happy face in her notebook.

Deus didn't like that, but after sending a fulminating glare around the table, he made an elaborately mocking bow, and said, "I beg your august pardons if my impatience has pricked your respective prides. What you may think of as boorishness is simply my enthusiasm for joining the weyr."

"Why?" Drake asked, his fingers steepled as he watched Deus.

That question clearly took Deus by surprise. "Why do we wish to join the weyr?" he asked.

Drake inclined his head in acknowledgment.

"The weyr has long been held before us as an example of how dragons can live peaceably," Deus said after a minute during which a variety of expressions crossed his face. "Why would we *not* wish to join it?"

Worry stabbed Bastian. Deus's aggressive attitude might be explained away as nervousness or bravado, a misguided attempt to present himself as equal to the wyverns, but what couldn't be explained so easily was the lack of preparation. Why would the tribe come to the *sárkány* without having prepared for even the most basic of questions?

"The weyr is for septs," Kostya pointed out, his jaw set. Next to him, Aoife put a hand on his arm, no doubt reminding him that the wyverns had agreed to treat Deus with the utmost politeness. "If you want a governing organization for you and your tribe, why do you not simply form one of your own?"

Another interesting parade of emotions passed Deus's face: irritation, chagrin, anger, and something that looked remarkably like guile. "The tribes …" He made a vague gesture and started again. "The masters of the tribes have not always been willing to work together. Some are at war. Others stay to themselves. But there are a number of us who see how dragons can work together, how they can become stronger, and we seek that bond."

Bastian had to admit it was a good answer, and one that had the smell of truth to it.

Truth or lie? Charity wrote on her notebook.

Bastian traced the letter *T* on the table, then after a moment's thought added a question mark.

"The weyr was formed not just for septs to take strength, but to bring them together, against foes outside the dragonkin, and those within," Gabriel said slowly, one hand teasing the back of his mate's neck. "If you were to join us, what would your tribe bring to the weyr?"

Deus didn't like that question. Ire flashed in his eyes, but he quickly schooled his face into one that expressed nothing but earnestness. "I would think that was obvious: The bulk of my tribe is made up of former members of the blue sept. They would return to your fold, and could resume ties with family that had been severed."

"Ties that were destroyed by their own hands, not those who remained in the sept," Bastian said with a calmness that did not match the fury that roared to life within him. He suppressed it, clamping down on it with steely resolve. It would take far more than a pushy dragon to make him lose control again.

I don't like him. I don't trust him, Charity wrote. *Do you?*

Bastian hesitated, then made a slight negative gesture.

Deus did not meet his gaze, keeping his attention on Gabriel as he said, "You asked a question, and I answered it. I am not here to debate the placement of blame for the history of your septs."

Aisling, Ysolde, and May all looked very much like they wanted to say something, but they had all promised cooperation in allowing the proceedings to run along much more formal lines than was normal, and leave the questions to the wyverns.

"You are familiar with the canon?" Bastian asked, deciding to let the matter drop.

"I am," Deus said, glancing briefly at him.

"Then you must know that all applications for membership in the weyr are required to show proof of respect to our ancestors, and to the First Dragon, by the possession of a dragon relic."

"That is so," Deus agreed, and reached into his jacket pocket, pulling out a small orange-red silk rectangle. "Knowing this, I have brought my tribe's most valuable item, a ringsel."

The silence that followed that statement was broken only by the whisper of Charity's pen on paper.

What's a ringsel?

Bastian didn't answer her, feeling somewhat stunned.

"A ringsel? You have a ringsel?" Drake asked, glancing at Baltic, who was looking particularly inscrutable.

"How did you get it?" Kostya asked.

"*Where* did you get it?" Constantine asked immediately after.

"Which ringsel?" Bastian felt obligated to ask, still half-doubting that Deus could be speaking the truth.

"I hate to be the only one at the table who is clueless, but what, exactly, *is* a ringsel?" Aisling asked.

The other mates all looked as confused as she did.

No one spoke until Ysolde elbowed Baltic.

He scowled. "Mate, do not continue to poke me in such a manner. I am a wyvern, not a mound of bread dough that must be so attacked."

"Aisling asked a question, and I am one hundred percent certain that you know the answer, so please put us all out of our respective miseries and tell her. *Us.*"

He looked like he wanted to sigh, but instead said simply, "It is a relic of Iceni, the Life Mother."

"Oooh," Aisling said, her brows rising. "That's serious stuff, then, assuming the Life Mother was … er … the goddess who gave birth to the original four dragons?"

"Five," Constantine said, his expression black.

"Ah. Yes. Sorry, five," Aisling murmured, casting him a sympathetic glance.

"The ringsels contained the ashes of the Life Mother," Drake said, his thumb stroking Aisling's fingers. "Next to the shards of the dragon heart, they are the most powerful relics of all dragonkin. It is said that the First Dragon, in order to keep them from being abused, bound them to the twelve hours of the Underworld."

"I believe the locations of only three are known," Constantine said, turning his gaze onto Deus. The latter took a step back. "They remain safe where the First Dragon placed them."

"Which leads us to this ringsel you have," Bastian said, aware that his dragon fire was reacting to the object Amadeus held. Whatever it was, it definitely had an affinity with dragons.

"I would be in my rights to resent the implication that I have stolen this artifact," Deus said, his expression smoothing out to one of apparent ease. "But as that is not the case, I am willing to share the source of the Cantref Ringsel. It was given to the first master of the Chaos Tribe, and thus given to me when I became master."

"Given by whom?" Bastian asked.

"Gil, goddess of the third hour, bestowed it to the Chaos Tribe in repayment of a life debt," Deus answered after a few seconds of silence. A muscle twitched in his jaw. "It has been held in reverence ever since that time. You are the only ones outside of the tribe who have been fortunate enough to be in its presence."

The wyverns all stood as he peeled off the silk wrappings and laid bare a small golden torque inscribed with runes that Bastian did not recognize.

"Ooh, pretty," Aisling said.

"Although none but members of my tribe have been allowed to see it, I will allow you to examine it, in order that you might rest easy about its veracity," Deus said in a voice that reeked with satisfaction.

Bastian wondered about that for a moment.

Is it real? Charity wrote.

"The others may examine it, if they like," Bastian said, retaking his seat even though his fingers itched to touch the precious gold relic. "But I can sense its authenticity from here."

Charity made a face.

"I agree," Gabriel said as the other wyverns sat down. "I can feel its power, untainted and pure. It is no doubt a relic of the Life Mother."

"Then you will accept the Chaos Tribe." Deus made it a statement, not a question, as he wrapped up the relic in its protective silk, and tucked it away in an inside pocket.

Bastian glanced at the other wyverns. He knew what decision he would make about the application, but he had to think of the weyr, rather than his own desires. "The matter is one of importance," he said after a moment's silence. "There is no precedence for a tribe wishing to join the weyr. We will discuss the matter. My guards will escort you to a room where you may wait in peace."

Luca and Gio moved immediately, but Deus, with a curl of his lip, spun around and marched out of the room before the two men could reach him. At a nod from Drake, his two lieutenants followed, no doubt to safeguard the house.

The second the door closed behind them, a cacophony broke out, everyone speaking at the same time, talking over one another, the wyverns demanding to know where the ringsel had come from, and the mates making statements about their impressions of Deus.

Only Charity and Bastian sat silent.

Charity watched the others for a few minutes, her fingers tracing absently on her notebook before she turned to Bastian and asked softly, "What will you do?"

He knew exactly what she was asking—not whether they would allow the Chaos Tribe to join the weyr, but how they would structure the joining. "I will suggest a provisional membership."

"I don't think Deus will like that," she said, her gaze back on her notebook. She underlined the word *asshat*.

"He will not be able to complain if we present it to him as being due to the restructuring of the weyr with the coming renaissance," Bastian answered, dread filling his belly.

She nodded, and returned to watching the others, many of whom were now arguing.

Bastian remained where he was, feeling a weight settle on his shoulders, pulling him down into the earth.

He didn't trust Deus and the blue dragons who had abandoned their kin to follow Fiat, but there was no reason he could give for refusing them access to the weyr. He'd simply have to make sure they did no harm.

His inner self shook his head at the naivete of thinking there was anything he could do to prevent it.

SIX
THE DOUBLE DATE

"Good goddess, you look like complete and utter hell, Phil. Ha! *Hell.* I made a pun. Jord! I punned! Did you hear?"

"Yes, darling, but I thought it much better not to acknowledge it. Phyllida, despite what my uncouth and clearly raised-by-badgers sister says, you look charming. Perfectly charming." The tall, slender man in a maroon Victorian smoking jacket made me a little bow before drifting toward the stairs. Jordan Armstrong always drifted—he was the personification of Victorian homosexual male beauty, all languid grace, richly hued velvet garments, and shoulder-length auburn curls, although considering the fact that I had caught him on three separate occasions ogling my cleavage, I wasn't ready to lay down a wager on his sexual preference.

"Thank you, Jordan," I answered with a pointed look toward the woman who just dropped a massive black-and-white striped bag onto a chair before grinning at me. "I might look like hell, Lin—and yes, I got the pun, hellerune … hell … very punny—but you look as gorgeous as ever. I'd ask you how you do it, but I suspect it's going to be some skin-care regime that is beyond me."

"Bah," she said, leaning in to give me an air-kiss on either cheek before moving over to the windows on the ground floor. "It's just good genes. *Grand-mère* was a sun fairy, and she had the most gorgeous skin you'd ever see. She glowed, positively *glowed.* If you got close enough at night, you could read a book by her glow. So, are you going to wear that?"

I looked down at the pair of yoga pants and T-shirt that I had pulled on that morning. "Do I have a stain somewhere? I could have sworn they were clean when I put them on."

"I meant out. Are you going to wear that out?" She paused before the big dormer window that overlooked a pocket garden, tracing an intricate pattern of symbols that resembled—to my mind, at least—complicated Celtic knots. The symbols glowed golden in the air for a moment before dissolving into nothing. Lin moved over to the next window, each redrawn protection ward leaving me feeling as if I were Jacob Marley obtaining another link of the chain that bound him.

"Out?" I asked, wondering if I shouldn't have Lin and Jordan ward the windows and doors of my cottage more than once a week. Since the renaissance of the Otherworld was almost upon us, wouldn't it be more prudent to have the entrances warded twice a week?

"To lunch? Philly! You didn't forget, did you?" She looked disappointed when it was obvious that I had forgotten. "Our double date. The one we made three weeks ago when I told you that Clarice's brother was going to be visiting her, and he would be just perfect for you, since he's an artist, and you're an art historian, and he's divorced, and you're not seeing anyone."

"Oh, that." A little skittle of fear rippled through me, a sadly familiar sensation. Part of me wanted to protest that there wasn't anyone who interested me other than a blond dream lover, but there was no way I was about to admit that my brain had provided me with what life had denied. It was just too pathetic for words. "I *had* forgotten about our arrangement. Er … maybe now isn't the best time for meeting new people. Could we have the double date another time?"

"Double date?" The light, lilting voice came from the small, dark room that I referred to as the library. "We're having a date? With whom? Why didn't you enter it into the calendar? I've told you and told you that you simply must enter all engagements into the calendar if you expect me to be able to attend."

Lin shot a sour look at the woman who appeared in the doorway. She was short, with a brown pageboy haircut, little round John Lennon glasses, hazel eyes, and very straight eyebrows. She also wore what seemed like a perpetually harassed expression, one I had become quite familiar with in the last two years since she had become my gaoler.

"Phil and I have a double date," Lin said with a sniff. "There's no reason for you to come with us. I'll be with her, so you can take the day off."

Seawright Pendleton pulled herself up to her full height of five foot nothing, and attempted to look down her nose at Lin. "It doesn't work that way, as you well know, because I've personally explained it to you at least fifty-seven times in the last two years, four months, and thirteen days. I am a junior scribe third class. She—" Seawright pointed to me with the stylus she used to write on her ever-present tablet computer. "She is my appointed charge. According to Otherworld Directive 842: *Any person, being, or minor deity deemed dangerous to the Otherworld, and/or the mortal world at large, but not directly subversive or malignant or otherwise considered nefarious, shall be accompanied by a scribe who shall ensure that said person conducts no actions that are in violation of the rules of the L'au-dela Committee herewith.* Which means that where Phyllida goes, so goeth I, up to and including blind dates, not that I hold with that sort of thing."

"You don't date?" Lin asked her before I could stop her.

Seawright squared her shoulders. "I am a junior scribe third class. Junior scribes are always asexual beings so that we might better serve the Committee without pesky libidinous thoughts and desires clouding our ability to do our job."

"Wow," Lin said, shaking her head. "That's some serious fuckery going on right there, but never mind, I suppose if you're going to throw a hissy about coming along on our date, then you'll just have to come with. But for the love of all the sun motes and moonbeams, don't mess this up for Philly. She doesn't have a whole lot of alternatives."

"Gee, thanks," I said drily, sighing to myself that she was absolutely right, my dream would-be lover notwithstanding. Although if he was really Xavier in disguise … I gave a mental headshake at that thought. Despite my initial fear that Xavier had found a new way to torment me, I had a hard time believing my mental lover was him. Bastian felt … warm. Hot, even. And so, so sexy. Whereas Xavier was made up of shadows and smoke and fear.

"Again, as you well know because I've met you once a week for the last one hundred twenty-three weeks, I do not interfere with, hinder, or otherwise influence in any way the life of my subject, unless she undertakes an action that would be in violation of the Otherworld Directives," Seawright said with a self-righteous sniff before turning to me, her stylus poised over the tablet that she wore slung like a bandolier across her chest. "I will let this incident pass without requesting corrective action by the Committee despite the fact that you are, in fact, required to give me twenty-four hours' notice of any and all appointments, meetings, and other forms of assignations outside the secure domicile, but in the future, I must insist that you abide by the rules to which you agreed."

"I was less than three years old when the agreement was signed, and it certainly wasn't by me," I told her, unable to just let her officiousness roll off me as I usually did. Immediately, I felt guilty. It wasn't Seawright's fault that my life sucked so hard. "I apologize if that sounded ruder than I intended. I know you are simply trying to do your job, and given the alternative, I'm grateful that you're here."

She gave me one of her rare, tiny smiles before tapping quickly on the tablet. "We will consider the subject closed, then."

"I don't know how you can be grateful to have someone always dogging your footsteps," Lin commented, moving over to another window. "Although I will admit that Screen-writer Peddleham Jr. is far better than that abomination you had before her."

"I am *Junior Scribe* Seawright Pendleton," my shadow corrected Lin. "I am prepared, in the course of my duties, to be referred to simply as Seawright so as to further the impression by non-Otherworld citizens that ours is a friendship instead of a working relationship, but I must insist you use my proper name."

Ignoring Seawright, I said slowly, "Lin, I think that given the situation, this double date is a bad idea. This isn't a good time for me to go anywhere."

"Of course it's a good time," Lin scoffed, moving to a fourth window before warding the front door. "You're just being your usual antisocial self. Besides, Clarice says Jack will be going to Alaska to see the in-laws—mine, not his—on the weekend, so we only have today and tomorrow. Why don't you pop upstairs and pick out something a little more suited to going to lunch at the Greek Pamplemousse with a hunky artist while I finish up down here?"

"The Greek Pamplemousse?" Seawright asked, tapping quickly on the tablet. "That sounds exotic. Do they provide gluten-free foods? I am very sensitive when it comes to gluten, although in a pinch I can bring my own starch-based products. Merciful codifications! Their prices! Informal wear clearly will not be suitable for this restaurant. I will have to change." She shot me a pointed look before doing an about-face and marching into the library, the door closing behind her louder than normal.

"Tell me you're going to get rid of her," Lin said from where she was ensuring my front door didn't allow anyone of a dark nature into the house.

I made a face, and tried frantically to think of an excuse other than the obvious, which had never impressed Lin, and probably never would. "If I make a fuss about her, they'll just stick me with someone worse. Seawright aside, we're so close to the renaissance that I think it's better to stay put."

"Bah." She waved away my excuse, and headed for the kitchen. "Clarice and I will be there to guard your pristine self against anyone trying to force you to unmake magic. And I suppose if your geeky shadow insists she can't leave you alone, even for a couple of hours, then she can help protect you."

"Seawright is better than a lot of my gaolers, but I honestly doubt if she cares if I live or die so long as I don't give her any trouble. In fact, considering the pained way she's always reciting Otherworld Directives at me, I have the distinct feeling she'd be happier if I was gone and she could move on to someone less troublesome."

Lin gave a one-shouldered shrug. "You're not troublesome. You're just … problematic."

"I know. I always have been," I said, unable to keep from feeling particularly martyred, thinking of Bastian. What had he meant when he said he couldn't visit me? What sort of games was my brain playing with me?

"You know full well I meant your life is problematic, not you personally. And stop fussing—you'll have Clarice and me, so go change, and we can head out as soon as I'm done with the windows and doors. Clarice and Jack are meeting us at the restaurant."

"Lin, I just think—"

She spun around and gave me such a pointed look that I found myself halfway up the stairs before I realized she'd used some of her inherited fey abilities on me. "Drat the sun elves, anyway," I grumbled to myself, feeling all shades of grouchy at the inevitable outing.

"I'd say amen to that, darling, but *Grand-mère's* blood is what lets me do my job without sacrificing demons," Jordan said, emerging from my bedroom, his hands trailing little tendrils of black nothingness that I knew came from drawing banes, another powerful protection symbol.

"For which I'm eternally grateful," I said, pausing, knowing full well I was procrastinating, but I always enjoyed chatting with Jordan, even if he did leave me puzzled about his personal life. "How did you get started doing this?"

"This?" He gestured toward the bathroom door, the black smokelike tendrils evaporating with the movement of his elegant hands. I nodded. "After *Grand-mère* went into the Beyond, we had to do something to make ends meet. This was before Lin met Clarice, you understand."

I nodded again, and propped up one hip on a small half-moon table that sat against the wall.

"It turns out that we just happened to be very adept at drawing wards, so we decided security would be as good a job as any to take up."

"Well, I'm very glad you did go this route," I said, rubbing my arms. "Protecting my house against intrusion by beings both mortal and immortal is the only thing that lets me sleep at night."

Not that sleeping brought me any comfort, or even relief.

Especially when it came to Bastian and his delicious body, which even now I craved.

"We always aim to serve all our customers, but we both take particular care of you," he said with a little smile that might have been amorous in nature.

I studied him for a moment, unsure if he was flirting, or if I was so desperate for romantic contact with Bastian that I misinterpreted Jordan's quirky personality. "Er … thank you."

"Darling, much as I love chatting with you, if you don't move, I won't be able to get to that octagon window," he gently chided me, causing me to hurry forward until I stood at the threshold of my room.

"Oh, sorry. I was just … er …"

"Fascinated with me?" he asked in his usual light, slightly drawled tone. Once again, I stared silently at him, unsure of what he was implying.

"Doing as your sister compelled," I said after a few seconds' struggle. In the end, it didn't matter whether Jordan was flirting with me or not—I wasn't in the market for a man, no matter how empty my nights were.

Nights that were too often filled with terror, the result of loneliness that was irrevocably etched into my life.

If only my brain would send Bastian my way again. He had a way of banishing both fear and loneliness.

"What—oh, the big lunch date. You'd best get ready, then, hadn't you?" Jordan turned his back to me in order to draw complicated symbols, using a dark power to manifest a layer of protection across the large octagon window.

"Against my better judgment, yes," I told his back, and retreated to my bedroom to consider the contents of my closet.

Fifteen minutes later, I trotted down the stairs to find Jordan standing before one of my floor-to-ceiling bookcases, the pride of my booklover's heart, his hands clasped behind him as he hummed softly to himself. "I see you have a copy of the *Pretiosissimum Donum Dei* in English, but it doesn't look at all similar to the one in the British Library. Is this a different translation?"

"Yes, my godmother sent it to me. It's not a commonly known version. I suppose one of these days I should share the translation." I did a twirl for Lin, who was texting a message on her phone. "Suitable enough for the Greek Pamplemousse?"

"Adorably so," she said, putting away her phone. "Jack is going to fall head over tits for you."

"I hope not, for a variety of reasons, but mostly because I hope he doesn't have anything but the most manly of breasts." I raised my voice and directed it toward the closed door to the library. "Seawright! If you're coming with us, you'd better shake a leg. We're ready to go."

"Your godmoth—ah. The former Venediger." Jordan, who had been about to reach for the *Donum Dei*—a fifteenth-century alchemical text—snatched his hand back as if it had been made of hellfire. "Just so."

A muffled explosion of oaths drifted out from the library, followed by what sounded like several large trunks being moved.

I sighed. "My gaoler is clearly having wardrobe issues and is going to take a few minutes. I'll follow you to the restaurant, if you don't mind," I told Lin, who'd moved over to take the book and flip through a few of the pages.

"It's no problem to take you and the pedantic one with me," she said, her eyebrows rising at a page before she hastily slipped the book back onto its shelf.

"I don't want to make you late," I said before turning and bellowing, "Seawright! I'm walking out of this door in thirty seconds. Honestly," I added in a more reasonable volume to Lin, "I like driving. It's not an imposition at all."

"You may like driving, but you get nervy when you go out," she pointed out when the door opened behind me, and Seawright appeared in a short maroon dress that ended midthigh, with a square neck and a formfitting bodice. She also wore black-and-white striped tights, a pair of Mary Janes, and what looked like a matador's hat on her smooth bob.

I stared at her for a moment.

"I'm ready. It just took me a bit of time to find my good hat. I hope we are traveling separately. The Committee frowns on hellerunes traveling in groups of more than three people."

"Considering there are only two hellerunes on the planet at any one time, I don't see how they can be worried about us grouping up," I said, deliberately misinterpreting her.

Her brows pulled together. "According to the Concordance of Constantinople 1423, a hellerune '*shall have full and entire liberty to propound and direct her life as fitting and proper, in each and every circumstance save those carried out within the circle of beings both immortal and mortal, should the number of that circle be greater than three, lest the hellerune be likewise free to carry out acts of unmaking.*' Which I pretty much think says it all."

This was the payback for trying to play verbal games with her, I realized. "Do you have a photographic memory or something that allows you to remember all those bizarre and seriously annoying directives?"

"Yes. I'll pilot the car," she said simply, and walked out the door.

"Not until you get a proper driver's license you won't. No, that one was given to you in 1924. Traffic laws have changed since then. Seawright, please!" I sighed to myself. "This is going to be a different sort of day than I envisioned when I woke up. You guys ready?"

Lin and Jordan followed when I went to the door. They were still engaged in a quiet conversation, but when I paused to lock the door behind me, I heard Lin whisper to her brother, "Who's her godmother? That book was seriously tinged with dark power."

"A powerful mage who died a few years back. Killed by a demon lord."

"Ouch." Lin lifted her voice as she noticed me moving over toward my car, saying loud enough for me to hear, "Are you sure you don't want to ride with me, Concordance of Constantinople notwithstanding? I don't want you arriving stressed because someone looked at you while you were at a stoplight."

Jordan, with a languid wave, rode off on the motorbike that was oddly anachronistic with his smoking jacket and general air of having been best buddies with Oscar Wilde.

"I'm not quite that bad," I said, smacking her lightly on the arm before pointing at Seawright, who, with an exaggerated sigh, got out from behind the steering wheel and moved over to the passenger seat.

"This from the woman who now has her groceries delivered to her porch because she said someone tried to kidnap her in the dairy department of the local store," Lin pointed out.

I made a face. "I've told you more than once that the employee who almost kidnapped me was up to no good. I'd seen him putting expired yogurt in the front of the dairy case."

"Does yogurt expire?" she asked, her nose wrinkling in an adorable manner that I would never be able to achieve. "I thought all that good bacteria in it kept it from going bad."

"It has to go past its prime at some point in time." I took a quick look around my tiny yard, then the street. No one was lurking suspiciously behind convenient trees, cars, or the one-fifth-sized replica windmill that my neighbor insisted on decorating for whatever season was upon us. Right now it sported a family of plastic ducks with yellow slickers and nor'easter hats, each duckling bearing a bright pink polka-dot umbrella. "Everything does."

"You don't," Lin said, flashing another smile before getting in her car.

I made another face and followed suit, taking pleasure in my little VW Bug even if it did contain Seawright, now typing madly on her tablet. It might be a small car, but it felt like a protective shell around me while I followed Lin to the restaurant a few miles from my house. "Kind of a traveling suit of armor," I murmured, giving the car a fond pat.

"Suits of armor are, for the most part, very uncomfortable. They pinch and can cause chafing," Seawright murmured, reading something on her tablet.

I digested that for a minute. "Sometimes I forget just how old you are, not that I knew they made suits of armor for women."

"I wasn't always female," she replied, her attention still on the tablet.

It was on the tip of my tongue to say that explained a lot, but instead, I turned on the radio, and enjoyed the pleasure of going out in public. It wasn't often I had the opportunity to see the small town in which I lived, and notice all the little changes that had been made since the last time I'd left home. All too soon, I turned into the parking lot of a low, vaguely Mediterranean-themed building.

"Coast is clear," Lin told me when I got out, putting an arm around my waist in what I knew was a gesture of support. "Just to be sure, I warded the restaurant two days ago."

"That was very thoughtful of you," I answered, a sudden wave of panic washing over me. The pattern was always the same—at first I was excited to be out and mingling with others, but after a few minutes, nerves got the better of me, and I wanted nothing more than to race home and close out everyone. It took a few moments, but at last I reminded myself that it was ridiculous to be suspicious of everyone just because one man existed who felt entitled to cause destruction and suffering. "I appreciate you going to all that trouble for me."

"Naturally, I would have seen to the protection of the restaurant had I been told about this visit," Seawright told me in a voice tinged with both annoyance and affront. "I must point out for the fifteenth time this year that the directives set down by the Committee are not negotiable, and as such—"

"Yeah, yeah, heard the lecture, got the T-shirt," Lin said, pushing past us to wave at the front of the restaurant. "There they are. Clarice, love, you are not going to believe it—Phil has a *Pretiosissimum Donum Dei.*"

A tall, elegant woman who, like myself, was of mixed ethnicities rose to greet us when we entered the restaurant. She had a lovely warm-brown skin tone, bright gray eyes that always seemed to be smiling, and a halo of black curls that made me profoundly jealous. "How very interesting. Hello, Phyllida. And I see you have your protector with you. It's a pleasure to see you again, Seawright. May I introduce my brother Jack? He's visiting for a few days before going to see our parents in Alaska."

"You may," Seawright said, leveling Clarice with a stern eye, "although to avoid any uncomfortable expectations, I will state that I am not currently engaging any lovers. As a junior scribe—"

"Third class," Lin murmured sotto voce.

"—I am not allowed to engage in sexual shenanigans or take a lover, although I am permitted to write love poetry and prose in my spare time," Seawright continued. "To date, I have completed three novels with an asexual female protagonist who finds happiness with an equally asexual male, after much soul-searching, and consultations with pertinent members of influence in each character's life. I hope that someday the novels will find favor and be published."

Jack gave Seawright a wide-eyed look that he slid over to his sister before murmuring a polite greeting. "Er … indeed. I'm afraid I know nothing about books. I'm an artist, you see."

"So was my male protagonist." Seawright stared at him without blinking behind her little glasses. "A sculptor, in fact. He liked to make phalluses out of genital-friendly probiotic material that encouraged healthy flora in the appropriate female parts."

Jack looked even more startled.

I sighed an inner sigh this time, just to shake up my habit of sighing out loud whenever Seawright was around, then gave Jack an apologetic smile when I shook his hand. "It's a pleasure to meet you. Please excuse my friend; she is a little eccentric. Clarice, you look as lovely as ever. How nice of you to invite us to lunch."

Since the restaurant was packed, we were obliged to remain in the waiting area and exchange polite chitchat. Several people cast curious glances at Seawright, but she blithely ignored the attention to focus on her tablet. I sat next to her, uncomfortably aware that the restaurant was doing a booming lunchtime business, with people streaming in and out of the building. I felt like I had a target on my back, and it was only a matter of time before someone took aim at me.

"And you're an art restorer? Do you paint, as well?" Jack asked after a few minutes, his face as open as his sister's, although his eyes were more hazel than gray. He seemed like a perfectly nice man, intelligent, interesting, and polite, and yet I was too distracted to pay him much attention. I glanced around the room, wondering at the sensation that continued to make me feel nervous. Was something wrong there that had pinged my inner alarms, or was I just being overly paranoid? I rubbed at the back of my neck and tried to focus on the conversation with Jack.

"I do some restoration, but am not an artist," I explained. "I prefer to handle the cleaning and physical restoration, and let others do any necessary artistic touch-ups."

"And you?" Jack asked Seawright politely. "Do you write full-time?"

"I believe I mentioned that I was a junior scribe just a few minutes ago," Seawright answered after giving him a long, considering look. "Do you have short-term memory problems? If so, I will preface all comments to you with reminders of subjects we've already discussed."

"Er … no, I don't." Jack cleared his throat, obviously ill at ease.

I took pity on him, aware of a breeze swirling behind me when a couple of people entered the restaurant and paused at the now-full waiting area. Since Jack—although mortal—knew there were other beings in existence, I gave him a short overview. "A scribe is what people who are set to watch others are called, because in the course of their duties they take copious notes. Seawright has been assigned to me mostly to act as an arbiter of magic."

I swear Jack's eyes glazed over. I gave his hand a quick pat before adding, "She is for lack of a better word my gaoler. She keeps me from doing anything I'm not supposed to do."

"Because you're some sort of a magic breaker? How does she keep you from doing that?" Jack asked softly. I had the feeling he wanted to run away, which just made me heave another mental sigh. What was I up to? Four sighs for the day? Five?

"Hellerunes aren't really breakers of magic—we just convert it. But that detail doesn't matter—just think of Seawright as being here to make sure that no converting goes down." The fine hairs on the back of my neck prickled at the same time my peripheral vision caught the flicker of two men. They were heading away from me down a side hallway, one that clearly led to restrooms. Absently, I noted that both men were tall and blond, one with hair down to his shoulders, the other with strands of dark amber hair swept back in a style that reminded me of men in 1930s movies.

Something about that hair seemed familiar.

"What does it convert into?"

I frowned at the men, still rubbing my neck, wondering why my inner warning system was going off so strongly.

"Danger." Seawright set down her tablet to answer. "I monitor Phyllida and ensure that if she uses some of the limited power the Otherworld allows her to have—uses it in a manner not specified by the contract she signed—the Committee is immediately informed so that they can lock her away as is right and proper."

"Er … " Jack said, shifting enough that he blocked the sight of the men heading into the hallway. I tried to peer over his shoulder, wanting to pinpoint just what had me so uneasy. I dug through my memory, but I had no male acquaintances who were blond.

Except, of course, the sexy man in my dreams.

I gave yet another mental headshake. That was just something my frustrated body and mind did when I was asleep.

"Hellerunes are the most dangerous beings in existence," Seawright added in another blithe comment before picking up her tablet again. "Personally, I don't think they should be allowed to exist, but four hundred and thirty-one years ago, it was decided not to put hellerunes to death when they were born, and instead allow them to live in captivity."

Their conversation dimmed into muffled white noise while I looked between Jack and Clarice toward the hallway beyond them. At last I caught a glimpse of the two men. The one with the familiar hair paused and scanned the restaurant. Even across the restaurant, I could see the blue of his eyes—a startlingly pure blue.

I stepped back, my breath caught in my throat, feeling as if I'd been struck.

Jack turned to his sister, blocking my view of the man, and when I shifted to the side, he was gone, obviously having disappeared down the hallway.

I wondered for a second if I wasn't having a very realistic dream. Why else would I see Bastian? A real-life version of him, not the dream lover. No, it couldn't be him. I rubbed my temples, panic rising in me as I tried to resolve the two disparate images—the man my brain conjured up, and the real, live person, exactly as I'd pictured him.

"—had to accept the position, of course, since I live to serve the Committee, but you can imagine how onerous a job it is keeping Phyllida under the strictest of controls. And then there are others who want her. Or rather, the three percent of the magic she retains. It's why we don't go out much. It's quite, quite dangerous for her to be in public like this, which is one of the seventeen reasons why she is supposed to schedule outings with me in advance. I mean, anything could happen without precautions being taken. Mortals like you could die. What sort of art do you make if you don't sculpt?"

I glanced back at them to note that Jack looked dazed about the eyes, but I had little attention to spend on the effect Seawright was having on him.

I had to find out if the man I'd glimpsed was Bastian. I had to know if he was real, or if I'd completely lost all hold on sanity.

I had to find out what was going on.

"—did a year in Paris, which I know is so stereotypical for artists, but when you wish to worship at the feet of the Postimpressionists, that's the place to go. After that, I went back to Austin, and have lived there ever since. So, that's the story of my life in a nutshell. How about you, Phyllida?"

I blinked at Jack a couple of times before reminding myself that I was supposed to be paying attention to him. And it was at that moment I realized that although he was a perfectly nice, normal man, we would have no future together.

He was mortal, and I was not.

He had a future. I had mere existence.

He was not a sexy blond Italian who had a way of touching me—even if it was just in my dreams—that thinking about it made my temperature go up at least five degrees.

"That's so interesting," I said with a bright smile I didn't in the least feel. "I would love to talk to you about your time in Paris—I've only been once, to attend the funeral of my godmother—but if you would excuse me a moment, I need to visit the ladies' room."

"She has irritating bladder syndrome," Seawright told Jack in what she mistakenly assumed was a confidential tone, and prepared to rise.

I waved her back. "I do not have irritable bladder syndrome, and thank you, I'm able to use the bathroom by myself. You can stay here and watch who comes in."

Seawright, who was about to protest, sat back down and nodded briskly. "Very well, but do not attempt to escape. I had another subject who vanished from a ladies' room, and I will not fall for that sort of misbehavior again. It is against three separate Otherworld Directives, as you well know."

"It should only be a few more minutes before our table is ready," Lin added, clearly having seen me slip away and head for the hallway where I'd last seen the Bastian look-alike.

I lifted a hand to indicate I heard, all the while lecturing under my breath, "What on earth do you think you're doing? Chasing after some stranger like this … it's not Bastian. He's made-up, not real. OK, maybe you saw a picture of someone who looked like him, and your brain has chosen that image to use for your smutty fantasies, but that doesn't mean this man is him. And if he is, that means he's Xavier in disguise, because no other dragon can walk in dreams like that. You should be running in the opposite direction, not putting yourself in a position where—*unf!*"

I rounded a corner at the end of the hallway and slammed up into a warm, solid form that was speaking in Italian. "—is there no one else we can call to track her? She has to be somewhere around—"

"Mille scuse," I murmured automatically, backing up when the man I'd run into turned around, surprise and anger quickly fading to an expression that was outright stunned. "Sorry. I didn't know you were there. Er … this is going to sound crazy, but do I know you?"

"Phyllida?" He studied my face for a moment, his sapphire gaze seeming to sear its way down to my soul. A lock of his hair had fallen forward onto his forehead. For a moment, I felt breathless, as if time itself had stopped. My fingers itched to push back that lock of hair, to slide my fingers through the rich amber gold of it, but before I could tell myself to stop being so ridiculous, the world seemed to shift back into place.

"Bastian," I said softly on a breath, joy flooding every morsel of my being until I realized what that meant. "Holy shit, you're real." I turned around to bolt, desperate to get away.

If Bastian was a living, breathing person, then I was in danger.

Heart-pumping, blood-surging, world-ending danger.

SEVEN
THE MAN WITH BLUE EYES

"Phyllida!" Bastian grabbed my arm, keeping me from dashing away. "What are you doing here? It *is* you, yes?"

Fear gripped me, and for a moment, my fight-or-flight instinct decided that fighting was an awfully good idea. If I screamed, Seawright and the others would come running, and I would be safe, protected from whatever heinous pretense Xavier was trying to pull on me.

But as Bastian held my upper arm, a scent teased my awareness, a warm, sexy scent, like a summer afternoon in an alpine field.

Xavier never smelled like a field, alpine or otherwise.

I peered into Bastian's gorgeous eyes, desperately trying to find traces of the cunning that never seemed to leave Xavier's face, but there was nothing there but surprise … and pleasure.

Warmth washed up from my chest, heating my cheeks as I said softly, "You're hurting me."

Instantly, his grip on my arm relaxed, his fingers now caressing my flesh. "I did not expect to find you here. I was going to hunt for you, yes, but to find you here—" He stopped, an odd mixture of emotions visible, dismay chasing the pleasure that had so warmed me, followed by a flat, cold look that I recognized as suspicion. "What is it you are doing here?"

"I live in this town." The words were out even before I realized how stupid it was to give away my location. But if he wasn't Xavier, then … "You're a dream walker."

His hand dropped as he took a step back, almost as if I'd struck him. At the same time, his expression went blank, totally blank.

"But you can't be," I continued, shaking my head. The other blond man with him stood watching us, silent. I cast him a quick glance, but his expression told me nothing. "You're a dragon, and Xavier said he was the only dragon who could dream walk. There were no others, no one who could save me."

"Save you?" Bastian repeated the words, then stiffened. "You don't deny that you sought me out? That you called me to you and attempted to seduce me? You wanted me to protect you?"

Yes! Yes, protect me from Xavier! my brain yelled, startling me with the intensity of emotion that followed the words, a heady cocktail of lust, loneliness, and, oddly, a feeling of security. Instead of throwing myself on his chest—of which vivid details remained locked in my mind—I backed up a step. "I didn't seek you out. I didn't even know you were real, because you can't be real. That is, you can't be a dragon and a dream walker. And yet … you *are* a dragon, aren't you?"

"Bastian is wyvern of the blue sept," the other man said stiffly. I had a feeling he wanted to say more, but he bit back whatever it was.

I rubbed my forehead, as if that would make thinking any easier.

It didn't.

"And you're not … you don't know …" I stopped, and got a grip on my errant emotions. There wasn't the feeling of Xavier around Bastian. I needed to move past the suspicion that he was somehow my tormentor in disguise, and deal with the situation before me. "I'm sorry that you think I've tried to seduce you, but I will point out that if you are indeed a dream walker, then you invaded my dreams, and not vice versa. So if anyone has a complaint about the fact that you rubbed your stubbly cheeks all over the underside of my boobs, and flaunted your chest and thighs at me until I couldn't help but touch them, driving me insane with really smutty thoughts about biting your butt, and touching all your dangly parts, and even rubbing my cheeks on you … er … I lost the point I was trying to make. Oh! If anyone has the right to complain, it is me, the dreamer, not you, the walker. So you can stop accusing me of trying to seduce you, when it was you who marched into my nonexistent Italian flower shop and seduced me."

I stopped, panting just a little, both at the run-on speech and at the memory of all the things that Bastian had done, and what I had wanted to do to him.

"There is another who visits your dreams?" Bastian asked, his gaze now wary. "You entertain others?"

The laugh that erupted from my lips was short and harsh. "Entertain? No. Stalked, yes. By a dragon, as a matter of fact." I hesitated a second, remembering something Xavier had once said. "Well, he used to be a dragon."

"This lover, this Xavier you mentioned?" Bastian took a step closer to me, his eyes blazing with a strange light. I couldn't help but notice a little spurt of flames around his feet.

"He was my lover at one time, yes," I said, wondering why on earth I was telling something so intimate to a man I had effectively just met. "But it did not take me long to realize he was not interested in me romantically, and instead became my stalker, tormenting me in my dreams."

"And this is why you seek my protection," Bastian said, giving a sharp shake of his head. "I told you before that I cannot risk my sept. Not for you, not for anyone. You will release me from your hold."

I glanced down at my hands. "I'm not touching you."

"Your hold on my mind. You will stop calling me to you in your dreams." He tipped his head back ever so slightly, like he wanted to look down his nose at me, but stopped himself in time. "You will cease enticing me. I do not find this sense of mystery with which you wrap yourself intriguing at all. I cannot protect you. I cannot save you. You will forget I am a dream warrior."

"Dream ... what?" I stared in the sort of confusion that came from absolute ignorance.

For a second, he looked horrified; then quickly, the expression faded to one of resolution. "I am not your savior."

I felt oddly hurt by that statement, so bald and clear. And yet, what had I expected? That the dream lover who turned out to be real would rush to my side and protect me from Xavier's torments?

Yes, the little voice in my head said on a sob. *Yes, I need help. I need someone. I need hope.*

"Fine," was what I said, ignoring the despair and emptiness that once again filled me. "I'm not a weak little Gothic romance heroine who needs a big strong man to save her."

Although that sure would be nice. Especially if he was blond and had a chest that made me drool, and thighs that had my hands tingling with a need to touch them.

"Good," he said, giving a quick nod. "Because I am not that man."

"Fine," I repeated, raising my chin to show him that I, too, could adopt a haughty mien. "I'll take care of my own problems, and you take care of yours. I hope you find whoever you're looking for."

I made it two steps down the hallway before a hand was on my arm again, this time spinning me around to face two narrowed, suspicion-filled dark blue eyes.

"How do you know I am looking for someone?" Bastian asked in Italian. Behind him, his buddy loomed, a menacing expression on his face, as well. "Are you the messenger? Are you with Deus?"

"No," I said, wriggling my arm from his grip. He let me back up, although he fairly dripped with a sense of coiled power on the verge of being released. "I don't know anyone named Deus, nor do I know anything about a message."

"Who are you?" he asked, his gaze once again searing me.

"You know who I am," I answered just as his cohort's phone played a brief tune. "I'm no one. That is, I'm someone. I'm a person, and I have value. I'm just … well, me. Phyllida. And I heard you say something about finding a person before I bumped into you. That's all."

"And yet you called to me, pulling me to your dream," he said slowly.

His light brown eyebrows pulled together as he was clearly about to say something more, but his buddy stopped him by holding out his phone.

"He insists on speaking only to you," he said in Italian.

Without taking his eyes off me, Bastian took the phone. "Bastian Blu. Yes. We can meet you if you are sure."

I started to edge away, determined to salvage my tattered pride and remove myself from the presence of the sexy, but somewhat annoying, Bastian and return to the safety of my friends.

Except there was no comfort to be had there.

To my surprise, Bastian took my chin between his thumb and forefinger, and tipped my head up slightly to gaze down into my eyes. I was so startled that for a moment I just stood there and let him.

"This must stop," he said, leaning close enough that his lips fluttered against mine when he spoke. "I cannot tolerate this need I have for you. Later, when I am not distracted. Then I will pay homage to your body as you deserve. But I can't save you. I won't be responsible for more deaths, more failure, more madness."

Gently, I bit his lower lip, then moved backward out of his grip. "I don't know why you feel it so necessary to emphasize the fact that you don't want to help me, but it's fine. I'm fine. Everything's fine. I don't need you."

He gave me a long, long look that basically laid my lies bare, but said nothing, just moved past me, his friend on his heels.

I sagged against the wall when both men left, feeling as if all the air in the restaurant had suddenly been sucked out in Bastian's wake.

What on earth was I thinking exposing myself to a stranger like that? "Of all the stupid, foolish, foolhardy acts. Anything could have happened! Haven't you learned?" I shook my head at my own inexplicable actions before returning to the main room of the restaurant.

An hour and a half later, I hugged Lin and Clarice, and offered my hand to Jack, who gravely shook it. "Thanks so much for a wonderful lunch. I'm so sorry about Seawright insisting on telling you how one goes about skinning a behemoth, and hope you get to enjoy your doggie bag lunch later, after your stomach settles down. Lin, I'll see you next week, yes? Remind me then that I want to talk to you and Jordan about coming out twice a week instead of just once. Ready, Seawright? Good-bye, all."

I was well aware of Lin's pointed look when she murmured her own good-byes, but I couldn't remain behind to placate her. The itchy feeling I'd attributed to the sexy Bastian had continued even after he'd left the restaurant, the sensation ramping up until I found it difficult to sit still.

"I think that went well, given that you did not conform to the rules and alert me ahead of time of our outing," Seawright said in a voice close to satisfaction. "Your date was a very interesting man, despite being mortal, and not at all conversant with sculpture. I wouldn't mind seeing him again, so if you would like to set up further dates, I will have no objections."

"Gee, thanks for the permission," I said, torn between wanting to laugh and cry. We got into the car, and after I made sure there was no one in the parking lot who had designs on me, I started the engine. "I doubt, however, if Jack feels the same way."

"Possibly," she said, typing on her tablet. I glanced over and saw the heading SUBJECT PHYLLIDA BLIND DATE WITH MORTAL and decided I didn't want to know what sorts of notes she was taking. She glanced up to ask, "Is something wrong with your nether region? Is your irritating bladder syndrome bothering you?"

"What?" I took the opportunity of being stopped for a light to glance over at her. "My nether bits are just fine, thank you very much, and I've told you that there is no such thing as irritating bladder syndrome, nor do I have a UTI, which I suspect would be your next question. Why on earth would you ask that?"

"You were positively squirming in your chair the entire time," she answered, complacent as ever.

I was silent for a moment, but I had such little contact with others, I couldn't help but blurt out, "Do you know anyone by the name of Bastian Blue?"

"Blue like the color?" She shook her head. "Should I?"

"No. I don't know. It is an odd name, isn't it? I wonder what he was looking for?"

Seawright paused to give me a long, questioning look. "Who is this Bastian? Someone you met online? Have you made an assignation with him, about which you haven't told me? Otherworld Directive number 788 says—"

"I don't care what it says, and no, I have not made any assignations. Bastian Blue was outside the bathroom at the restaurant—ack! Seawright!" The last was in response to her grabbing the steering wheel and jerking it so that we careened into a parking lot for a tire repair place. I fishtailed a little on the wet pavement, but managed to get us into a parking spot safely so that I could put the car in park before turning on her. "What the hell?"

"You went to meet a man?" She positively snorted with outrage, her fingers typing madly on the screen of the tablet. "This is a grave offense indeed! I am willing to overlook the situation with the blind date, but to use me in this way—I know our relationship is official and not personal, but it still is hurtful that you could deliberately use me in order to meet secretively with a man. What sort of magic did he ask you to unmake? How many illegal acts did you perform? How much dark magic did you release?"

"I did nothing," I answered, my heart beating wildly in the aftermath of adrenaline. "I didn't break any magic, nor do any other act considered illegal by the Committee."

She glared at me. I lifted my hands and repeated, "I didn't break magic. I don't even know why you're asking, since you'd know if I did."

Her frown slowly faded as she stopped typing. "That's true, I would. If you did not go behind my back to meet a man and perform magic, then why were you so nervous that you could hardly sit still?"

"I wasn't nervous, not in that way," I said, relaxing back into my seat, my heart rate slowing bit by bit. "I wasn't on edge because I was guilty over doing something wrong, but because something there was … not right."

The suspicion in her face was tinged with thoughtfulness as she chewed that over. "I did not sense anything amiss, but I am not gifted in that area. Still, this is what comes from circumventing proper rules and dictates. Anything could have happened, and all because you did not schedule the date in the proper method, so that due care could be taken at the location."

"I know, I know, and I'm sorry. I forgot about the whole thing," I answered, rubbing the back of my neck.

"Was it the blue man who made you nervous?" She tapped on the tablet. "He could be a troll. They are often blue."

"No, I don't think it was him. The feeling remained after he left." My nerves once again calm, I pulled back out into traffic.

"Otherworld Directive 9921/C/2 as stated in the contract which you signed specifically states that any and all threats must be recounted to your scribe at the earliest available time," she said, her attention focused on the tablet. "Please remember that."

I wanted to point out yet again that I hadn't breached my

contract with the Otherworld, because I had never agreed to one, but it was a moot point, and we both knew it.

The memory of the intensity of Bastian's gaze, and his lips brushing mine, remained for many hours afterward.

To my regret, he held true to this words and didn't visit my dreams that night.

I was still thinking about him the following day, when I stood gazing through the rivulets that streaked down the window. This part of Oregon received more than its fair share of rainfall, leaving everything lush and green, but prone to sogginess.

"And that's how I feel," I said to no one, my spirits as damp as the minute garden outside. The fact that I was so down irritated me, causing me to go into self-lecture time. "Come on, Phyllida—snap out of it. So you met a handsome man and he wanted no part of you. So you can't go out without feeling itchy and worried and anxious. It's just a few days until the renaissance, and then things will be kick-started and you can go back to your normal life. And what a depressing thought that is."

"I thought you liked a quiet life? Your biographical data stated that you were an introvert by nature, not just by circumstance. Was that incorrect? I am happy to edit the information if something is not right," Seawright asked, entering the kitchen, where I was enjoying my pity party. "I, myself, prefer a lifestyle that isn't quite so shut-in, but I understand the threats that face you every time you step past the protections woven into your house. Perhaps you need more exercise? I have heard that there are machines that one can use to emulate the riding of a bicycle. Would you like me to look into that for you?"

"I don't need an exercise bike, thanks," I answered, and tried to rally my sodden spirits.

The rally fizzled out due to lack of interest.

"As you like. Your phone is ringing," Seawright said in what I was certain she thought of as a helpful tone.

"Where would I be without you?" I murmured, pulling out my phone. Normally, I didn't answer calls when the number was unknown to me, but a desperate hope that it might somehow be Bastian calling drove me to answer when my phone burbled a bit of Vivaldi at me.

"Phyllida?" My hopes rose at my name, then instantly crashed to the floor when I realized it was a woman who spoke it, a woman whose voice was so breathless I couldn't identify her.

"I shall go file the weekly report," Seawright informed me, taking a cup of tea from the microwave. "And update the calendar retroactively for yesterday's lunch."

"Yes, I'm Phyllida," I answered the caller, closing the kitchen door so Seawright wouldn't overhear. "Who's this?"

"It's me. Sandy. I need help. I'm in a bad situation, and you're the only one who can get me out of it. Are you at home? Can you get away? Oh, goddess, I hope so, because I don't think I'm going to get the opportunity to call again."

"Sandy?" I sat down suddenly on a hard wooden chair, not expecting that the unknown caller was my former roommate. "What's going on? I haven't heard from you for … it must be going on three years now. Where are you? What's the bad situation? Are you OK?"

"Not really, no," she said in the same breathless, hushed tone. "That is, I'm fine right now, but if you don't help me get out of here … well, I don't know what the dragon is going to do, but it won't be pretty."

"Dragon?" I shook my head, wondering why all of a sudden my world was filled with them. Until Bastian, I'd had little dealings with any dragons.

Except one.

I pushed down the fear that chased that thought, and focused my attention on a knot in the wooden floor. "How did you get mixed up with them?"

"Customer," she said hurriedly, her voice dropping until it was almost inaudible. "Please, please say you'll help me. I'm trapped at the dragon's camp, and I can't get through the magic binding the doors of the cabin. I'll be lost if you don't say you will help me get out."

"Of course I'll help you," I said automatically, my inner self recoiling at the idea of leaving my safe haven again.

"Really? You don't sound sure," she said in a whisper that made the fine hairs on the back of my neck rise.

"You know me," I said, wanting desperately to explain, but at the same time hide away from what she was asking. I swallowed hard, hating the apologetic tone in my voice. "If I sound reluctant, it's not because I don't want to help you—far from it, given the debt I owe you—but … well, you know who I am, and what the dragons would do if they found out about me. What is it you need, exactly? To get away from a bad customer? I'm sure I could hire someone to do a little knee breaking if needed."

"No, it has to be you, don't you see?" Her voice was tinged with fear, enough that it stirred my own, like seeking like. "There's magic everywhere. Binding wards and banes and goddess alone knows what else."

"If there's just magic on the doors and windows, perhaps someone could chop down a wall or something," I suggested, trying to keep panic from choking me. "I can hire someone big and strong who can help you. A handyman or contractor. One who has a chain saw, and who could get you out of wherever you're trapped—"

"I don't need a handyman!" she interrupted, the words tumbling out raw with emotion. "Phil, please, I need *you*. I need a hellerune. You're the only one who can break the magic that's holding me captive."

"I'm not," I answered, miserable. I felt caught, trapped just as surely as Sandy was. For one wild moment, I thought of finding a demon lord and paying him to break the magic that evidently had been placed on Sandy, but even in my desperate state, I knew just how impossible that was.

"You're the only one," she repeated in a half sob. "Please, Phil. I'll promise you anything, just please help me."

My mind scrambled madly for any solution to the situation but the one that Sandy asked for. Maybe if I hired a group of people, they could overpower the dragons and get

Sandy free? "How many dragons are there?" I asked, moving over to the computer to see if there was a handy "get your friend out of a horrible situation" service to be hired.

"A lot. The whole tribe of Chaos dragons are here, a few miles north of the California border. Phil, I know I've been incommunicado the last couple of years, but if you have any fondness for me, please say you'll help. I've pissed off the dragons, and there's no one else I can turn to. In fact …" Her voice cracked on the words; then a whisper came accompanied by a rustling sound as if she was pulling a blanket over herself. "I think one of them is outside the cabin. I can hear voices. Oh god, I hope it's not the master. He's … Phil, I swear I'll do whatever it takes to pay you back—"

"No," I said, pushing down all the emotions that were twisting around inside me. I had no choice. I couldn't turn my back on someone who had risked so much for me, not when now she needed my help. I got up from where I'd sat down at the computer, and scanned the room for my coat and purse. Seawright's door was closed, but I knew there was more to escaping her surveillance than just walking out of the house. "You don't owe me anything. I, however, owe you my life, and I'm not going to let you down now. Where exactly are you?"

I took down her hastily dictated directions, my heart beating wildly at the thought of what I was going to have to do, but there was nothing for it. Once, many years before, Sandy had taken me in when I escaped Xavier. Now it was my turn to return the favor.

I just hoped the world would survive such an act.

EIGHT
THE FIND

"She's there. In Oregon."

Three days before he had been stunned to see Phylli-da in the flesh, Bastian had finally found that which he'd sought so long. It was a struggle to leash the emotions and keep his voice neutral, but he had long experience in doing just that.

"Alessandra is in the US?" Rey shifted, obviously trying to get more comfortable in the oversized armchair. "This surprises me. She has never mentioned desiring to visit the West Coast. I will ask Marcel what he has heard."

"Marcel?" Bastian sorted through his memories, not finding one for the name.

"My cousin. He is a bit scatterbrained about many things—he is human, after all—but there is no one better at hacking into databases than him. I will have him verify this information. Not that I am casting aspersions on it." Rey slid him a look from the corner of her eye. "You, of all the blue dragons, are the best at reading mortals' minds. But it can't hurt to verify the details, yes?"

"It can't hurt," he agreed, shoving down the guilt. Rey might be one of his closest and oldest friends, but she did not know everything about him. If she knew that he was unable to ascertain even the tiniest morsel of thoughts from a mortal, she would decry him, mock him, demand that another take his place as wyvern.

He could not stand that. Not again.

"I'll have Marcel check Sandra's mobile phone, assuming it's the same number as it was a few years ago," Rey said, punching in a text on her own phone. "He can check the pings or whatever it is the TV detectives trace."

Bastian was silent, absently noting when Rey again shifted in the chair, her large belly obviously giving her some grief. His emotions were as volatile as ever, but he put on a placid expression, refusing to give power to the fire that always burned in his blood.

"And now, what about you?" Rey asked.

He eyed her, unsure of what she was asking. "What about me?"

She waved a hand at the activity going on around them. "How are you coping with all this? You aren't sleeping at all. You seldom eat. You swear the woman in whose dreams you walked holds no sway over you, and yet you seem ..." She hesitated for a few seconds, her gaze uncomfortably piercing. "Sad."

"My daughter is missing, possibly being held against her will," he pointed out, avoiding the fact that his emotions were a tangled mess. He couldn't face thoughts of Phyllida. Not now. Later, once he had resolved the biggest problems facing him, then he'd find her. But until then, he would put her out of his mind.

"That's frustrating. Irritating. Worrisome. But not sad." Rey put her feet up on a three-legged stool, her head to the side as she rested her hands on her belly. "You are sad."

"I am not," he corrected her. "I am worried about Alessandra. I am furious that we lost so much money in the last few years fighting the demon lords and the red dragon hybrids that I must liquidate our sept holdings. I am sweating because this part of Italy now appears to be residing on the surface of the sun. And I am sexually frustrated, but in none of those items does sadness enter."

Rey's dimples blossomed at the mention of his last aggrievement. "You should visit this woman who captured your attention."

He shook his head, unwilling to discuss Phyllida. "No."

"Ah, well, then perhaps you need a mortal. A temporary girlfriend?" Rey asked.

"If I knew of a mortal who could withstand my dragon fire, do you think I would not have bedded her and saved myself many nights of onanism?" He reflected for a moment on the time spent since he'd first found Phyllida. "Not to mention mornings. And showers. So many showers. The cost of body lotion alone that I used to keep from going insane with lustful thoughts would have saved at least one painting."

Rey laughed out loud. "Now I know you are right, and I am wrong, for you would not joke about your masturbatory needs if you were truly sad. But the truth remains that you need a woman, and I will do what I can to find one for you, even if she is not the one of your dreams."

"It's not as if I am averse to finding a woman," he protested, feeling the weight of all those showers, and all those bottles of body lotion. Had it really been only four days since he'd first found Phyllida? "Women do not gag upon seeing me, so I don't believe my appearance is what is keeping them away, although if you have suggestions on how I might make myself more attractive, I am willing to hear them."

"You are one of the handsomest men alive, and you know it," Rey said with another dimpling of her cheeks. "More than once, I have seen mortal women pause as you walk past them, and watch you with lust in their eyes."

"It may be in their eyes, but it doesn't last long," he answered, absently brushing a hand down his shirt, and wondering if he needed a haircut. "As soon as I speak, they seem to lose interest."

"Ah, but that is because you don't know how to talk to the women of today," she said, still laughing, although her expression turned thoughtful as she repeated, "Women of today. Yes, I think that's it."

"What is? I am conversant with women. I have watched that British show—*Real Housewomen of Cheddar.*"

"*Real Housewives of Cheshire,*" Rey murmured.

"I am not unaware of what it takes to engage a woman," he said, pulling dignity around him. "I just have bad luck with those with whom I choose to do so."

Except Phyllida. She was the only one who had greeted his awkward flirtation with delight. She didn't seem to mind how he conversed with her.

"Uh-huh." Rey smiled at him, a warm, genuine smile that bathed him in a gentle glow of affection. "Bastian, you were born six hundred years ago. For the last hundred, you were locked up, so at best, your manners are still roughly in the Victorian era. You may think that you are Real House-wives up-to-date, but I don't think you are. For one, you say whatever is on your mind."

"That is honesty," he said, his shoulders twitching. "Women like honesty. I saw that in a magazine. There was some sort of a quiz to determine how honest the quiz taker's man was, and when I took it, I rated twelve out of twelve."

"You told a woman who cleans for us that her shape was pleasant," Rey said, her lips twitching.

"She was comely," he answered, thinking back to the in-cident a few months before. "Women like compliments. I was complimenting her on the form her body took. How is that wrong?"

"Remember the discussion we had regarding what is and what isn't allowable to say?" she parried.

He thought for a moment, his shoulders drooping. "Re-ferring to a woman's body—"

"Anyone's body," Rey corrected.

"Referring to anyone's body shape without express per-mission to do so is considered inappropriate." He grimaced, then added, "If someone told me that my body pleased them, I would not be offended."

"No, but you're not a person who has been the subject of the male gaze," she said.

"I have, but not in recent years." He brushed a small bit of fluff from his sleeve.

Rey laughed. "Like I said, you're as handsome as the day is long, so it doesn't surprise me that you attract attention from men as well as women, but that's not my point, and you know it. Maybe we should do a little role-play to help smooth out your rough edges. Let's say I'm the cleaner with the big breasts."

His fingers spasmed as he thought of Phyllida's breasts, so perfectly made. "If you like."

"So, I'm the cleaner, happily dusting the drawing room, and you come in. What do you say to me that does not involve the shape of my body?"

Bastian thought for a moment, pulling together the knowledge he'd gleaned from various TV and media sources. "Being near you makes my cock hard. I would like—"

"No!" Rey's scream was part laughter. "Bastian, you can't say that!"

"I did not refer to her body at all," he protested. "Surely I am allowed to mention my own?"

"Yes, but not your genitals." She waved a hand toward his groin. "That is outright sexual harassment. Now try it again, without any mention of your body parts."

He sighed, and once again shifted through his thoughts. "It seems far too much trouble to find someone if I can't speak the truth. Very well. I will try this: *Good day. You are skillful in the arrangement of my objets d'art. I like the way your hands flutter while you dust.* I can mention her hands, yes?"

"Yeees," she drawled, looking mildly suspicious.

"*Their movements are graceful,*" he continued.

"So far so good," she said, leaning back in the chair.

He thought for a moment. "*I enjoy watching your hands at work. I can imagine them stroking me.*"

"Oh, I give up," Rey said, laughing again and shaking her head.

"If I cannot even sway you, then I am lost," he said, seeing the humor in the situation nonetheless. It occurred to him that Phyllida would not have a problem with him telling her that she made his cock hard. He had a feeling she'd be just as interested in that fact as he, himself, was.

"You're not lost—you're just unfiltered, which I happen to like, but women today ..." She paused to glance at her phone when it pinged at her. "They get a bit twitchy when it comes to unfiltered men. We'll have to work on smoothing out your approach to mortal women just as soon as we're done here. Ah. Marcel is on the case for us. He says he had a preliminary look at her cell phone data, and it was definitely located where you said it was."

Beyond Rey, a handful of blue dragons carefully tagged the furniture in the main salon of his villa. Two others were taking photographs, while in the background, a trio of auctioneers moved from piece to piece, closely examining each before making notes and taking their own photos. "There are no blue dragons on the West Coast of the US. Why would she be there?" Bastian asked, puzzling over the information he'd gained by paying a thief taker.

"That I can't tell you, since Marcel couldn't extract phone numbers from the data. He might be able to with time, but he said the encryption was pretty strong, and he wasn't sure he could break it." Rey was silent for a moment, her gaze on the men as they moved around the main salon, but Bastian suspected she was chewing over the mystery of what Alessandra was doing. "Bastian, does it strike you as odd that she has not called you in the last six months?"

"That is a very good question," he said slowly, locking away pain and frustration. "I don't know the answer any more than I understand why my daughter would choose to remove herself from her kin. She has no reason to hide from her family."

"There is something ..." Rey shifted a third time, distracting Bastian.

He wondered at what point he would have to step in and demand that Rey rest for the remainder of her pregnancy. The fact that her mate allowed her to do as she pleased both delighted him—she deserved a man who adored her as much as her mate, Cole, did—and annoyed him that the very same man not demand she stay home and rest as was right and proper with women who were close to their birthing time.

"Something that bothers you?" he asked. "I knew you should not have made the trip here. The heat is too much for you. I will call Cole and have him take you home, where you may rest and be more comfortable. Your midwife is ready, yes?"

Rey leveled Bastian a look that he would not have tolerated in anyone but his oldest friend. "You know that I love you as much as the brother you should have been, but no one, not you, not Cole, is going to nag me into bed just because I was due yesterday. And stop looking at me like I'm going to pop. It's just a baby!"

He watched her rub her belly as she spoke, wondering how hard she'd hit him if he called Cole regardless of her protests. "If it is not the babe causing you distress, what troubles you?"

Her expression changed from a fond annoyance to that of wary concern. She was silent for a few moments, clearly picking her words with care. "There are no blue dragons on the West Coast of the US, that is true. But there *are* dragons living there. Lots of dragons, especially in the Northern California and Oregon areas. I could not help but wonder if they might have been what drew Alessandra. Now that the Chaos Tribe is part of the weyr."

"Alessandra is my daughter," he said, his shoulders twitching again with a prickling sensation that left him itchy. "She would have nothing to do with the Chaos Tribe, not that they are full members of the weyr. She has no reason to go to them even if the circumstances were different. She is a member of the sept first and foremost."

"One who is a noted diviner," Rey said softly, her gaze skittering away when Bastian narrowed his eyes on her. She lifted her hand to stop the protest that he was about to make.

"I do not say that Alessandra would betray you or the blue dragons. I simply point out that she has worth to others as well as dragonkin."

Bastian thought that over for a few seconds. Fury that someone would harm his mercurial child caused the dragon fire within him to roar to life, instantly demanding an outlet. With an effort, he clamped down hard on both the emotion and his fire, but not before a little curl of smoke slid between his lips. "You agree with me that someone is holding her prisoner? Exploiting her abilities?"

"I don't know the answer to that," Rey said, frowning and snapping out a harsh word when one of the dragons inventorying dropped an antique book. "I simply suggest it as a reason why she would be in that area. Or why she hasn't phoned you or any sept members in the last half year. It is said that the number of tribes is growing. No one knows where the dragons are coming from."

Bastian turned from the dismantling of his salon and strode out to the upper garden, the water of Lake Como sparkling and glistening like so many dancing diamonds. He loved the light, loved the sunshine of northern Italy, never failing to find solace outside where the air was fresh and crisp. He could deal with much—had dealt with much over his lifetime, including incarceration, the severing of his sept, and later its decimation by demonic beings until only thirty-seven blue dragons remained—but he didn't have to watch as his possessions were taken away to be sold. "Why does she shun contact? If she needs aid, why would she not seek it from me? From her kin?"

"Stubborn pride?" Rey had followed him out to the patio, one hand on the small of her back as she stretched. Her words were harsh, but there was amusement and affection in her eyes when she gently pinched Bastian's arm. "She is very like you in that regard. Do not let this distress you, Bastian. We will find her. If she is being held captive by some unscrupulous person, we will free her, just as we will rescue her if she has fallen in with an ouroboros tribe. That I pledge."

Bastian smiled, and gently herded her over to a comfortable chair in the shade. "If there is anyone who can find her, it is you, the best of all the blue dragon trackers. But I would not have you undergo such a long trip when you are so close to your birthing time. There are others who will help. Now, do you have need of anything? Water? Are you hungry? You should put your feet up again."

"If I wasn't, at this very moment, willing to give everything I own for a foot rub, I would tell you to stop patronizing me. But as it is …"

"As it is, you will do as your wyvern orders, and sit here and allow your mate to attend to your needs," Bastian interrupted, catching sight of a dragon who appeared at the edge of the patio. Dark-haired and dark-eyed—an anomaly amongst blue dragons—Cole gave Bastian an apologetic grimace when he hurried over.

"Don't make me punch you," Rey said, her smile growing several degrees warmer when she caught sight of Cole. "I'd love a lemonade if you have some, but I'm not really hungry. Well, I could eat a little fruit, say a few grapes. Is there any of that delicious sharp white cheddar? Perhaps a small selection of meats? Oh, and those stone-ground crackers. I love those crackers. The ones with the rosemary, not the garlic ones. The baby doesn't seem to like the garlic ones."

Bastian made an exaggerated bow, relieved that Cole was there to worry over Rey's health so he could focus on watching his belongings being auctioned off to the highest bidders while fuming over the situation with Alessandra. "Luca!" he called to his guard after he gave Rey's order to his housekeeper. "You have kin in Canada, yes?"

"My son Dante is in Vancouver." Luca made a face that had Bastian laughing to himself. "He wishes to become an actor. *My son!* Have you ever heard of such a thing as a dragon demeaning himself in front of a camera? And for what? The adulation of mortals? Bah. He is deranged, that one. I washed my hands of him long ago."

Bastian knew full well how proud Luca was of his son despite his words to the contrary, and confined himself to saying, "Does he know anything about Oregon?"

"I don't know. Possibly. He takes acting jobs wherever he can get them, although he seldom goes into the US. Why?"

A beautiful Rubens, the pride of the blue dragon sept, was lifted off the wall so the auctioneers could examine it closer. Bastian ignored the stab of pain at the loss of his favorite painting. "Get us a plane to Oregon. Alessandra is there."

"You found her? That is a relief," Luca said, pulling out his phone. "What airport do you wish to fly into? There are several."

Bastian hesitated, turning when a dragon called his name. Beyond him, one of the auctioneers stood consulting his tablet computer. "The largest airport. And hire a local tracker. I don't know the exact location of Alessandra's whereabouts, and Rey is too close to her time to travel."

Luca very much looked like he wanted to comment on that fact, but he had been with Bastian long enough to know the value of keeping some thoughts to himself, and instead went off to book a plane to the US.

Bastian dealt with the auctioneers' questions, and watched in silence while the Rubens was carefully crated and removed along with the other valuables held by blue dragons down the ages. He thought for a moment of his badly depleted lair, now empty of all but a few items, and sighed.

He had done what was needed in order to protect his sept, and the others in the weyr.

Three days later, he strode into a restaurant located in a small town outside Portland, and glanced around for the messenger who had news of the men who were holding his daughter. "Where is he? Do you see him?" he asked Luca, who accompanied him.

"He said he'd wait for us in the back, out of sight," Luca said, nodding toward a hallway that led past toilets, to what were clearly administrative offices. They started across the restaurant, filled with mortals happily enjoying their meal, but just as they reached the hall, an awareness that had prickled Bastian's flesh since he'd entered the building became too much, and he glanced back to see who was causing it, but saw nothing.

The messenger wasn't in the back areas as he had said he'd be. Just as Bastian was about to demand Luca make contact with the man, someone bumped into him. When he spun around, he was astonished to see a tall woman with pleasing curves, and a riot of blond-tipped chocolate curls that were pulled back to a blob on the top of her head. But it was her eyes—pale mossy green—that registered the same surprise, then delight that he felt.

It became clear after a few minutes that something was not right. How had Phyllida found him? *Why* had she found him? She had to have sought him out because somehow she knew he was a dream warrior.

"That is not happening," he growled to himself when he stalked out of the restaurant, his penis singing a dirge about leaving her behind.

"This woman, it was she who you visited her in your dreams?" Luca asked slowly, his expression guarded.

"It was her dream, not mine," Bastian answered. He almost returned to Phyllida to demand what it was she wanted from him. He badly wanted to find out if she was keeping something from him—not to mention indulge in more lovemaking—but all those years of confinement had taught him one thing: he was master of his emotions, not vice versa. He kept walking, determinedly pushing thoughts of her from his mind.

"Is it not a very large coincidence for her to be here now?" Luca asked.

"No. Yes. I don't know, and I don't care," he lied, wrapping himself with grim intent as they headed to the car they'd rented upon arrival in Portland. "She has no impact on the situation facing us. The messenger had better be telling us the truth. I have little patience for playing games, and if what he says is true, then we will have grounds for kicking Deus and his band of villains out of the weyr."

"The thief taker is fey, and they find it difficult to lie," Luca said, getting behind the wheel, and after a quick consultation with his phone set off to a nearby town. Thankfully for Bastian's peace of mind, he let the subject of Phyllida drop. "He didn't outright say that Alessandra was seen with Deus and the Chaos Tribe, but there are no other dragons in this area. I think he was telling the truth. He told me that it wasn't safe here, and he was taking his life in his hands by going against Deus's tribe members."

"*Peste,*" Bastian said, unable to keep his anger from rising. "A week. It's been only a week since Deus begged to join the weyr, swearing an oath to support us against all other claims, and yet now we see the truth. They are little more than a thugs, and Deus is the worst of them all. Once we have Alessandra free from their grasp, we will have to see to it they do no harm to any other dragons."

And then he'd be able to focus on Phyllida. That thought brought him both a rush of desire and a lump of dread in the pit of his stomach. What if she learned the truth about him? What if she knew how he had failed as a dream warrior? Could he survive the accusation and condemnation in her eyes?

"Seeing them removed from the weyr will give me great pleasure," Luca answered. "Dante said that he heard from some green dragons residing in Vancouver that the tribes' populations have erupted on the West Coast. Perhaps the weyr could make a deal with them concerning the Chaos Tribe?"

"The weyr's power concerns only those septs that are members of it," Bastian answered absently, ignoring the pain that followed his dark thoughts. Instead, he wondered why he sensed fear when Phyllida mentioned her former lover. What had she said? A dragon who was not a dragon, but who could dream walk? He shook his head at that idea. He was the only dragon who had the ability to do such. It was an ability given by the First Dragon, and he'd never heard of any others who could do it. She had to be mistaken … but that didn't negate the fact that she was scared of something. Or someone. Why else would she summon him to her dreams? "A conundrum," he said softly.

"The ouroboros tribes?" Luca asked, giving a one-shoulder shrug. "I suppose they are, although mostly I assume they are troublemakers, cast out of their respective septs for misdeeds."

He wondered why Phyllida's dreams were different from the few others he had seen before his disastrous attempt to be the dream warrior the First Dragon wanted. "Most mortals' dreams are a confusion of emotions and impressions, their way of sorting through issues."

"Oh?" Luca asked, a faintly puzzled frown pulling his brows down. "I suppose that makes sense."

"The indigenous people of Australia have something they call a dreaming track," Bastian said, dredging from his memory long-forgotten facts. "It marks the route taken by their ancestors in the Dreaming."

Luca shot him a quick look, his gaze flickering between the road and Bastian. "Mortals or immortals?"

"Both. Some mortals—not only those from Australia—share a similar ability with a songline of their own. That traces their path through life, tied to both the past and future. Those who have songlines dream differently from others." Phyllida's detailed dreams definitely belonged to the songline group."

"Do they." Luca's voice was completely without expression.

"Their dreams are more storylike, complex and filled with emotion." Bastian was silent for a few minutes, thinking of the depth of Phyllida's dreams, the way her skin felt, how her scent had teased him, and the taste of her as he took delight in her body. "Joy and happiness in those dreams are a thousand times more potent … as are fear and despair."

"And … erm … I assume that goes for other emotions. *Sexual* ones." Luca seemed to have trouble getting the words out, his jaw flexing a few times as if he was holding himself in check.

"Yes, that, too, can be heightened." Bastian shifted in his seat, aware that an erection was threatening to blossom wholly to life at the memory of Phyllida, but he willed it away.

Or tried to. His penis had never been one to take orders well.

Silence filled the car for a few minutes, before it struck Bastian that perhaps Luca was concerned about the effects of visiting Phyllida.

"I did not intend to dream walk again," he said, his gaze on the passing buildings as they headed for an interstate highway. "I swore a hundred years ago that I would never again put the sept at risk, and I held true to that oath. What happened with Phyllida was … unprecedented. If you worry that I will lose control, you need not fear."

Luca was shaking his head even before Bastian finished his statement. "I never thought you would endanger the sept, but then, I never thought you went insane all those years ago. I do not profess to know what happened, or why the First Dragon put you in a position where you were accused of being mad, but my faith in you has never wavered. You are the wyvern we were meant to have, not—"

"We will not speak ill of the dead this time," Bastian said, guilt lancing him at the thought of the devastation his nephew had wrought throughout the weyr.

"What I would like to know, if you do not mind talking about it, is how walking in dreams differs from our ability to read mortal minds. If dreams are merely extensions of mortals' waking thoughts, the jumble of images and concerns you spoke of, why can you not simply view them remotely as we do with mind reading?"

"Unfortunately, it's not that simple." Bastian pulled out his phone and checked for any new messages. "And irrelevant. I am not a dream warrior. No matter how enticing Phyllida is, I will not destroy the sept a second time."

"You didn't destroy it the first time," Luca stated with a stalwartness that warmed Bastian almost as much as his devotion. "It was Fiat who betrayed you. Us."

Houses flashed by as they drove out of town, but Bastian said nothing.

He knew the truth. Fiat betrayed him, but there was no one but himself to blame for the loss of his sept. He might not be much of a wyvern, but the blue dragons needed a leader, and he would give his life to protect them. He couldn't do that if he gave in to the failure that lay buried deep in his soul.

Dream warrior, whispered in his mind. *Phyllida needs you.*

He refused to acknowledge the voice.

That way lay madness, destruction, and death.

NINE
THE HUNTED

"Again, you try to hide. This would be amusing if it was not so futile."

The subway was crowded, very crowded. The sort of crowded where people were crushed up against one another, a mass of humanity with a million arms and legs, moving as one entity.

I was in Tokyo, I realized with an odd sense of relief. My dreams the last few years had been a mixture of memories—reliving each second of each day with Xavier—and locations where I successfully hid from him. During the last six months, I'd only had one memory of my time with him, and the rest of the dreams were formed on my terms, not his.

Including the ones involving Bastian.

Was Xavier losing his hold on me after all? I dared not speak aloud as I was pressed backward, against the slick tile of a Tokyo subway wall, men, women, and children squeezing their way through the dense crowds to various train platforms. I hunched down so as not to make it obvious where I was, my fingernails biting into my palms while I tried to find something safe for my mind to focus on.

"It will do you no good. It never has," his voice said, rolling around and through the bodies that pressed around me.

Desperately, I scanned the crowd, needing something to distract my brain and thus keep Xavier from finding it. I'd learned early on that if I didn't give in to his taunts and threats, he had much more difficulty invading my unwilling mind. He could speak to me in dreams, but only speak. It would take someone far more powerful in the ways of dreaming to do more than that. "Dream walker," I whispered to myself, my brain grabbing at Bastian as a suitable distraction. "Dream walkers are people who can interact with others in their dreams. They can participate in dreams, shaping them, instilling in the dreamer memories that never really happened. They can affect personalities, and bestow either calm or chaos in the host's mind. They are outlawed by the Committee, just as hellerunes are outlawed."

"Hellerune …"

I closed my eyes for a moment, dismayed at the slip I'd made. "Dammit. I didn't mean to say that. He always knows when I say that word."

"I know everything you say or do," he answered.

I shook my head, moving as best I could down the slick ceramic tile wall. I didn't like staying in one place too long, not when I had no idea if Xavier's dream walker self was nearby. "He doesn't know. Ignore him. Think about dream walkers. There was a famous one last century, a Frenchman. My godmother told me about him. He was special. What was his name?"

Wind whirled around me, whipping my hair out from the hoodie that confined it. Despite the press of bodies, minute bits of paper as small as raindrops spun up and around us.

Beyond the mass of humanity, a long gleaming metal train pulled into the station with a soft hiss of its air brakes, stirring the raindrop-papers even more. For a moment, I stopped forcing my mind into the focused pathway that would keep me safe, and stared in wonder at the paper drops as they twirled upward in a helix, unnoticed and unaffected by the people streaming past it.

"It's so beautiful," I murmured, my eyes dazzled by the twirling, spinning flecks of paper.

"As are you. There are times when I wonder why I let you leave." Cold touched the back of my neck. I twisted where I stood, kept in place by the mass of bodies around me.

Xavier stood behind me, his black eyes filled with amusement.

"Bastian!" The scream woke me up, echoing through my brain. I sat bolt upright in the chair into which I'd dozed off, looking around me with a profound sense of disorientation. Why wasn't Bastian here? Why hadn't he appeared in my dream, driving off the horror that was Xavier?

It took a few seconds before I could shake the clinging tendrils of the dream from my mind, and realize I was sitting in my living room, my phone at my feet, and the soft patter of rain hitting the window.

Slowly, my speeding heart calmed as I slumped back in the chair, checking my phone to make sure that it hadn't been accessed while I was hiding in my dreams. I had to get out of there. I'd lost only twenty minutes to the unexpected nap, and that meant I had less than two hours to rescue Sandy. First, though, I had to get away without Seawright knowing.

Two minutes later I tapped at her door.

She opened it, dressed inexplicably in a Victorian girl's sailor suit. "Yes?"

I kept my gaze firmly affixed to hers. "I just wanted to let you know that I am going to my room to rest."

Seawright was many things, but didn't have any magic abilities. She did, however, have an exceptionally good lie meter, so I was careful to confine myself to absolute truths.

"All right." She pulled her tablet out. "Did you wish for me to note a migraine? Or are you simply depressed? Have you taken any medication? Alcohol?"

"No, no, no, and no. You know I don't drink. I'm just tired, and want to curl up and go to sleep for a day or three."

"Hmm." She wrote with the stylus, saying as she did so, "*Subject Phyllida displays no signs of narcolepsy, but seeks extra sleeping periods during the day.* Very well, you take your rest. Tonight is my night for making dinner. I will make a vegetable soup filled with antioxidants so as to help boost your immune system. Does that meet with your approval?"

"Yes, that'll be fine." I gave her a wan smile, and tried to anticipate how long it would take me to get out to Sandy and return. "Although please don't wake me for dinner if I'm not up. My sleep has been disturbed lately, and I could really use the rest. I'll heat the soup later if needs be."

"As you like," she said, her gaze narrowing on me, something setting off her warning system. Evidently it wasn't enough to push her, because she said nothing more as we made our way upstairs. I stood aside so she could check that both the window wards and the electronic security system were in place and functioning. The former would keep things out of the house, but the latter … well, that was there to alert Seawright if I tried to escape.

"I think I'll put on one of those meditation videos," I said, kicking off my shoes and sitting on my bed.

"Meditation … videos … " she noted on the tablet before leaving, the door clicking closed softly behind her.

I waited five minutes after she went downstairs before slipping off the bed and padding to the door. I listened with my ear against it for a minute, was satisfied by the silence, and turned to consider the closet.

"And here's a toast to Anthony the builder who managed to get a door cut into my closet during the times you made me sit at the dentist watching while you had a tooth replaced," I muttered to the absent Seawright when, after dressing in a pair of black leggings and matching hoodie, I donned a pair of tennis shoes and carefully pushed aside my clothing to reveal a small hinged panel. I punched in the code that unlocked the door, and eased it open.

Cold, damp air rushed around me, while rain dribbled down from the leaves of the handy maple tree next to the house. I reached out to catch the branch that Anthony had assured me would hold my weight, and carefully shut the door with one of my feet before swinging my way forward until I felt a lower branch, one that had been cut so it didn't brush the house.

Ten minutes later I was running down the street, my hood up, half-braced to hear Seawright's demands I return when she discovered I'd slipped out. By the time I jogged through my neighborhood and onto a main cross street, I was a nervous wreck, twitching every time a car accelerated or decelerated near me.

Ahead, at a public library, I saw a car waiting that matched the one shown on my ride-sharing app, and after comparing license number and driver, I approached with a greeting for the driver on my lips. "Thanks for picking me up. You know how to get out to the address I want to go to?" I asked her.

"The Narmar Oasis? Yeah, I've taken people out there before. It's a fancy place, lots of woo-woo talk about chakras and opening third eyes, but eh. To each their own," she answered.

I murmured something noncommittal and, pleased to see that the car had tinted windows, opened the door to the back seat.

Seawright sat with her tablet propped up on her knees, softly speaking as she wrote. "—*said subject arrived at two fourteen p.m. in a rideshare vehicle she booked earlier, without the knowledge of Seawright Pendleton, thus violating Otherworld Directives 43, 112, and 441.*"

My shoulders slumped and my mouth hung open a few seconds at the sight of her before I squared the former, and snapped closed the latter. "How on earth did you find me? How did you know I booked this ride? And what is Otherworld Directive 441?"

"*Subjects shall not purchase, hire, or steal vehicles where the intended purpose is to escape the supervision of assigned personnel without said personnel's express knowledge and permission,*" she quoted, signing her tattletale report with a flourish before looking up at me. "And as for the other questions,

I am charged to ensure you do not break the terms of the contract you currently hold with the Committee, a contract, I feel morally obligated to remind you, that provides you with their protection and services, up to and including safe harbor, financial support, and appropriate magics applied to your domicile. All of which you have just forfeited the right to by engaging this woman to drive you out to some expensive meditation camping spa without clearing it with me first. Not that I would have sanctioned such a thing, but still, the point remains that you are legally obligated to do so, and yet, you did not."

I took a deep breath, prepared to argue with her yet again that I was three years old when the contract with the Committee was signed, but the driver, glancing up from her phone, asked, "You going to get in the car, or just stand there and squawk at each other? I'd like to get back before it's dark, so if you could get a move on, I'd appreciate it."

"We aren't going anywhere—" Seawright started to say, opening her door.

"You may not be, but I most certainly am." I dashed to the other side of the car and climbed in, snapping on the seat belt with a defiant look at my gaoler. She heaved a dramatic sigh and closed her door again. "I'm ready. Let's go," I told the driver.

"This isn't going to look good, you ignoring the dictates of the Committee when I've informed you of your violations," Seawright told me. "You can't even claim ignorance, as you have the one hundred and seventeen other times you have violated the rules."

"I'm ninety-six years old," I told her, looking out of the window, and wondering how on earth I was going to get rid of my persistent little shadow. Maybe I could bribe the ride-share woman to drive off with her after depositing me at the Narmar Oasis? "If I didn't get some time to myself now and again, I'd go stark, staring mad. Besides, you don't know the situations for the first one hundred and eight of those times. You've only been around for two years."

"I assure you that as a representative of the Committee, I thoroughly acquainted myself with your file before I agreed to take on your case. To do otherwise would be the sheerest folly." She rustled around in the messenger bag that was always strapped to her petite person. "I took especial note of the three years when you remained outside of the Committee's supervision."

A little shudder ran down my spine. "You know full well I was being held captive during that time."

She gave me a long, unreadable look. "In the end, yes, that was true according to statements offered by impartial witnesses. But the documentation also states that you willingly went away with your captor."

I took a deep breath, reminding myself that old sins always had a way of coming home to roost. "That's neither here nor there. I'm not running away to meet a lover now."

"No, but you did attempt to evade me, which is why you only have yourself to blame for the extreme measures to which you have driven me."

I leaned my head against the cold window of the car, her words taking a second to filter through my frantically scrambled thoughts. Perhaps if I could disable her somehow. Wasn't there some sort of a karate chop that knocked people out? Or was that the Vulcan Nerve Pinch? And just how did one go about learning how to do—I straightened up and was just turning to ask Seawright what extreme measures she meant when a cold metallic sensation enclosed my left wrist. *"Deo damnatus,"* I swore in Latin, jerking my hand up to stare at it.

"If you are damned by a god, it is only because you insist on running amok all over the sensible—and quite practical, when you think about them—laws set down for the careful governance of hellerunes and similar beings of such a dangerous ilk," Seawright said with satisfaction as she snapped shut a handcuff on her right wrist.

"Take it off!" I demanded, shaking my wrist and struggling to force the handcuff off. "This is outrageous, Seawright! I won't stand for it."

She lifted her chin and gazed serenely out of the window. "You don't have much choice, and it is in no way outrageous. It is a direct action taken to ensure that your amokness will be limited until such time as my supervisor can arrive to take you into custody."

"What?" My gaze of outright disbelief moved from the handcuff—which solidly encircled my wrist despite my attempt to remove it—to Seawright herself. "You called your boss on me? Wait, custody? What sort of custody? I'm already in custody!"

"No, you are monitored," she said blithely, rubbing a spot on the car window. "There is a difference, which you will shortly find out."

"Here's the thing about hellerunes," I said quietly, glancing at the driver, but she was singing along to a tune on the radio. "We may not wield magic that can harm people, but we *can* defend ourselves when cornered, and you, Seawright Pendleton, junior scribe third class, have just backed me into a corner you're going to wish never existed."

She didn't even look mildly worried by my not-so-veiled threat. "Oh?" She took up her stylus and opened a new document on her tablet, her hand poised over it as she asked, "What exactly do you intend to do to me?"

I thought for a moment, discounting any number of highly satisfying, but equally unlikely, options, and ended by leaning forward and saying loudly, "Hello! Do you happen to know if there's a locksmith on the way to the Narmar Oasis? My … er … friend here got a little crazy with her bondage fetish." I held up my wrist for the driver to see.

Seawright *tsk*ed, and pulled my hand down, making a note.

"No, but I can find one if you really want," the driver answered, giving us a wary look in the rearview mirror.

"There's no need," Seawright piped up. "A locksmith won't be able to open these restraints. They are … er … unique."

"Unique how?" I asked in an undertone as the driver gave a little shrug of dismissal and began to sing again.

"One of the many facts that has been gleaned about you by the scribes assigned to you in the past has been your ability to remove handcuffs. Thus, when I was sent out, a special pair was created just for you. A mortal locksmith will not be able to open it any more than you will be able to slide your hand out of it by relaxing your thumb joint," she answered, complacency fairly oozing from her.

I swore again, but quietly, my mind still racing around, chasing first one thought, then another.

I couldn't take Seawright with me to help Sandy, but neither could I get free from her, not if the Otherworld people had done something to the cuffs to keep me from sliding them off. Without looking at Seawright, I gave another attempt at sliding the metal over my fingers, but although it was loose on my wrist, it refused to budge.

I could magic her. ... Even as those words formed in my brain, I dismissed them. My abilities, limited such as they were, did not include harming people.

Not directly, anyway.

If I couldn't get the cuff off so I could somehow ditch Seawright, then I'd simply have to get her to release me.

"What would it take—" I started to say.

"There is nothing," she said, recoiling from me until she was pressed against the car door, her face red and her voice shaking with emotion. "*Nothing* anyone could offer would cause me to betray my oath of office to the Committee."

I sighed.

"It is sacrosanct. I am appalled that you would even think that I could be so bribed."

The mental squirrels chasing thoughts in my head scattered, leaving one in sole possession of a thought: if I couldn't get rid of Seawright, I'd just have to sway her to my side.

"The position of junior scribe third class is a sacred trust!"

I bit my lower lip. Which meant I'd better come to an agreement with her so that she didn't actively hinder the rescue of Sandy from whatever dragons were keeping her prisoner.

"It is one I have aspired to ever since I made junior scribe sixth class," she said, her hackles obviously still up. It was clear she was prepared to continue her outraged state, but I didn't have time to let her work through all the indignation she'd stored up.

"All right, all right, I'm sorry, I didn't mean to impugn your devotion to the Committee," I said, then cleared my throat to smooth out the irritation in my tone. "Nor would I ask you to do anything illegal. Which is why I'm willing to scratch your back, if you scratch mine."

She blinked at me, and wriggled her shoulders. "My back doesn't itch. If you are attempting to convince me to release your hand so that you might scratch yourself—"

I took a deep breath, reminding myself that patience was a virtue, and all that crap. "It's a phrase that means I will work with you if you return that consideration."

"Work with me how?" Seawright asked, her eyes narrowing. "I have notified the head of the Committee about your escape, and he has assured me that a thief taker will be sent out to reclaim you, so really, it's just a matter of time before you will be incarcerated. You assisting me in some manner will have no impact on the completion of my duty in that regard. Otherworld Directive 278 states—"

"You know," I interrupted, holding up my free hand, and forcing a smile that I didn't in the least feel in an attempt to be pleasant, "I really don't think I can take another Otherworld Directive right now. I don't know how you found out I escaped the house—"

"I had a tracking device installed on your mobile phone."

The smile slipped a few notches, but I held on to it. I also made a mental note to buy a burner phone. "—but you might ask yourself why I left the safety of my own home, safety that I very much need, cherish, and appreciate to the fullest extent."

"Well ..." She frowned in thought for a few seconds. "I did think it was a bit odd, since the renaissance is almost here, and you are extremely vulnerable for the time between it and the re-forming of the Committee."

"I'm on a rescue mission, one I tried very hard to avoid," I told her, and quickly explained about Sandy's call, and my obligation to help her. "Sandy initiated my escape from the man who tormented me, so naturally, if she's in a situation where I can repay her kindness, I can't turn away her plea for help."

To my surprise, Seawright didn't immediately dismiss my statement, instead almost bouncing in her seat as she scribbled wildly on the tablet. "Your friend's situation sounds just like something in *Dragon Heart*."

I blinked a couple of times, hoping that would clear my mental fuzziness. All it did was loosen an eyelash, which fluttered off to adventures unknown. "What's *Dragon Heart*?"

"A puzzle game that I and three other junior scribes play. In our designated off time, of course," she said, adding the last in a self-righteous tone. "It's like an escape room, but in digital form. Last week we started *Dragon Heart*, which features a highly valued captive being held by thuggish dragons bent on world domination."

"I don't think dragons are thuggish," I said slowly, moving away from a mass of memories that lurked in the back of my mind to dwell on Bastian. He was sunshine and warm, sexy man compared with the fear and darkness that Xavier represented. "Have you ever met dragons? They're thought to be pretty urbane, on the whole."

"I haven't, but everyone knows how powerful they are, and with power comes danger," Seawright said in the voice of one pronouncing a sage thought. She was silent for two minutes before adding, "I have given your proposition some thought."

"My propo—oh, my offer to help you if you help me? Really, all I want is your cooperation so that I can get Sandra out of whatever fix she's in."

"I will bring the collective mind of the junior scribes to you," she continued, just as if I hadn't spoken. "If we can't solve the problem of your friend, then she is in an untenable situation indeed. Just give me the pertinent facts, and I will message the scribes."

I wrestled with my need to keep myself removed from danger, which fought with the desire to help Sandy. In the end, I gave in to the inevitable: I told Seawright everything I knew. She sent the info with a note of explanation to her buddies.

"I appreciate your help," I told her a few minutes later, when the driver indicated we were almost to the entrance of the Narmar Oasis. "But I don't quite see how your friends are going to be able to advise us on this situation. This is real life, not a game engineered to have a solution, after all."

"Pfft," Seawright declared, waving away my objections as she scooted forward in the seat, peering avidly through the window. "You underestimate the power of the Scribe Collective. Is that it?"

"It looks like it," I said, glancing at a discreet sign that sat at the entrance of a graveled track leading off the main road. I lifted my hand and shook it to catch her attention. "If you could take these off, then we can get started."

"Oh, I can't remove the restraints," she said. "It would be against three different Otherworld Directives." She paused, and thought. "No, five if I consider you having performed misdemeanor offenses, which, of course, I do."

"You want me to drive up to the lodge, or stop here?" the driver asked when she pulled up next to a second sign that informed visitors that only guests were allowed onto the grounds of the Narmar Oasis.

"Here is fine," I told her, shooting a quick glare at Seawright before continuing. "You'll be here in an hour, yes? We'll have a friend with us, and we will definitely need a ride back to town."

"You booked it—I'll be here," she said, giving me a cheery smile and a thumbs-up when I thanked her.

Seawright didn't wait for me to do more than pull out my phone to give the driver a tip before she started off down the track, dragging me behind her like a reluctant sack of potatoes.

"Will you slow down?" I hissed, stopping so that I could take stock of the situation, aware that there might be people lurking in the bushes. Or worse, dragons, who in general had a very good sense of hearing. "We need to have a game plan."

"We have the Junior Scribes Collective for that," she said, trying to get me moving again.

"Much as I value any help in saving Sandy, I think we need to rely on our own judgment." I eyed the gravel drive that curled around a stand of pine and fir trees, indecision gripping me so strongly I couldn't move. "Dammit, I wish I'd thought to ask her whether or not there were dragons hidden around the camp. Right. Let's brainstorm a plan."

She sighed loudly and, grabbing my wrist, hauled me into a particularly large laurel bush. "Fine, but we can't plan standing out in the road where anyone can see us. Let's tackle this properly. Why is your friend being held prisoner? Has she contravened Otherworld laws, too?"

I let that slight pass, chewing a little on my lower lip as I thought. "No, she's not that sort of person. It has to be something to do with divining. She's a diviner," I added unnecessarily.

Seawright shot me a look that said she expected better of me. "Then it truly is just like *Dragon Heart*. The innocent victim there held secret knowledge about the Grand Garibaldi, dread dragon lord, and his plan to control the world. We can use that." She consulted her tablet, but evidently her friends hadn't responded yet, because she tucked it away in her bag again.

"The problem is how we're going to free Sandy if any of the dragons are around," I mused aloud, dismissing any number of outrageous—if daring—plans. "It seems impossible when ninety-seven percent of my power has been locked down by the interdiction. I guess our best bet is to find her, and just deal with whoever is holding her prisoner."

We paused for a second; then as one, we flung ourselves onto the ground, trusting the laurel to hide our prone forms. A car's engine grew louder, then faded as it passed by on the main road. I picked a startled beetle from my arm and waited for the count of fifty before I led us back to the gravel drive, where we continued to creep from tree to tree, scanning all the while for signs of life.

"I suppose that is a reasonable plan," Seawright said, the corners of her mouth turning down. "I would be remiss in my duties if I did not point out to you that although you do have access to three percent of your powers, it is highly forbidden for you to use them, and any attempt to do so in front of me will force me to take extreme measures."

"What extreme measures?" I asked in a whisper as we crept along the edge of the road, ready to dash into the wooded stretches on either side of it at the approach of a car or person. "You've already handcuffed me, which I would like to point out yet again is going to make any rescue operation that much harder."

"Taser," she answered with a complacence that had me pulling up and spinning around to stare at her.

"You have a Taser on you? Why in the name of all that's good and green didn't you tell me?"

"You didn't ask," she said, and I had to admit she had a point.

"Is it charged up and ready for action?" I asked as we crept closer to a clearing. Through the trees I could see red roofs of what must be the cabins.

"Of course. You don't think I'd go out after a desperate criminal without a fully charged Taser."

I narrowed my eyes at her. "Are you talking about me, or the people who are holding Sandy? Wait. Don't answer that. I don't think I want to know. Sandy said she's in cabin fourteen. Let's go along the back of the buildings so we have less of a chance to be spotted."

We circumnavigated the edge of the camp. There were several cabins laid out in a gentle curve, encircling a center area that held a fire pit, a large stone slab that had a horrible look of a sacrificial altar to it, and oddly what looked like three portable massage tables. Beyond the circle of small cabins, a larger log cabin lodge sat.

"I'll say this for them," I murmured a short time later, after we'd identified cabins number six, eight, and twelve. "Dragons know how to do camping right."

"Hot tubs," Seawright said, nodding and checking her tablet. "Hammocks filled with blankets and pillows."

I pointed to the roof of the nearest cabin that we were skulking behind. "Satellite antennas and solar panels. It must cost a small fortune to stay at this place. Whoa."

We both stopped and plastered ourselves against the back wall of the cabin when radio static burst into the silence. "—camera was tripped. Dominic, check it out," a hollow voice said.

I gestured to Seawright for silence and, crouching, peered around the edge of the cabin. A man with his back to us stood about five yards away, looking toward the lodge.

"It's probably just game," the man said, his voice rich with an Eastern European accent. "Elk. Deer. They've been triggering the cameras for the last few days."

"It's set off more than one camera," the person on the radio answered. "Go check it out. Deus will be here soon, and he'll have your heart on a plate if anything goes wrong."

The man in front of us turned and stalked off beyond the fire pit and sacrificial altar, muttering under his breath in a language I didn't understand.

"Dragon?" Seawright whispered, her tablet in hand.

"I think so," I whispered back. "Let's get Sandy out quick while he and his friend are focused elsewhere."

"If they have cameras watching the north side," she said softly as we hurried down the line of cabins, careful to check each time we emerged from protection before dashing to the next building, "they may have had one on the drive."

"They would have come after us," I said, and pointed at the number on the cabin just in front of us. I put my finger to my lips before sidling along the side, carefully peeking out to make sure no one was in the center common area.

Without waiting to consult with Seawright, I hustled up the two steps to the door, twisting the handle and hurtling inside, closing the door just as swiftly behind us before turning to assess the interior.

"I knew it," Seawright said, her voice fat with satisfaction as she held up her tablet to take a picture before tapping quickly on it, obviously sending the picture with a message. "It's just like *Dragon Heart*."

I stared in shock for a few seconds at the figure of Sandy, bound to a center pole that held up the roof, her hair almost reaching to the ground as she slumped over.

She lifted her head as I paused, gasping at the sight, my heart beating so loud I was certain Seawright could hear it.

"Don't move." The words were spoken in a rasping tone that made my throat ache in sympathy. "Don't … net." She slumped forward, her hair swinging with soft little swooshing noises on the wood floor.

"Sandy—" I started forward despite her words, wanting to help her, to free her from where she'd been bound, but Seawright yanked me back before I had taken more than a step.

"Look," Seawright said, pointing at the ceiling.

Although the log cabin had a vaulted ceiling, an odd square metal grid apparatus hung down from it. Pinpoints of red lights appeared to move as the metal grid swayed slightly, no doubt with the breeze generated by the door opening and closing.

"Lasers," Seawright said.

"Yes … laser grid." Sandy's head lifted again, her face white and gaunt with strain, her eyes, normally a clear blue, now clouded with pain. Her words came out in short, breathy bursts. "They heard me. They knew I called someone. Called you. They wanted to punish me. They want …" Her shoulders slumped and her head dropped as she sagged forward again.

"We have to do something," I said, shaking the handcuffs. "Unlock these, Seawright. We can't possibly navigate that laser with them on."

"Not under pain of death will I take them off," she answered, squinting first at the grid hanging overhead, then at the wall opposite us. "Does the lettering on that laser grid say ALP1414 or is that L4L4?"

"I've never growled at a person in my life," I told her, so frustrated I could scream. "But I'm about to go feral if you insist on bringing up that Committee crap. Take them off!"

"ALP1414 or L4L4?" she asked again.

"Gah!" I wanted to yell, but mindful of possible dragons outside the cabin, I confined myself to pinching her on her arm. "It's 1414, and if you think I won't remember this when we're out, you're dead wrong. I'll be firing off a report about you putting Sandy at risk so fast it'll make your head spin."

"I've tried spinning my head, but it just ends up in muscle strain," she murmured, tapping on her tablet.

It was a struggle, but I managed to take a couple of deep, calming breaths. "If you take the handcuffs off, I can rappel down to where Sandy is bound, and release her. I promise you can slap these obnoxious things back on my wrist once I have her, OK?"

"No." She scooted along the wall, pulling me after her, keeping her back firmly pressed to it as she skirted the edge of the laser grid. "Not only would I be in violation of two laws, but something might happen that would keep you from honoring your word. Besides, you don't have rappelling equipment, and it would be almost impossible for you to get your friend out without it. It'll just be easier to destroy the power box to the laser grid."

"I swear to you that I won't run—what?" I stopped thinking up persuasive arguments, and moved with her. "What power box?"

She waved the tablet at me. "The one I looked up. The ALP1414 Destructo-Laser Trap III has a wall-mounted box, and is not battery operated like the later models. If we destroy the power supply, the laser will turn off, and we can rescue your friend secure in the knowledge that we have contravened exactly zero rules governing the Otherworld, and specifically any acts contained within your contract. I think that's it there, screwed into the wall next to that lamp."

I turned my gaze from Seawright to the small black box that was indeed screwed onto the wall, and then back to Seawright. "OK, I take back several of the unkind things I was thinking about you being pedantic and overly delighting in minutiae like the Otherworld laws."

"Oh, I do love minutiae," she said with a little frown. "How could I not? But I will accept your retraction of unkind thoughts. Hmm. This power supply appears to be quite sturdily made. I don't suppose you have a screwdriver handy?"

"I am not Doctor Who, so no," I said, glancing back at Sandy, but she was still slumped forward. My anxiety was growing with each passing second, the skin on my back almost twitching with the need to free Sandy and get the hell out of there. "That dragon might be back any minute. Or others who will check on Sandy, so if you're going to do something, do it now—otherwise you can take the cuffs off me, and I'll try swinging out on that big overhead beam. I might be able to reach the grid there."

"That would be the sheerest folly, since you have not—according to your dossier, which I again remind you I studied at length—displayed any sort of acrobatic ability, and if your stiffness and inability to conduct even the simplest of poses taught by the caprine vinyasa class we attended last year was anything to go by, I doubt if you have acquired such since then."

"Oh!" I said, momentarily distracted. "That's not fair. I had pulled muscles in my back a few days before, which is why I was taking that yoga class to begin with. It's not my ineptness that kept me from doing a proper downward dog."

"Your goat kept falling off," she pointed out, then, after rustling around in her bag, added, "After which it abandoned you. You were the only one in the class shunned by them. This is not ideal, but I believe my scissors will allow me to pry off the back of the box."

Stung as I was by her reminder of my failure at the goat yoga class we'd taken, I stifled my protestations that it wasn't anything to do with my abilities, acrobatic or otherwise, that cut short the class, and watched as she tried first to pry apart the box, then to stab it into submission.

"I don't think that's going to do anything," I told her after a few seconds. "Except possibly electrocute you, and since we are connected by a piece of metal—really, I swear upon anything you'd like that I would not run away if you took them off—I'd appreciate it if you avoided that situation."

She sighed, and dug out a small hammer. "I will be sure to write a stern letter to the manufacturer," she said just before lifting the hammer up high.

"You know, I don't think—" I started to say, but that's all that I managed to get out before her hammer connected with the box, and a brilliant red light filled the space in front of us.

The concussive blast sent both Seawright and me flying backward, into an inky abyss that sucked us in and swallowed us whole, leaving nothing but insensibility.

TEN
THE MATING

"Hrn? Flrt." The noise of a voice wafted gently through the mass of clouds that seemed to fill my mind. It was counterpointed by a shrill barrage that slowly resolved itself into angry words being spat out with the velocity of bullets.

"I don't recognize that language," a voice answered nearer than the shouting person. "And since I am familiar with seventy-two languages, both extant and extinct, including the four you speak, I don't believe they are actual words."

Images drifted in and out through the mind clouds, until the latter suddenly dissolved into nothing, and I sat up, exclaiming, "Sandy!"

"—you almost killed me!" Sandy yelled. "Can't you see that I'm bound here? Why do you want me dead? I thought you were my friend, and yet you bring in that insane … insane … *goblin*, and let her blow me up!"

"I am *not* a goblin," Seawright said with a near snort. "I am a junior scribe third class."

"Same difference," Sandy spat. "You could have killed me!"

I looked around us. Two of the cabin walls were still standing, although blackened and charred. Seawright, who was on her knees next to me, was checking the contents of her messenger bag. She also was blackened and charred with a faint curl of smoke rising lazily from a clump of her hair that poked out at odd angles.

I reached out to touch one of the clumps, but it fell off and hit the ground with a soft noise.

My eyes widened as hastily I pushed the hair behind her while she was focused on her bag. "Er … are you OK?" I asked her.

"*I'm* not OK. *I'm* nearly dead, not that you asked, which is a miracle considering the fact that the goblin tried to blow me to smithereens," Sandy said, sniffing loudly.

I gave her a quick glance, but far from being harmed, she appeared to have been sheltered from the blast that left everything else in the remains of the cabin coated with soot and singed about the edges. I assumed the laser grid was enhanced by a protective magic that kept the occupants from being reached by things outside its bubble, and turned my attention back to Seawright. I touched her arm, asking again, "Are you OK?"

"Yes, of course," she answered, without looking up. "I'm a junior scribe."

I didn't see what that had to do with the situation, but evidently, junior scribes were heartier beings than I had given them credit for. I touched my own hair, wondering if I wore the same "fork in a light socket" look that she had, but although it felt dusty and out of sorts, it didn't seem to be smoking. "I'm glad to hear that. What happened?"

"Your goblin tried to break magic," Sandy said, narrowing her eyes on Seawright. "Which you of all people should know isn't going to end well. What on earth were you thinking?"

"Ah, excellent. No one need panic," Seawright said, her voice filled with relief as she sat back on her heels. "All is well."

"Is it?" I asked, rubbing my face. It felt gritty and hot, like I had been out in the sun too long.

"Yes. The tablet is unharmed," she answered, showing it first to me, then to Sandy, who was struggling with her bonds. "I'm so glad I heeded the warning of the junior scribe who attended to you before me, and insisted on getting the blast-proof case for it."

"Blast?" I asked, my brain still drifting a bit. At a tug on my shackled arm, I glanced down at myself, and realized what had happened. "You blew us up?"

"Of course not. That would be counterproductive." Seawright got to her feet, yanking on my arm until, with zero grace whatsoever, I clawed my way upright.

"She did. She totally did," Sandy said, outrage dripping from her voice. "Just look at what she did to the cabin! I'm lucky I'm still alive. *Dio*, Phyllida! If you didn't want to help me, you could have simply told me so, not sent a goblin to destroy me."

I glanced quickly behind us at the wall that lay splinted and smoking. From the part of the cabin that remained upright, it was evident that whatever Seawright had done, it caused a massive explosion that had we been mortal, would no doubt have ended with our deaths. "How did a simple hammer—no, never mind. You can explain it later. We need to get out of here before someone comes to investigate."

"And about time!" Sandy said. It was obvious she was about to say more as I staggered toward her, hauling a slightly resisting Seawright with me, but Sandy, who had opened her mouth to speak, suddenly gave a moan and slumped forward again.

"I suspect the power supply had several highly effective protective wards on it," Seawright said as I reached out to Sandy with my free hand.

Seawright jerked me back just as a pain sizzled across the flesh of my arm. I yelped and looked down at the red line above my wrist.

"We didn't turn off the laser grid," she said, nodding upward, to the part of the roof that remained overhead.

"No, you didn't," a man's voice said from behind me, heavy with an Eastern European accent.

I froze into a block of Phyllida-shaped ice, fear swamping me at the same time a wave of chill swept up my spine, making goose bumps ripple down my arms.

I knew that voice.

I knew that accent.

A shadow fell across me even as I weaved, causing Seawright to reach out and grab my arm, no doubt to keep from falling.

I knew that shadow.

"I see you are as inept as ever in the use of your magics," the voice said, and the last shred of hope I desperately held that I was wrong about the origination of the voice dried up and floated away as Xavier strode past me to stand with his hands on his hips while he surveyed the damage. He didn't even acknowledge me as he added, "I will have to lesson you in that, as well as other things. Deus, turn off the grid and take the woman."

"What—" My voice came out more a croak than a word. I licked my lips and swallowed down the sudden ache of tears in my throat. Only Xavier triggered such a reaction. Only Xavier caused my brain to shut down with the sheer unadulterated horror of his presence.

Only Xavier hunted me like the helpless prey that I was.

"What are you doing here?" I managed to ask, trying hard not to look at him, but my gaze was drawn against my will.

I hated the sight of him, hated that he filled me with such impotent fear, and hated myself most of all because he still had such an effect on me.

"I told you that I would find you," he said, his black-eyed gaze brushing over me in an impersonal manner that I didn't for one second believe. There was nothing impersonal about the man who had betrayed me. "Deus, do not make me repeat myself."

A little spurt of anger warmed my belly, and I cherished it, fanning it to glow hotter. I'd learned long ago that the only weapon I had against Xavier was contempt. I realized then that he wasn't alone; three other dragons accompanied him.

"There is a disturbance to the north," one of the men answered, holding a phone to his ear. "The trail cameras were destroyed, and several members of the tribe are not answering when called."

It was fleeting, but I managed to catch a spasm of irritation that crossed Xavier's face. His hair was as black as his eyes, sweeping back in a way that I used to admire, just as I'd allowed his angled jaw and high, Slavic cheekbones to lead me to believe he was the handsomest man I'd ever met.

A mental image of Bastian flashed through my brain, and I realized there was no comparison. Bastian's fire and golden light cast Xavier in the shadows, where he belonged.

"I did not ask you what has happened to the tribe. Remove the woman." His gaze flickered over to Seawright, then down to where the handcuffs connected us. One eyebrow rose a fraction of an inch. "Really, Phyllida, this is a new side to you. Regardless of your new lifestyle, your … whatever it is … must go. Deus, attend to it, as well."

Seawright straightened up and gave Xavier her haughtiest look. I mentally applauded both her gesture and the fact that she could hold his gaze and not crumble before it. "I am not an it. You may refer to me with they/them pronouns if you wish, although as I am currently in female form, I also accept she/her. My name is Seawright Pendleton, and I am a junior scribe third class. I assume you are a dragon?"

"One of the L'au-dela," he said, using the formal name for the Otherworld. His tone was as dismissive as his glance before he asked the other man, who I assumed was Deus, "Do you have the ringsel?"

Deus had his back to Xavier while he spoke rapidly into his cell phone in what sounded very much like Magyar to me. I wondered at that, since I knew Xavier was born many centuries ago in what was now Kazakhstan, and he had— at the time I had been with him—surrounded himself only with dragons from the same area.

"Take care of it," Deus said in a near growl. "The sire is here, and we don't have time to be chasing after mortals who've decided to tweak your nose. He wishes for the ceremony to take place immediately."

"I grow impatient," Xavier said in a soft voice, one that sent another round of shivers down my back and arms. Deus spun around, and snapped a rude word into the phone before hanging up, bowing to Xavier.

Seawright shot me a curious look, saying softly without moving her lips, "You know that dragon?"

"The one with black eyes, yes," I answered out the side of my mouth, my gaze darting between Xavier and Deus. "You read my file. You know what happened to me years ago."

Her eyes widened as she gazed at Xavier. "This really is just like *Dragon Heart*. He is a dead ringer for the Grand Garibal—"

Xavier, who was snarling at Deus and an underling to cut down Sandy, spun around to glare at us for a few seconds before turning back and continuing to harangue the men now clustered together.

"—di," Seawright finished in a whisper.

Deus, a tall man with gaunt angles on his face, which somehow seemed familiar, strode past Seawright and me, not even sparing us a glance. He had long auburn hair and muddied-gray eyes, but it was the orders he snapped out that made me feel like a rug had just been pulled out from under me.

"Turn off the lasers," he told a woman, who hurried forward to start drawing symbols over the power supply.

"Not a dragon," Seawright whispered, watching her with interest.

"Not if she's undoing those wards, as it looks like she is," I agreed.

"We'll have the ceremony immediately," Xavier told Deus, then, without a word or glance my way, strode out of the remains of the cabin and disappeared into the center common area.

"We'll take the mate out now," Deus told two dragons who came forward, then, with an annoyed expression, jerked his phone out of his pocket and snapped a, "What?" into it.

"Mate?" I stared at Sandy, who was still slumped against the ropes, dread filling my belly. "Oh, holy hellballs. He's going to bind Sandy to him."

"Oooh," Seawright said, still watching the woman at the power box, who evidently managed to reverse the wards, because she toggled something on the box, shutting down the laser grid. "That's not at all what happens in *Dragon Heart*. It's one of the outcasts who sacrifices herself to Garibaldi."

"Well, I'm not going to let Xavier add Sandy to his victim list," I said, fighting down the nausea that I knew came from the fear of what Xavier had planned for me. I had no idea how he'd found me, but assumed it was the slip in my last dream. "I don't suppose you have any martial arts experience?"

"No, although I have taken a self-defense class with a really intense troll who dislikes mortals."

"That'll have to do. Ready?"

"For wha—"

I grabbed Seawright and rushed forward, spinning around to kick at the nearest dragon who was approaching, fortunately nailing him right in the chest. Sandy's head snapped up as I grabbed the ropes binding her, and used them to lever myself up, slamming my foot into the dragon who had jumped at me, connecting with his jaw in a satisfying manner. He fell back onto his friend who was in the act of rising.

The woman who had worked on the power box made an *eep*ing sound and, skirting us, dashed out of the remains of the cabin.

"Cut her loose," I ordered Seawright, twisting as best I could given the handcuffs, and waving my fist at the third man.

He, however, didn't come into range of my feet, as I had hoped. He sneered and, with a shimmer of the air, morphed into the shape of a stout, dirty-gray dragon.

"Oh, shit," I swore, knowing what was going to happen even before it did. I'm not normally prescient that way, but at that moment, I knew without a doubt that the dragon had shifted in order to blast us with dragon fire so that he could drag Sandy out to be bound to Xavier.

A memory of a few days ago wiggled in the back of my brain, causing me to yell, "Hurry!" to Seawright before I spun around, my bound arm wrapped around my body as I put myself between her and the dragon.

He roared and blasted us with fire, causing Seawright to jerk my arm hard.

I turned my head and closed my eyes, focusing on not fighting the fire but allowing it to simply be. It skittered down me, little tendrils of smoke wisping out of me, but although the fire was just on this side of being painful, it didn't actually burn.

I wasn't about to wait for the dragon to realize that, though. I unwound myself, spinning out, and caught this dragon in the groin, knowing that even in dragon form the males were vulnerable at that spot. When he roared again, this time to double over, I slammed my fist into his snout, and followed up with a kick to the chops. He fell to the ground, swearing in Russian, writhing with pain all the while casting dire threats.

"Got it," Seawright said, panting a little as she cut free the last bit of rope. "That was very interesting. I've never seen dragon fire up close. I will have to write up a report and share it with the other junior scribes."

"Can you walk?" I asked Sandy, my free arm around her as I half dragged, half escorted her toward the back of the cabin. "There's a car that should be waiting for us. We have to get you away before Xavier notices."

"I'm afraid I can't allow that," a voice said, and Deus appeared before us. "Xavier would not be happy to see his chosen one leave before the ceremony was complete."

"Over my dead body," I said before I realized that I had spoken. For one moment, my mind was horrified that

I would risk myself for Sandy, but instantly, I was ashamed of myself. She was my friend. She had done much to help me when I'd broken free of Xavier, and if I could repay that debt, then I would. I moved out in front of her, glaring at Deus. "Seawright, you remember us talking about that thing you had with you that I didn't know you had with you? Now would be an excellent time to bring it out and introduce it to Deus."

The dragon gave me a look that spoke volumes, none of which were complimentary. He simply gestured, and two dragons who had been behind him moved forward.

"No!" I said, struggling when one of the men headed toward Sandy. "Leave her be! Take … I can't believe I'm going to say this. … Take me, instead."

Deus and the other descended upon me, easily avoiding the kick I tried to land. Deus yanked me forward, spinning me around so my unbound hand was twisted up behind my back, hissing, "See that you behave yourself in front of the sire," into my ear.

Seawright squawked when she was jerked forward. She'd been rustling around in her bag, obviously trying to find her Taser, but the other dragon, at a word from Deus, simply slung her over his shoulder.

"I protest this manhandling most strenuously," I heard her say as Deus marched me forward. It was awkward walking with one arm still attached to Seawright, but I was more afraid for what was happening to Sandy to pay much heed to my discomfort.

Xavier stood with a handful of people around the big stone table that gave off the uncomfortable sacrificial-altar vibes. My bile rose when I saw a dragon behind Sandy, herding her forward to Xavier.

"I have been awaiting you—" Xavier started to say.

"Stop it," I yelled, taking Deus by surprise when I charged forward to Xavier, my free hand gesticulating when I demanded, "Whatever it is you have planned for her, just stop it. She's innocent of this stupid vendetta you have against me. I don't know what you want with her, but whatever it is …" I took a deep breath, bits of my soul crumbling at the thought of what I was doing. "Whatever it is can be negotiated."

I held my breath, praying that I had spoken the magic word. Dragons, I had found during my ill-fated time with Xavier, loved nothing more than negotiating terms to something they sought, and in this, Xavier was no different from his kin.

He froze for a few seconds, then slowly turned toward me, his eyes half-closed as he gave me a thorough once-over, one that left me feeling like I had been wiped down with an icy glove. I shivered in response, but kept my head held high. I'd survived him before. I could do so again.

But you almost lost yourself in the process, a voice whispered in my head.

"An interesting proposition," he said, and I could swear amusement lit the unholy darkness of his eyes. "What terms do you have to offer?"

I glanced at Seawright, who was now standing next to me, her eyes round as she split her attention between Xavier and me. "I am bound by the terms of the contract with the Committee, as you know."

Xavier made a *tch*ing sound, and waved that away. "What do you offer me to leave the diviner in peace?"

"This is stupid," I heard Sandy mutter, but I wanted desperately to keep Xavier's attention off her. I literally waggled my hand in the air to make sure he was looking away from her. My stomach turned over as a result of his attention, and it took me a few seconds to fight down the resulting nausea. "If you let Sandy go free without any compulsions or other restrictions, then I will take her place."

"You cannot do that," Seawright objected, clutching her tablet to her chest. "Otherworld Directive number—"

"Silence that," Xavier said, nodding toward her.

I jumped in front of her, holding her behind me with my bound hand. "You touch one clump of smoking hair on her head, and the deal is off. She is my gaoler, nothing more."

There was definitely amusement in his eyes now as he glanced again at the handcuff, but he gave an elegant twitch of his shoulder. "Very well. I accept your terms. Alessandra, it would seem I owe you an apology. When you proposed this plan, I thought it unnecessarily convoluted, but it has worked just as you said it would."

"Apology?" I said stupidly, my brain feeling as if it were filled with dense cotton candy. "Plan?"

"Sorry," Sandy said, strolling past me to stand next to Xavier, kissing him on the cheek as he continued to watch me with obvious amusement. "I knew there was no other way you'd leave your hidey-hole unless it was to help me, and it really is important that you be here." Her gaze shifted to Xavier. "I'm sure that one day you'll get over the sense of betrayal I feel boiling around inside of you."

"Betrayal?" I repeated, my mind unable to process what she said.

Seawright sucked in a deep breath, her brain obviously much swifter on the uptake than mine.

"You … betrayed me?" I asked, shaking my head at the absurdity of the question. Sandy couldn't betray me. She was one of the few people I trusted, part of a tiny group who knew what I was, and what danger the world was to me. She knew how Xavier had abused me.

She was my friend.

"It really is for the best," she said, a little smile lifting the corners of her mouth.

A rush of emotion hit me in the form of a flush washing upward from my chest. "You were my friend. You knew what I'd been through. Friends don't betray."

"Sorry," she said again, her shoulders rising in a half shrug. "If it helps, think of it more as a necessary evil. You have to be here now, with Xavier, in order for the blue dragon sept to be destroyed."

I stared at her open-mouthed with horror and denial and disbelief, wondering for a second if I'd gone mad. "But *you're* a blue dragon."

"Yes, well, sometimes, you have to let go of the things you love," she said with another half shrug, then addressed Xavier. "Are we leaving?"

"As soon as the ceremony is over," he answered, his gaze shifting around to the few dragons who had gathered.

I wanted to sit down and cry. I wanted to scream and yell and hurl profanities at Xavier. I wanted to hurt Sandy as badly as she had just hurt me.

Instead, I stood there, tears burning the backs of my eyes, refusing to allow them to fall.

"You don't need me here. I'll get my things and meet you at the helipad," Sandy said, and, without a glance toward me, spun around and marched off toward the most distant cabin.

My heart broke at the knowledge that someone I had trusted, someone whom I had risked all to help, had cast me over in such a callous manner.

"Life sucks," I said under my breath.

Seawright pursed her lips.

"Time and time again it keeps telling me that I can't trust anyone. And time and time again, I forget that, and this is what happens." My fingernails bit into my palms. I would not break down. I would not let anyone see how I had been hurt.

"A harsh lesson, to be sure," Seawright answered, casting a glance toward Xavier, who was in the middle of berating Deus over something. "But you are a hellerune. It's your lot to be alone."

I bit back the urge to say something rude to her, knowing it wasn't her fault. My soul wept, though.

"It's my worst nightmare come to fruition," I said softly, but not softly enough.

"Your *worst* nightmare? Ah, but we've shared so many that were much more exhilarating," Xavier said before turning to survey the dragons who had gathered around in a semicircle, and was apparently unhappy with what he saw. His voice, normally as smooth as velvet, was full of spiky irritation. "Where is the rest of the tribe? Why are they not here to witness the mating?"

Mating? I glanced at the stone, my skin crawling at the idea that he intended on having extremely public sex. Panic hit me hard, driving out the pain of Sandy's betrayal and making it impossible for me to catch my breath.

"They have not returned from checking on the cameras," Deus said in a low voice, the flash of irritation across his face immediately smoothing out to submission. "I warned you of that."

"Call them back. It is important that the Chaos Tribe see the claiming."

"Hell's bells," I said softly, my spirits plummeting even further. Could life get any worse?

"I have tried, Xavier, but they do not answer my call." Again, a flash of emotion was briefly visible on his face, this time anger. Deus clearly didn't like being put on the spot by Xavier, a fact that I made note of.

"Then we will do this without them. Record it for the rest of the tribe." Without looking at me, Xavier grabbed my hand and hauled me over to the sacrificial rock, Seawright squawking as she was forced to follow. She had been holding up her tablet, clearly filming Xavier and me, no doubt as proof of whatever violation she would file against me.

That was the least of my worries. The panicked squirrels that made up my brain ran around waving their hands in the air as I tried to find a way out of what Xavier had planned, but in the end, I had made my bed.

I just wished trying to save Sandy wouldn't end in my destruction ... or that of the mortal world.

"Dragons of the Chaos Tribe," Xavier said loudly, facing them, still holding my wrist. "Witness as today I name Phyllida Hall as mate."

Silence met that pronouncement.

Horror crawled over me like ants, my throat aching with the need to cry.

But I would not give him that pleasure. I blinked rapidly and tried to swallow down the lump in my throat.

"Acknowledge the honor I do you," Xavier demanded, turning to me.

"I … what?" I was unsure of what he expected me to say.

He sighed a martyred sigh. "You must swear fealty to me in order to complete the mating." His eyes narrowed. "Or do you wish for the more old-fashioned method of sexual claiming, instead?"

"No," I said, pushing down the need to vomit. "May the world forgive me for what I do here today, but I … against my will, I do so swear fealty to you."

He smiled a fat, satisfied smile, then promptly dropped my hand, and gestured to Deus. "Go find your kin. Then join me. We have much work to do."

"That's … that's it?" I asked, so stunned that the words were out before I could stop them.

Xavier paused as he passed me, his eyebrows raised in an obnoxious show of innocence. "Did you expect more, *meelaya*?" he asked, making me want to curl in upon myself at the term of endearment that I'd heard so often in the past. "Do you miss our bedsport so much that you would demand it of me now, in front of Deus's tribe?"

"Goddess, no," I said, once again without thinking. There was nothing Xavier disliked more than having his ego pricked, and the knowledge that he made me sick just being near me would do more than poke at his pride. I tried to recover as best I could, lest he lash out at Seawright or me. "I have never been an exhibitionist, as you know."

His lips twisted in acknowledgment, but to my extreme relief (and no little confusion), he simply nodded and strolled out of the camp, Deus and a couple of his flunkies following behind.

"That was interesting," Seawright said, filming until Xavier and Deus disappeared around the bend of the road. "I will have to check with the Compendium of Directives, but I believe hellerunes are not allowed to be mated without permission from the Committee. I'm not sure the question has come up, since most hellerunes—"

"Don't live long enough to find a life partner, yes, I know," I said, sighing to myself before glancing around. The remaining four dragons were clustered together, speaking. I took a step backward, watching to see if they'd notice. "Part of my mind is screaming at what I've done, and the other part is telling me that I deserve it because I believed Sandy was my friend. Goddess. Could life get more horrible than it is now?"

I took another step back. Seawright looked up when she felt the movement, glanced at me, then at the dragons when I tipped my head toward them.

"Ah," she said, and, pursing her lips, slid her tablet into her bag, turning so that she stood next to me facing the dragons.

We took two steps backward.

The dragons continued to pay us no attention.

"Let's get the hell out of here," I whispered, and after moving backward a few yards, we skirted one of the cabins, still keeping our eyes on the dragons.

One of them got a call, and the others clustered around to listen.

"Now," I said, and, grabbing Seawright's arm, spun us around, bolting around the corner of the cabin.

Straight into the arms of Bastian.

ELEVEN
THE BETRAYAL

"You're certain?" The words were spoken softly, but Bastian pinned his lieutenant back with a hard look.

Luca nodded, and flipped through screens on his phone, holding up a text message for Bastian to read. "The others are Chaos, but these three are from the Blood Tribe."

"Peste," Bastian swore, looking down at the five dragons who lay inert before them. Gio emerged from the shrubs, holding up yet another remote camera. "What are they doing here? This is supposed to be the camp of the Chaos Tribe. The Blood Tribe is …"

"Mythical?" Luca asked.

"Hardly that." Bastian dredged through his memories of the time before the madness. "There were rumors of the Blood Tribe when I was young, but they were believed to reside in Asia—Kyrgyzstan and Kazakhstan. I have not heard that any members have been seen recently, though."

"What will we do with them?" Luca asked, idly prodding one of the unconscious men with the toe of his boot.

"Leave them here." Bastian's lips tightened to a line for a few seconds. "Their tribe has no claim upon the weyr, and I would not have it said that blue dragons took the lives of others without due cause. Use extra zip ties on them, though, so they remain bound out and out of our way until their kin can find them. Have you seen any sign of Deus?"

"No," Luca started to say, but was interrupted by an obviously excited Gio.

"I have! There were three males hunting for this camera, and one of them received a call. I could hear the man speaking on the phone, and it was definitely the master Deus. He was angry, very angry, and swore at the men that by not returning to the lodge, they were shaming him before their sire." Gio frowned before continuing. "I do not understand that. One of the males was a blue dragon—former blue dragon—while the other two were green. They could not all have the same sire, since the blue dragon was Stefano. Do you remember him? He used to be Fiat's personal guard—"

Luca shot the younger man a warning look. "Do you forget yourself? You do not ask a wyvern if he remembers one of the sept members, even those who are no longer with the sept. To do so is to insult Bastian."

"I meant no slur against you," Gio said quickly, turning a pleading expression on Bastian. "I just thought that perhaps since you were confined so long, you might not remember Stefano—"

"I would have a word with you," Luca said, sighing loudly as he none-too-gently grabbed Gio's arm and hauled him off a few yards to speak quickly and quietly in his ear.

Bastian stifled a desire to laugh at the chagrined expression on Gio's face and, after a quick glance at the map on his phone, headed to the south, where lay the camp of what he'd been told were the Chaos Tribe.

He badly wanted to find Deus. If what the messenger told him was true, and Alessandra had been seen in Deus's company, then it was quite likely she was being held against her will. Nothing else made sense.

Ten minutes later, Bastian and his two lieutenants skirted an oval composed of several small log cabins, a cleared center area, and a large wood and white stone lodge at the far end.

He held up his hand as they approached the nearest lodge, hearing the faint rumble of masculine voices.

"Kin," he said after listening hard.

"Sounds like Saverio and Dario," Luca said softly, naming brothers who had been particularly devoted to Fiat. "What are they doing here with the Blood Tribe?"

"I suspect we will find that out shortly. You and Gio go to the left. I'll go right. We will meet by the lodge with a tally of how many dragons are present. If you see Deus, do nothing; just note who he is with."

"And if we find Alessandra?" Luca asked, his eyes steady on Bastian.

"If she is in peril, rescue her. If not, report to me her circumstances. I will not having us running blindly into what could be a trap set by Deus to cause trouble in the weyr."

"Ah, so that's what you are thinking," Luca said, nodding; then with a sharp gesture at Gio, they slid silently into the foliage surrounding the camp clearing.

Bastian followed suit in the other direction, making sure to keep hidden amongst the shadows of the cabins as he drew closer to the dragons who were still talking in the center of the clearing.

"—unfair to blame us," Saverio was saying angrily when Bastian paused behind the cabin nearest them. "It is the Blood Tribe's problem, not ours."

"And yet we are the ones the master is angry at." That had to be Saverio's twin, Dario. Bastian's memory of them was of sullenness and petulance. They were young, like Gio, but clearly had bought into the story that Fiat had presented the sept. "I will not stand for being any man's scapegoat, not even the sire's!"

A third man hushed them, warning, "Quiet, you fool. The master has ears everywhere. No, do not fire up at me. I like the situation no more than you, but our opinions matter little. We must do as ordered and keep our heads down until such time as the sire leaves."

Bastian wondered about who was this sire that the men referred to, but just as he was about to peer around the corner of the cabin to assess the location of the three dragons, a whirlwind slammed into him, sending him reeling backward two steps.

Only his presence of mind kept him from uttering a loud, "Oof!" when he found his arms full of the lush form of a woman.

"Wh—" He had a hand over the woman's mouth before she could do more than take in breath preparatory to gasping in surprise. For a moment, he stood staring down in familiar mossy-green eyes before the fear in them clicked in his brain. A second shape moved into place behind Phyllida, but as it was a smaller woman, he simply stepped backward two paces, taking Phyllida with him.

"What are you doing here?" Phyllida asked in a whisper when she pulled his hand from her face. Her eyes clouded, her brows pulling together when she asked, "Are you with them? With him?"

"Deus? No." He glanced at the smaller woman for a moment, noticed the handcuffs binding her to Phyllida's left wrist, and wondered just what the hell was going on.

"Not Deus. Xavier." The last word was spoken so softly he almost didn't catch it, but once again he sensed fear in her, a deep, abiding fear that stirred the sense of protection in him that he thought of as his wyvern side.

"Your lover?"

"Former lover," she said quickly.

"I do not know him. Why are you here? Do you have business with the Chaos Tribe?" he asked, studying her. Her face was flushed and she seemed both fearful and triumphant, an odd mix of emotions that nonetheless stirred the warrior inside of him.

She cast a glance over her shoulder. "Dear goddess, no. Or rather, yes, but hopefully not any longer. Not if we can get away from those bastard dragons. Come on, Seawright."

"Do you know this man?" the smaller woman asked even as Phyllida pulled herself from where he was holding her free arm, and sidled past him, taking care not to disturb the tall ferns that all but brushed against the back wall of the cabin.

"He's the one I saw at the restaurant," Phyllida answered after an obvious hesitation.

Bastian frowned at her for a second, but before she had taken more than ten steps, he had texted to Luca that he would be delayed a few minutes, and hurried after the women as they dived into the woodland surrounding the camp.

Phyllida paused next to a tall fir tree, shooting him a look filled with both ire and disbelief. "Are you following me?"

"Yes," he answered, taking her arm and pulling her forward, away from the camp. "But I would not need to do so if you would explain why you were in the camp of the Blood dragons."

"Yeah, well, that would take more time than I have right now," she answered in an annoyed tone. "And I don't think they are the Blood Tribe. Seawright, stop pulling on me! My wrist is getting rubbed raw."

"I am not pulling on you. I am simply sending a notification of my abduction—and yours—to the watch, so that they might send out an officer to rescue us." She shot Bastian an assessing glance, then tapped again on the tablet she held in her cuffed hand. "Or maybe two. Three would probably be better. Your boyfriend looks like he wouldn't stop at taking out a couple of watch officers."

"Boyfriend!" Phyllida gave what Bastian thought of as a ladylike snort, and glanced upward as if she was seeking affirmation of what she had to put up with. She also pulled her arm free from him a second time, striding forward with a set to her shoulders that made him want to smile despite the mild insult. "He's hardly that. I mean, a little nooky in a dream or two doesn't constitute boyfriend status. Especially when the last time I saw him, he more or less said he couldn't stand to be around me for some mysterious reason that he never came right out and explained. Not to mention he accused me of seducing him, which is just way out of line, since he's the dream walker. Where's the road? We don't want to be going in circles. That Lyft lady should be back by now."

"I did not accuse you of seducing me. I accused you of calling me to your dreams to protect you, which I explained—in detail—that I could not do," he said, feeling self-righteous. "As for our activities, they were enjoyable. Greatly enjoyable. But until I have taken care of the situation with Deus and my daughter, I cannot return to finish the activities we started. You did not answer the question of what you were doing with the Blood and Chaos Tribes," Bastian said, moving alongside her lest she decide to run. He didn't think she was part of a trap set by Deus, but he had been wrong before—very, very wrong—and he would not allow himself to be fooled now simply because Phyllida was a lovely woman.

"You get a gold star for noticing things," she answered. "But that's it, because I didn't summon you—"

"I feel obligated to warn you that to leave the scene is to bring down upon your head even more charges," the smaller woman interrupted, jerking her arm in a manner that caused Phyllida's arm to move at an awkward angle.

Bastian frowned. "I don't know you, or why you are desirous of setting the watch upon me, let alone some sort of charges, but regardless, I wish you would stop moving your arm in that manner."

Both women continued to march forward, although they turned identical confused expressions on him. "Why?" Phyllida asked at the same time that the smaller woman said, "I wasn't talking to you. And my name is Seawright Pendleton. I am a junior scribe third class."

"Because it looks painful," he answered Phyllida.

She paused for a moment, her eyes widening, her pupils dilating, all the while her lips softened and curved into the beginnings of a smile. "That's—thoughtful of you. I take it you really aren't with Xavier? You weren't lying, or trying to fool me, just so you can hold me prisoner and use me?"

Bastian found himself blinking twice, a habit he deplored as being unworthy of a wyvern. "I have yet to hold any woman prisoner, let alone one to whom I wished to make love. Also, I do not lie."

"Really? Then you are a paragon among men," she answered with a little grimace. "Just as a point of fact, I wasn't actually referring to sex when I asked if you weren't going to hold me prisoner and use me. Although, if I was absolutely honest, that isn't a horrible suggestion. Yours, that is, not mine."

She finished with a blush that delighted Bastian. Before the wise side of his mind could remind him of his better intentions, he asked, "If I told you that my cock wishes to know you better, would you be offended because you consider that an inappropriate statement, or would you appreciate it as a compliment on the fact that you have the most beguiling eyes, and curves that make me hard contemplating them?"

"Wow. That's really ..." Phyllida stared at him with those lovely eyes, so clear and guileless he felt as if he could see to her soul.

The shadowed side of his mind pointed out he'd been very wrong about the innocence of others in the past, but he dismissed that thought.

"That's really ... you know ... out there. Er. Not your dick, your statement," Phyllida finished, her gaze dropping to his crotch for a fleeting second. "But on the whole, no, I'm not offended, although it's not a thing I'd suggest you say to just anyone."

"You are not just anyone," he said, and, without considering his motive, took her free hand to lead her forward, toward the road where Luca had left their car.

The small woman named Seawright gave a bark of laughter.

"No, that I'm not," Phyllida said with a little twist of her lips, glancing down at where he held her hand. "You appear to be holding my hand."

"I am. You get a gold star for noticing that."

To his complete pleasure, she gave a rusty chuckle. "Nice way to use my snarky comment against me. OK, let's try this—why, Bastian, are you holding my hand?"

"It is a nice hand. I like holding it. Also, I sense that you wish to escape, and since I would not recommend anyone being around ouroboros dragons, especially someone as tempting as you, I feel obligated to escort you to safety. Also, walking helps alleviate the erection, although if you keep curling your fingers into mine in that manner, it will simply become more painful."

"Is this flirting? Should I put this down as flirtation, or foreplay?" Seawright asked, still tapping on her tablet. "Or is it sexual harassment? Otherworld Directives 14-C and 14-E both have clear statements on what is considered sexual harassment, and I believe the holding of a hand without express permission, as well as untoward mention of a gentleman's personal dangler, qualifies in both situations. Phyllida, do you, at this moment, feel uncomfortable in the presence of your boyfriend? As an employee of the Committee, I am authorized to levy charges related to the general behavior of the denizens of the Otherworld. I will be happy to lay a further charge upon this man so that when the three watch members arrive, they will have even more reason to incarcerate him."

"You are odd," Bastian told Seawright. "And mistaken. No one will incarcerate me. Not again."

Phyllida, who had been striding along next to him with an amused expression, shot him a startled look before she said, "It is not flirting, nor foreplay. And might be considered sexually inappropriate by someone else, but I don't see it in that light, so you can just stop trying to have everyone arrested, Seawright. And while you're at it, please stop filing reports on me. You can call the watch all you want, but I'm not going to let them come near me."

"Are you escaping from Deus?" Bastian asked, wondering how she'd gotten tangled up with the Chaos Tribe.

"No. Well, maybe. Mostly, we're escaping from Xavier," she answered. He felt her peeking at him from the corner of her eye. "What are you doing here?"

He thought about asking her why she was with a former lover if she disliked him as she evidently did, but decided instead to be frank with her. He might not be able to rescue her as she desired, but there was no reason why they could not be together. Somewhat. At times. "I am searching for my daughter, Alessandra."

"What?" Her hand jerked in his as she came to a halt so quickly Seawright ran into her, sending her forward a step. "You're Sandy's dad?"

For a moment, his blood ran cold with fear; then his dragon fire roared through his veins and set his temper alight. He clamped down on it, releasing her hand as he spun her around to face him, his hands on her arms. "You know my daughter? Where is she? Does Deus have her? Have you seen her? Just what do you have to do with him? Are you involved with her capture?"

"No!" she answered when he gave her a little shake, her eyes filled with mingled fear and dismay. "I came here to rescue her."

He released her, once again the inner protector reacting to the deep well of fear that clearly had her in its grip. He made her a brief bow before saying, "I apologize for my anger. It slipped away from me. But I do not understand—you said you were trying to rescue Alessandra? You know her?"

"Yes." She glanced over her shoulder, hesitated for a second, then, with a mutter to herself that he didn't understand, took his hand and started forward again at a brisk pace. "I know Sandy. We were roomies for a few years when I was going to college. She's not here, so you can stop trying to pull me to a standstill. She left."

Bastian gave a mental shake of his head. He had been incarcerated when Alessandra was young, and did not have contact with her while she was growing up. Still, he eyed Phyllida with faint suspicion. Who exactly was she? Why would Alessandra ask her for help and not her own kin? Was it all a plot to confuse him? To trap the blue dragons in an aggression against the Chaos Tribe? He got a firm grip on his emotions, and did his best to keep his voice neutral when he asked, "When did she leave? Where did you see her? Here at the camp of the Blood Tribe?"

"They aren't Blood dragons." She slid him another corner-of-the-eye glance. "That is, Xavier is one, but the others—it sounded to me like they were some other dragons."

"Chaos dragons, yes, but there were Blood Tribe members here, as well," he said, trying to push down a variety of needs—to race back to the camp and demand to know of the tribe members where his daughter was, to rage and roar and burn down the forest with the strength of his anger, and finally to kiss Phyllida until her eyes went soft with passion.

He shook away all those desires, and focused on what she was saying.

"—she called and said she needed help getting away from some dragons, so I came out."

"Ahem," Seawright said, now marching alongside Phyllida. He wanted badly to ask her about the handcuffs, but decided that explanation could wait until he found out about Alessandra.

"Seawright came with me. Unexpectedly," Phyllida said with a sharp look at her friend. "When we got there—well, that's kind of a long story. The end result is that Sandy … er … left." She stopped when they reached the end of the forest and hit the gravel shoulder of the road.

"Left where?" he asked, throwing grammar to the wind. Once again, fear twisted his gut. It was not a pleasant sensation, but he had grave concerns about Deus, and wouldn't put it past him to hold Alessandra hostage for acquiescence of the blue dragons. "And with whom? How? Of her own accord, or was she under duress?"

"I don't know, with Xavier, evidently in a helicopter, and of her own accord. Very much so, in fact." She bit off the last few words as if they tasted sour.

Bastian didn't know what to believe—on the one hand, Phyllida's body language, combined with the almost palpable fear that all but dripped off her, told him she was speaking the truth, and yet, he sensed a mystery about her. She was clearly not telling him everything she knew, and that was a situation that he could not tolerate.

He needed to find his daughter and ensure her safety. If Phyllida had information that he needed, then she would simply have to be induced to part with it.

"I don't lie, either," Phyllida said, putting a hand on his arm. "Sandy was in the pink of health when she walked out of the camp, and she did so without anyone putting pressure on her."

He looked down at where her hand seemed to be burning into his flesh, and noticed her fingernails were on fire.

"Ack!" She jumped backward when she followed his gaze, frantically waving her hand as panic tinged the air. "Christos, what was that? Did you do something dragony to my fingers? I told you I wasn't lying! You don't have to set me on fire."

He looked at her with speculation, his concern for Alessandra warring with curiosity. Phyllida's reassurance that his daughter was not being held prisoner allowed a fanciful thought to push forward in his mind. "You permit?" he asked, holding out his hand.

"Sure," she said, giving him her hand. "But unless you're a doctor, or you have a burn kit secreted about your person, I don't know what you can do about burned fingers. Also, dude! That was so not cool. I don't know why—"

Her words died on his lips when he pulled her into an embrace, his body singing a song of pure joy when her curves caressed him, filling him with not just sexual interest, but a bone-deep satisfaction that he hadn't remembered having before.

He caught her gasp in his mouth as he kissed her, wordlessly asking her to open up for him, and sinking into the sweet depths when she did so.

"This is definitely foreplay," Seawright said, electronic tapping sounds following her words. "I am so noting it on the file. And then I'm going to look away, because I am asexual, and also there are some things that should be kept private between two people. I'll watch the road for the ride that you ordered, Phyllida."

She tasted of honey, of sunlight and warmth and long, languid summer days spent in the meadows near his home. She filled his senses, sending them spinning with mingled longing and a desire so strong that it shook him.

"I hope those bad dragons don't come after us. We're just standing here where anyone who drives down the road can see us, after all. I wonder when the watch officers will be here?" More tapping sounds followed. "Hrmph. Evidently, according to the watch supervisor, there's no one in this area who can undertake a trivial offense. Trivial! As if anything Phyllida does is trivial. Are you still—oh, you are. With both hands on Phyllida's derriere. Mercy."

Unsure of the wisdom of giving in to the hunger that claimed him, he allowed his fire to slip its leash, just a little, just enough to see if she responded to it in person as she had in her dreamscape.

"I am continuing to look at the road, and not at the fact that at this moment Phyllida appears to be wiggling in a manner that is most definitely illegal in at least three countries that I can think of."

"Hrn?" Phyllida said, jerking back from him for a moment, her eyes wide, the green in them misty with passion. She touched her lips, then pulled away, looking at the dragon fire that played on her fingers. Then with a sound that touched something deep in his chest, she grabbed his hair with her free hand and pulled him forward, her lips claiming his.

"I'm going to put on a podcast now. Just so I don't have to hear the moaning noises and kissy-face slurps that you two are making." A faint tinny voice began, describing some sort of video game that involved dragons.

Bastian had always tried to be a thoughtful lover—not that he'd had the chance to practice that particular skill in the last few years—and so he allowed her to dominate the kiss for as long as it took for her lips to soften on his, his body tightening with the gentle dabs of her tongue against his. And then his fire spun between them, moving from him to her, and back again.

A word sang in his mind even as he groaned when she wiggled her hips against his in an attempt to push him past all bearing. *Mate.*

No, not just a mate.

Wyvern's mate.

"No," he said, prying himself off her, and gently pushing her back. "I can't cope with that. Not now. Not until I've dealt with Alessandra and whatever it is Deus is up to. You stir too many emotions in me. It's not good."

"Oh, it was very good," Phyllida said, swaying toward him, her lips parted in a manner that just made him want to dive back into the depths of her mouth. "Better even than the dream. I'm going to risk inflating your ego and say that this was truly a silver-medal-level kiss."

"Not gold?" Bastian asked, oddly disappointed.

Phyllida smiled then, a long, slow smile filled with heat that he felt down to his toenails. "One or both of us have to be naked for a gold-medal kiss."

He thought about that for a moment, then nodded. "I agree to your terms."

"Huh?" Her eyes widened. "I wasn't making an offer—"

"However, I am unable to fulfill them yet," he continued despite her protest, feeling the need to take charge. It was only by doing so that he could tamp down his errant emotions that Phyllida stirred. He wondered briefly at that, then decided that was another thing he would have to ignore. "First, as I mentioned, I must locate my daughter, and determine her situation before deciding on a course of action. Following that, I will deal with Deus—assuming he has broken the terms of his provisional membership in the weyr.

Then I will be able to explore what it means that you are a wyvern's mate, and whether it will have an impact on my issue with … but we will deal with it then. My car is this way."

"Is it? Thrilling as that news is, I'm going to have to pass on seeing it for myself, which I assume is why you've once again taken my hand and are pulling me in a direction that I don't particularly wish to go in," Phyllida answered, jerking her hand from his. "We have our own car scheduled to pick us up, as it happens, and I really don't want to stick around in this area in case Xavier or his buddies come back. The longer we stay here, the more likely those guards he left will find us."

Seawright said sotto voce, "The six minutes and thirty-nine seconds spent kissing each other aside, of course."

"You have sought my aid in escaping," Bastian said, a frown pulling his brows together.

"I don't think I have, no," Phyllida said with a calmness that prickled on his skin. "For one, you yourself said you don't want to help me—"

"And now we're going to have a discussion," Seawright said, taking the phone that Phyllida had pulled out, and opened a rideshare app. "Once again right out in the open. If I were a dragon, and someone I was meant to guard had left, then I would most certainly search the nearest street for them."

"—not that I recall asking you for help," Phyllida continued. "I'm not saying I wouldn't take it, because Xavier is … well, that's another situation. But escaping from him and the others? We have that down. So really, I have no need of further interaction with you. Steamy kisses, as Seawright pointed out, aside. Yes, yes, Annoying One, I realize that we're standing here yakking when we should be getting away, but since the car is still four minutes away, I don't know what you expect me to do."

"The dragons from whom you escaped have no doubt been disabled by my men. That is why they are not seeking to recapture you." Bastian pulled out his phone and texted for

Luca and Gio to come immediately to the car. It was on the tip of his tongue to tell Phyllida she was his mate—for surely she had to be, since there was no other reason he would react as he had done—but spurred by the need to locate Alessandra, he ignored the fact that at long last he had found a woman with whom he was meant to spend his life.

"Possibly," she allowed, obviously hesitating.

"As I mentioned, I have never forced a woman to do anything she did not want to do," he said, struggling with the need to shove her into his car where she would be safe. "I try to protect those who are at risk, however. If you are at odds with the Blood Tribe, or with Deus and his Chaos dragons, then I am obligated to offer you such protection as the blue dragons have."

It was a nice speech, a very nice speech, and he was pleased to see the ire that had filled her eyes fade into a softer look as he finished. But then instantly she stiffened up, and her gaze dropped to where she was bound to her companion.

"That's ... I wish ... but it's all impossible, so thank you, but no. So long as you don't tell Xavier you've seen us, we won't trespass on your kindness. I think that's our car coming down the road, so we'll say good-bye."

Seawright lifted her tablet and snapped a few pictures of him. He gave her a long look before turning his gaze back on Phyllida. "I cannot allow this."

"Allow?" He could swear little flecks of fire lit her eyes. "Oh, you did not just say that. You did, didn't you? You said 'allow,' just like you have the right to tell me what I can and can't do. Well, let me tell you something, Buster Brown." She poked him in the chest.

"My name is—"

"I know what your name is," she snapped, and poked him again. "I was being sarcastic. Where was I? Oh, let me tell you that I do not take to being *allowed* to do anything. I've fought too long and too hard to keep from destroying the world to let the first handsome, blue-eyed dream-walking Adonis who is almost a gold-medal kisser to come along and inform me he's not going to *allow* me to do whatever I want."

She panted a little at the end of her speech. Bastian weighed the option of continuing to make her see reason, with the need to get her away from Deus and his tribe, and decided the latter was the best course.

He bent and slung her over his shoulder, ignoring the squawk of her companion as he turned and strode down the road.

"What the—why does everyone feel it's perfectly fine to ignore my autonomy?" Phyllida asked, slapping her free hand on his back, her legs kicking as she struggled against his hold. "Bastian! Put me down this instant! I will not be kidnapped! Do you hear? I refuse to be kidnapped and used!"

"I have no intention of using you without your consent. No, do not attempt to cast yourself off me. You'll only hurt yourself and your scribe."

"Seawright Pendleton, junior scribe third class," the other woman said somewhat breathlessly as she trotted to keep up.

"Oh, I like that. You're going to torture me for info about Sandy, aren't you? Boy, it's a sad day when you can't trust your own libido and end up kissing a torturing bastard of a dragon," Phyllida grumbled, still kicking her legs.

"Stop that," he commanded.

"Make me," she snarled.

He slid his hand up from where it had been clamping down on the backs of her knees, and pinched the lush curve of ass that was so temptingly placed next to his head.

For a second, she froze; then she sucked in a huge quantity of air. "You dare!" she all but roared, the sound thankfully being muffled by the thick line of forest that swept almost to the road. She pounded on his back with one hand, swearing in Italian now, profaning not just the name of his mother and father, but his ancestors back three generations.

"You are not very fluent in Italian and have made several grammatical errors," he told her when she got the worst of it out of her system. "But I appreciate the inventiveness and quality of the insult. The bit about my grandmother fornicating with a grapefruit is a bit confusing, but I will assume that is merely a vocabulary malfunction. Here is my car. Do not make me force you into it. It would not be pleasant for either of us, and I do not wish to feel any more guilt than has already stained my soul."

"Don't you passive-aggressive me with that 'don't make me do bad things to you' shit," she said, the words filled with flinty edges as he set her down next to the vehicle.

The car that had been approaching slowed down to allow the driver a good look but, at the sight of the glare Bastian turned on him, drove off.

"Dammit, that wasn't our car," Phyllida said, her lips thinned. "I'm going to have a thing or two to say to the ride company about them not arriving when they are supposed to. Stop it! I told you I don't want to be kidnapped."

"Your protest has been noted," Bastian said with a grimness he felt down to his toes as Phyllida struggled to get away from where he was attempting to ease her into the back seat of the car.

Luca and Gio came running from the woods at that moment, the former pausing for a moment at the sight of the two women.

"The woman from the restaurant?" Luca asked, eyeing Phyllida. "What … er …"

"She knows where Alessandra is," Bastian said. Then before Phyllida could do more than start to sputter protestations, he gently pushed her into the car, taking care not to harm her or her companion all the while avoiding the self-defense moves Phyllida was attempting. "We leave now."

"But we don't know what the Blood Tribe was doing with Deus—" Luca started to say.

"That's the least of my worries," Bastian said, gesturing toward the steering wheel. Urgency crawled over his skin like fire ants, but it was a desire to sit next to Phyllida that had him squishing himself next to her on the back seat.

He needed to get Phyllida away from the other dragons. He needed to learn what she knew about Alessandra's whereabouts, and her role in his daughter's imprisonment. He needed to interrogate her to judge if she was telling him the truth, and whether she really was a wyvern's mate.

He needed to kiss her again until the green of her eyes went liquid with passion.

He just needed her.

And that thought scared him more than anything else had since he had failed the First Dragon.

TWELVE
THE NIGHTMARE

"Why do you remain handcuffed to your companion?"

I decided I would stop pretending Bastian didn't exist, if only so I could send him a scathing look. "It's not by choice."

"No? Let me see," he said, holding out a hand. I had tried hard for the last fifteen minutes to ignore the fact that he was pressed against me from knee to shoulder, a sensation that I might normally enjoy if he hadn't completely disregarded my wishes and forced me into his car.

I fumed about that fact for a few seconds before holding up my hand. Why did everyone—every man—seem to feel that they had the right to force me to do things they wanted?

Seawright clicked her tongue at the movement. "Now you made me hit Next before I could read the clue in the apothecary's jar."

I thinned my lips at her. "You're playing your game? *Now?* When we've been abducted? Why aren't you rallying every watch member in the state to save us?"

She raised an eyebrow at me, not saying the obvious.

"Fine," I said in a near snarl. "But you could at least let your handlers on the Committee know, so they'd send out an authorized person to rescue us."

"I tried," she said, pulling my hand down so she could tap on her tablet. "There's no one available."

I wanted to yell that her precious Committee needed to get their act together and save me before something horrible happened, but I said nothing. Bastian and his two dragons were obviously listening to us, and the fewer people who knew what I was, the safer I'd be.

"I am not abducting you," Bastian said with a reasonableness that I found irritating. How dare he be so calm when everything around me was falling to pieces? "You were clearly in danger, so I removed you from that situation. Why do you have a scribe with handlers on the Committee? Why are you handcuffed together? You can't be a criminal, because the Committee would not allow you to roam at will."

"Of course I'm not a criminal," I said with a sniff that should have told him just how irritated I was. "And I'll answer your questions if you answer mine."

Seawright shot me a startled glance at my apparent offer to discuss my background, but having spent time with Xavier, I knew I was safe. Dragons loved to ask questions, but seldom wanted to answer them.

"How many questions?" Bastian asked, obviously switching into negotiation mode. "And what ratio of questions to answers?"

"One to one," I said, leaning back against the seat, trying hard to ignore the fact that my body was celebrating every inch that was pressed against him.

He pursed his lips and switched the subject, just as I hoped he would. "If you do not wish to remain bound to your scribe, I would be happy to set you free." His voice was all shades of sexy, smooth velvet. Just hearing it rumble out of his chest located so near me sent sensual shivers down my back, charging the air around us.

"If I could get the damned thing off, don't you think I'd have done so?" I said, deliberately shaking my hand just as Seawright reached to tap on her tablet game. She shot me a furious look. "This isn't my idea of fun."

"Let me see," he repeated, and I managed to drag my hand across my body so he could look at the cuff.

"It will do you no good," Seawright told him without looking up, her arm pressing awkwardly into my belly as Bastian bent over the handcuff. "It's been spelled specifically to not break by mortal means."

"Ah," Bastian said, releasing my hand (much to my inner self's disappointment). "Then I'm afraid I cannot help you, although I can contact a mage who might be able to break the magic."

I slumped in the seat for a few seconds before the last of his words echoed in my head.

Break the magic. I peeked at Seawright from the corner of my eye, but she was focused on her game.

What had she said about the handcuffs earlier in the day? I dug through my memory of the last hour. She'd said there was no way for me to slip my hand out, and that the cuffs would be impervious to mortal methods ... but she said nothing about the magic used to bespell it.

My gaze shifted from Seawright to the two men in the front seat. They were conversing quietly. Without turning my head enough to catch his attention, I slid my gaze toward Bastian. He was looking out of the window, speaking in Italian on his phone, evidently inquiring how someone's childbirth labor was going.

I half turned away from him, as if making myself more comfortable against the car seat, and prepared to do something that I had done only four times in my life. ... I was about to use the talent that had doomed me from birth.

The interdiction, normally a minor feeling that I could ignore, grew heavy on my chest and head as I allowed my energies to turn inward, reaching for that part of myself that the Committee couldn't stifle. Three percent of my power remained untouched, they had told me, but I was forbidden to use it. For a few seconds, my mind was filled with jubilation as I flexed my long disused magical muscles, reveling in the rush of power that came even from the minute amount that remained unbound. I opened myself to the magic that was woven into the fabric of the handcuffs, allowing my inner eye to examine it, staring deep into it on a granular level, understanding how the magic was bonded to the metal molecules. With deliberation, I allowed my power to delicately unpick the magic, breaking the bond until each molecule evaporated into nothing, gathering speed down the curved metal, the unpicking and evaporating happening so fast that the runes on the cold steel of the handcuff barely had time to light up in warning before the metal dissolved into a fine black powder.

Seawright, who had looked up the second I turned my attention to the cuff, suddenly squawked and lunged for me, one hand clamped across my eyes, while the other went inexplicably over my mouth. "No! You cannot! It is against seven different rules! I forbid you to contin—oh, no. What have you done?"

I yanked her hands off my face before rubbing my wrist, giving her a long, level look. Her eyes were filled with anger and irritation but, more worrisome, something that looked a lot like fear. "You know what I've done—something I should have realized an hour ago."

Bastian glanced at me and clicked off his phone at the same moment that I brushed the dark power residue from the magic being broken onto Seawright.

She shrieked, and shoved it back at me. It fell onto the seat between us, a darkly glittering fine powder.

"Is something—ah. You seem to have removed the handcuff." Bastian's eyes were now a deep midnight blue, his brows pulled ever-so-slightly together. "I want very badly to ask you how you did that. Would you be offended if I did so?"

"I certainly would be," Seawright muttered, shooting me a glare that might have stripped the hair from my head if I wasn't immune to such things. She tapped wildly on her tablet, no doubt tattling to her superiors.

I sighed to myself. It wasn't like I could get in much worse trouble than I was in. Xavier had bound me to him mere hours before the renaissance. Bastian had kidnapped me to force him to find his traitorous daughter. And I was helpless to change anything, wrapped in a life of sorrow and loneliness.

"Phyllida?"

The way Bastian's voice seemed to caress my name had me slumping back against the seat again, too tired now to even fight … and whether the fight was focused on the overwhelming attraction to him or the need to get away was a point I wasn't sure I wanted to investigate. "Why would I be offended?" I asked, the question not at all what I had intended on saying.

His brow furrowed a little more as if he was concentrating. "It is a personal question."

"No, I'm not offended by the question, but it's not something that I feel like explaining right now. Not unless you want to answer some of my questions."

Once again, the thought of doing so turned the conversation. "Very well. Despite the fact that you are a dragon mate—"

"How did you know that?" I interrupted, first startled, then suspicious. He'd told me he had nothing to do with Xavier, but clearly, he knew about the mate ceremony.

Dammit. I really had to get away from Bastian, sexy eyes, and gorgeous chest, and truly magnificent kissing abilities, aside.

"I am a dragon, a wyvern. You took my fire. Only a wyvern's mate can do that," he said in a matter-of-fact voice that cut through my direst suspicions.

"Oh, that." When I had been with Xavier, his fire had never manifested itself. It struck me odd now that I had never questioned that fact. "It didn't hurt me, so I assumed it was just part of you."

His gaze crawled over my face, the color in his irises lightening several shades until the blue was like the sky on an early summer morning, the power behind it holding me like a snared rabbit. "It is, but few can take it. What I find interesting is that you do not question the fact that you are a mate. All the other wyverns' mates did not fall so easily into that role. And yet you do not dispute my statement."

"I don't know what to say to that," I answered slowly, trying to pick my words carefully from profound confusion. Every instinct I had said that he was a danger to me, no better than Xavier in the way he forced me to do his will, and yet there was no air of evil around him, no sense of the darkness that was wrapped around Xavier. The part of my mind that refused to give in to the hopelessness of my life desperately clung to the notion that he was my dream lover, the man whom I'd waited so long for, and one who could end a lifetime spent alone and isolated.

No, I told that little kernel of hope. *He doesn't want to help me. He's said so repeatedly. He's no better than Xavier, desirous of using me for some need, but not wishing to bind his life to mine.* "I have met dragons before. Sandy had friends who visited her, people she said were kin."

"Indeed," he said, glancing beyond me for a second to Seawright. "That is something I wish to discuss with you later, but my first concern is the welfare of my daughter. Once I know she is safe, then we can revisit the subject."

Released from the intensity of his gaze, I sagged back, more confused than ever by my emotions, part of my mind relieved while the rest was irritated that he clearly didn't intend on kissing me anytime in the near future.

For the love of the ten goddesses, I lectured myself as we drove into the nearest town, *you really need to hire someone for no-strings sexy time if you're all bent out of shape your kidnapper isn't trying to kiss you again. Stockholm syndrome, that's what it is! You're deranged, Phyllida, quite, quite deranged.*

I made a little snorting noise at the mental pathways my mind was wandering.

"Pardon?" Bastian asked, interrupting a conversation he was having with one of the men in the front seats.

"Nothing," I said, waving away the question before closing my eyes and crossing my arms. "I was just snorting at myself because my mind is being unreasonable."

"Then we have more in common than I thought," Bastian answered, humor rich in his voice. It gave me another little sensual shiver, and I couldn't stop myself from responding to it, remembering what he felt and tasted like. There was still so much to learn about him. What spots on his body would be sensitive to touches and nibbles, and long, long licks of my tongue? What made him pant and moan and arch up in a moment of exquisite pleasure? "I, too, have an unruly mind that insists on thinking and saying things that I am told are inappropriate and unwelcome."

"Oh, I totally get that," I said, opening my eyes again. "My inner self is always thinking the most improper things."

"And we're back to flirting," Seawright said, flipping a screen on her tablet so she could type furiously. "I will so note it, although I draw the line at transcribing it, as I should."

I ignored her. "What inappropriate things have you been thinking?" I asked Bastian.

He eyed me, his pupils elongating slightly, reminding me of a cat's eyes. "Concerning you?"

"Assuming you have some inappropriate thoughts about me, yes," I said, wondering about the fact that despite our dream-lover experiences, he felt so familiar, so comfortable. He was a threat to my welfare, and more, to the rest of the world if he found out about me when the interdiction was broken by the renaissance.

I stared at his mouth, wanting badly to kiss him again.

"You won't be offended? Rey—she is my second-in-command—she tells me that women of today do not like to be told how comely they are, or of the erections that are caused because of their breasts and hips and legs."

Inner parts of me, parts that I had been very aware of since I had bumped into Bastian, blew up balloons, set up a punch bowl, and shook out a WELCOME BASTIAN banner before demanding I continue the conversation no matter how dangerous he might be. "Women of today?" I asked, trying to stifle the party going on in my underwear.

"Yes." He frowned. "It appears that my time incarcerated at a small villa has left me out of touch with women. Or so Rey would have me believe. If I said to you that I enjoyed the way your tongue twined around mine, would that be considered impolite?"

Next to me, Seawright sighed, and switched her tablet screen back to her game. I had a feeling she was trying very hard to ignore us.

"I wouldn't find it so, but then, I liked the things your tongue did, too," I told Bastian, feeling a particular freedom in being able to speak my mind.

"And if I said that your breasts tasted like sun-warmed flowers? That even now, I wanted to feel and taste them again, to gently draw my teeth across your nipples until you shiver with ecstasy?" he asked softly, his voice barely audible.

I felt a bit flushed, myself. "I'd say that was a pretty compliment, since my boobs aren't particularly spectacular," I answered in a whisper, moving my shoulders. "Also, I'm now very aware of my nipples."

We both looked at my breasts. Fortunately for my sanity, the shirt I was wearing was fairly loose, but I knew from the sensitized way the material of my bra felt over my nipples that they had joined the party in my pants. So to speak.

"And if I was to touch you here—"

"No touching!" Seawright almost yelled, accompanied by a stifled laugh from the front seat. "I draw the line at outright sexual congress conducted in front of me. I am the most tolerant of scribes, but there is a limit to even my patience. If you wish to sex each other, you must do so in a private space. A secure private space, one that I am allowed to verify is safe, first, but private it must be."

"She takes her job very seriously," I told Bastian, my various and sundry erogenous parts now sad when he drew back the hand that had been reaching for my pelvis.

"Are you ready to tell me what that job is? I have never heard of a scribe who feels it necessary or even beneficial to handcuff herself to the person for whom she is transcribing."

I waved away that very dangerous question. "It's just a legal thing. The Committee is overly cautious. Can I see your fire? Er … that is … if you can make it pop out at will."

"You just saw my fire on your fingertips," he reminded me, making me blush at the memory of the heat of that kiss, and how much more I wanted from him.

"Yes, but that was just … you know … fingers." I cleared my throat. "Can you do more than that?"

He smiled a slow, sensual smile. "All mates can share their dragon's fire, but only a wyvern's mate can harness it, and use it as her own," he said, lifting my hand and pressing my fingers to his lips before turning over my hand and blowing a little ball of fire onto my palm.

I stared at it in amazement, for one panicked second worried it would hurt me, but it immediately became clear that it was nothing more than warm on my skin. I prodded it with a finger, and it spread out on my hand before melting away into nothing. "OK, that is seriously cool. And I can use that?"

"You will if you are mated," he said, his pupils going back to their narrow cat-eye state.

I said nothing about that, thinking about the words Xavier had spoken earlier. Just what was he doing, claiming me as his mate only to abandon me seconds later? He had to know the renaissance was almost upon us, since obviously he tied me to him in order to use me. But that didn't make sense—if I was that valuable to him, why would he simply dump me on his men and go off with Sandy?

The name of my old friend brought with it a stab of pain at her betrayal. I gently chewed my lower lip, wondering how much Bastian knew about her. Could he have lied to me? Was he working with Sandy and Xavier? Was he even now planning to turn me over to Xavier?

I shook my head. That didn't make any more sense than Xavier walking away from me. I rubbed my head, hoping that would give me some clarity.

It didn't, of course.

"Are you tired?" Bastian's voice skittered along my skin as if he were stroking me with the softest velvet.

"No. Yes. More confused than anything," I answered with stark honesty.

"Ah. That is common to wyverns' mates upon finding out who they are," he said with a little nod, just as if it made sense to him; then to my surprise, he took my hand and twined his fingers through mine, resting our hands on his thigh. "But all will be clear soon enough."

Seawright gave another one of her disgusted half snorts, and I thought I heard an echo from one of the two men in the front seat, but I said nothing, just allowed myself to melt into the seat of the car, and turned my mind to how I was going to escape this sexy, handsome, intriguing man.

And whether I would survive long enough to regret it.

THIRTEEN
LIFE SUCKS

A half hour later, I sat in a hard, uncomfortable couch in a chain-hotel suite, and studied Bastian, trying for the demeanor of someone who was calm and collected, and hadn't, just a few minutes before, attempted to geld him with a grapefruit knife I'd found on the table next to the complimentary fruit bowl.

"You will now tell me everything you know about Alessandra."

"I don't think I will, no," I answered, and made a show of looking out the window.

We were in a town outside Portland, at the kind of hotel where, if your abductor has enough money, no one cares if you make a scene about being kidnapped as you are marched inside by a couple of big, extremely handsome dragons, and one bitchy junior scribe, third class.

I made a mental note to write a scathing letter to the hotel-chain administration.

Bastian didn't like my response. His lovely dark-honey brows pulled together, his eyes glittering with obvious anger. "Why would you be so obstinate?"

"For one," I said, holding up my hand to tick the items off my fingers, "your bark is worse than your bite."

His frown deepened.

"It's a colloquialism," I explained, wondering how long he'd been in the US. He had a distinct Italian accent, but spoke English with a fluency that was impressive considering my grasp on his own language was mostly limited to basic phrases and a few curse words. "It means that you may sound all tough and badass, but really, you're not."

"My ass is as bad as anyone's," he said, squaring his shoulders. "Badder, for I am a wyvern."

I allowed one shoulder to go up in a nonchalant shrug. "Right, but you kissed me a little bit ago."

His eyes narrowed. "I have a feeling you are implying that I am weak and ungoverned in the face of desire."

I allowed the other shoulder to make its own mini shrug. "I'm not implying anything like that. You didn't seem ungoverned at all. Quite the contrary—you were very much in control of that kiss. In fact, I might say you were downright bossy."

"Control," he said, a strange iciness creeping into his voice, "is not something I take lightly."

"Is that one of your hot buttons?" I asked, ignoring Seawright, who muttered under her breath. Before he answered, I continued, "Let me tell you one of mine—it's being kidnapped. So if you don't want me unpacking a basketful of whoop ass on you, you'll have your buddy over there move away from the door."

His eyebrows rose, and I got a distinct feeling he was stifling amusement. "Do you really think you could?"

"Could do what?"

"Unpack a basketful of whoop ass upon me. Not that I understand exactly what that is, but I assume it has to do with you beating me into submission. Such a thing will not happen, but it intrigues me that you think it might."

It was on the tip of my tongue to let him know I was a few days away from becoming one of the most powerful beings in the world, but that was the sheerest folly, and I hadn't lived a life of solitude and isolation just to blab the truth to the first handsome, blue-eyed dragon who sauntered his sexy self into my dreams and life.

Dear god, his jeans looked like they were painted on him, highlighting every delicious swell and tantalizing curve.

"Let's just take it as read that I could make a really good attempt, and leave it there," I said in what I hoped was a noncommittal tone. "And the reason I don't want to tell you about Sandy is because you aren't going to like what you hear, and I know what happens when powerful men find out things they don't like—the messenger is punished."

"I have a feeling you have just insulted me, and yet, I don't see why you should do so," Bastian said, seating himself on the coffee table directly in front of me.

I looked away as if I was trying to avoid meeting his sapphire gaze, but in reality, I was noting the location of the other two men. One, apparently named Gio, had left with a promise to return with food. The dragon named Luca was sitting at the table, a phone in his hand, although he shot me nasty looks now and again, the grapefruit knife a few inches from his hand.

Inexplicably, a giggle rose.

Bastian's eyebrows lifted a smidgen.

"Sorry," I said, rubbing a hand over my mouth as if that would stifle my weird sense of humor. "And I mean that—I apologize for trying to castrate you with the grapefruit knife. Being dragged through the lobby pushed me beyond my limits, but I realize I didn't have to try to make you a eunuch. I'm glad you have such fast responses to threats."

My brain couldn't believe what my mouth was telling him, but that was not a strange situation, so I moved past the fact that I was apologizing to my kidnapper for attempting to break free.

Definitely Stockholm syndrome, the disgusted part of my mind said. The bit responsible for throwing the underwear party disagreed, but I ignored both of them and tried to assess the situation.

"I appreciate the apology," Bastian said, his voice serious, but his eyes were filled with amusement.

To my left, Luca moved the knife to the other side of the fruit bowl.

"Now, about my daughter, Alessandra—"

Seawright sat next to me on the couch. I shifted so that Bastian couldn't see my hand, and tapped on her leg. She glanced up at me, then down to my hand, then over to Bastian.

"I don't know why you don't wish to tell me about your interaction with her, but I assume it is because of your friendship. I assure you that I only want what's best for her," Bastian continued, frowning a little when I gave him my blandest expression.

We escape, I tapped in Morse code. I knew she understood it, because she'd caught me tapping a Morse message to Lin a week after she'd arrived as my gaoler.

Seawright squinted at nothing, clearly concentrating.

When I jump, you tackle Luca. I'll get Bastian. Then go to door and run.

Bastian's frown grew at my nonresponse. "That is why I must insist that you tell me everything and anything that could help me find Alessandra."

Seawright rustled in her bag, clearly looking for something. I hoped it was something heavy she could use to disable Luca.

"Phyllida." The edge to Bastian's voice could have sliced fresh bread.

Now, I tapped, then flung myself up and forward, slamming my fist under Bastian's chin in a way that sent him rocking backward off the coffee table. He cracked his head on a wood and glass end table just as Luca leaped to his feet and turned to us, but not before Seawright had her Taser out, blasting him with it as we both headed toward the door.

Bastian swore in Italian, but in a somewhat garbled way that reassured me he wasn't harmed too seriously. Part of me wanted to apologize and make sure he was OK, but the other part, the sane part, knew I had to get out of there before my time ran out.

I had the door open as Luca hit the floor, his body rigid. Two paces from the door was Gio, his arms laden with takeaway packages, his eyes wide as Seawright and I flung ourselves into the hallway.

"What—" he started to say, but Seawright zapped him, too, even as I heard a piece of furniture overturning in the room. I had a horrible feeling Bastian had gotten to his feet and was coming after us.

"Run!" I yelled, suiting action to word. Seawright pounded after me as we raced down the stairs and out a side entrance, barreling into traffic and almost getting run down in the process. Sounds of pursuit trailed us, but we had a head start, and despite my body's unhappiness at killing its party plans, my brain knew better.

Ten minutes later, while lurking in a small convenience store, I managed to catch my breath and ordered another car to pick us up before turning on Seawright. "What the hell?"

"Abaddon, not hell, is the proper name, and what about it?" Seawright asked, paying for a bottle of water. She wasn't even breathing hard, damn her junior-scribe-third-class fit self.

I made yet another mental promise to start some sort of home exercise program, and honed my glare to the point where it could pierce metal. "Your Taser works? Why the hell didn't you use it on Bastian when he kidnapped us?"

"We had no other way to escape the dragons at the camp," she said calmly, sipping at her water. "It seemed expedient to use his vehicle for that purpose, and remove ourselves later. Which is exactly what we did."

I was itchy with the need to argue, but didn't have the energy. Instead, as we got into our ride when it arrived, I ignored her lecture regarding my actions of the last few hours, and thought about Bastian.

Had he hit his head when I knocked him backward?

Was he angry at me?

Did he feel the same sense of hollowness that gripped me?

I shook that last thought away. Why on earth would he feel hollow inside? He was a wyvern, surrounded by his fellow blue dragons, able to go out in the world without fear.

"He probably hates me," I said as we entered my house. "Who?"

"Bastian." I closed the front door and slumped against it, feeling a perverse sense of pleasure at the thought. "All he wants is to find Sandy, and I wouldn't tell him anything about her. He probably loathes me despite our dream sexy times and that killer kiss a couple of hours ago. But how can I tell him? How can I tell someone that his daughter is a rat fink of the highest order? How can I tell him she betrayed me? Would he even believe me if I did?"

"I don't know the answers to these questions, but I will note that you have asked them of me, just in case it comes up at your trial," Seawright said with the pedantic way she had.

"You do that little thing," I said on a sigh, still feeling prickly, but now with a dose of self-pity thrown in just to make my life more miserable. "Wait, what trial?"

"The one that will surely be called so that you might face the charges for the violations you have conducted today."

"I doubt if they will go so far as to hold a trial." I made a face at my reflection in the hall mirror. It gave me no sense of satisfaction. "Not now, when everything is about to be undone. They have much more pressing things to do than worry about me taking a Lyft without you."

"I will also notify the Committee that you are once again safely confined." Seawright pulled her tablet from her bag and marched into her room. "I believe I will suggest that they send a few protective forces to monitor the house, just in case your dragon decides to descend upon us."

"Bastian?" I shook my head. "He doesn't know where we live. Not that I think he would follow me."

"Not your boyfriend—the other. The bossy one."

I shuddered. "Why do you think Xavier knows where I am? He couldn't, or he would have showed up here in person to do that weird mate ceremony with me." I rubbed my arms against the goose bumps that rose at the memory of it, my mental confusion growing when I considered his actions.

Seawright paused at the door to her room to give me a gimlet glance. "Your girlfriend had your phone number. Which, I should point out, is a violation of two Otherworld Directives, one which we will address later this evening. Regardless, if he had your phone number, it's possible he might have found this house."

"Nope," I said, rubbing my arms again. I felt chilled, like I'd been out in the rain for too long, and the cold had seeped into my bones. Odd that I had felt warm and toasty when I was next to Bastian. It was as if the man exuded sunshine and heat. "At least, the man from the Committee who gave me the phone said the records for it were tied to an account located in another state, just for that reason. And he didn't say I couldn't give out the number to friends who had previously been vetted by them, like Sandy had been when I was in college. Hmm."

I wandered over to the door to Seawright's room, my mind turning over her statement.

"What is your *hmm* regarding?" she asked, her voice muffled as she was bent in half while digging through a waist-high rattan basket. She had three of them in the room, which she claimed housed her collection of security gadgets, although I'd never seen her produce any but the Taser.

"It's Xavier," I said slowly, trying to pull together thoughts and ideas that seemed to slide away whenever I tried to get a good look at them. "I just don't understand what he's thinking. Why would he force me into being his mate, and then turn around and walk away when he's a hair's breadth away from the renaissance? Why weren't his men more vigilant in watching us? Why did we escape from them so easily?"

Seawright straightened, emerging from her basket with what looked like a small virtual reality headset. "Are you implying those dragons allowed us to escape them?"

I leaned against the doorframe and gave it some thought. "I think so. It didn't feel easy at the time, but that's probably due to adrenaline and shock at Sandy's betrayal muddling my brains. No, hindsight tells me that we got away far too easily. Dragons aren't, as a rule, stupid, and the fact that we could melt away into the forest without them noticing isn't likely."

"Your boyfriend said that his men had disabled them," she pointed out.

"There is that," I said, trying to puzzle it out. "But even so, Xavier's dragons, or whoever they were, let us get out of their sight without batting so much as a single eyelash. That just doesn't seem right."

She looked thoughtful for a moment, then gave a sharp nod. "I believe you are correct. I am disappointed that I didn't realize that at the time, but like you, I was feeling the effects of the dragons dominating us."

"Which brings us right back to the question of why." I rubbed the back of my neck, trying to ease the tension there. "Why did Xavier leave? Why make me his mate if he didn't intend to stash me away somewhere until he can use me to unleash hell upon the world? Why did he use Sandy to set me up?"

"Perhaps he doesn't want to use your hellerune abilities," Seawright said, picking up a small screwdriver and adjusting something on her headset.

I rubbed an itchy spot on my back on the doorframe. "That makes even less sense than Xavier's actions. In his eyes, the only valuable thing about me is the fact that I'm a hellerune." I thought about the nightmares in which he'd stalked me. "Never once have I had the feeling he was pursuing me because of who I was. … It was always the potential I held."

"You would know best about that," she said noncommittally. I'd told her once that Xavier had tormented me in my dreams, but I suspected she thought I was exaggerating. "But it seems clear to me that he is showing little interest in your abilities." She paused for a second in her tinkering. "I will message my superior in the Committee, and inquire if dragons are able to use dark magic."

"You don't need to ask anyone. The answer is no, they can't. It's something in their genetic makeup. Xavier told me that once. ..." The sentence trailed away as a memory returned to me. It was years ago, when we'd first met, and he was wooing me. He'd told me that he wasn't a typical dragon, that centuries before, he'd remade himself and had intended on starting a new type of dragon, one who harnessed the power of demonic beings, but that he'd been sabotaged before he could finish.

"What did he tell you?"

Seawright's voice cut through the memory, returning me to the present. I glanced over my shoulder at the hall, very aware of the shadows cast by the lights that had automatically turned on as dusk settled in. "He said that normal dragons couldn't wield dark power. But he's not normal, Seawright. He's ... separate from the other dragons. He can do things that other dragons can't, like dream walk ... although now Bastian can do that, too. Maybe he's special like Xavier, too."

"Your boyfriend didn't appear to be special or separate to me," she pointed out. "His companions didn't exude anything but dragonness. Did you have a sense of darkness about any of them?"

"Not Bastian and his friends," I said slowly, still puzzling over what Xavier was doing. "Xavier is another matter, however. Even if he couldn't personally use dark power, it doesn't mean he wouldn't sell me to someone who could. What if he hands me over right at the renaissance? The interdict would be broken, the Committee would still be re-forming, and boom. I'm breaking magic left, right, and center, and filling the world with dark power."

She slid her headset on and I realized it was an old style of night-vision goggles. She moved over to the window to look out into the growing darkness, still fiddling with the knobs. "That is why I will contact the Committee for more security. It's really too bad you decided to break things off with your second boyfriend. If he can't use your power, then he would offer excellent protection against those who can."

I stared at her for a few seconds before slapping my hands on my thighs. "For the love of the seventeen goddesses, Seawright, Bastian isn't my second boyfriend. I don't have a boyfriend. And if I did—" I stopped, unsure of how I wanted to finish the sentence.

"If you did, what?" she asked, just as I knew she would.

I sighed to myself. The truth was, if I could have a man in my life, Bastian would be my top pick, even though I'd known him for such a short time.

"I know better than to let a dragon into my life," was all I said before I turned and went upstairs.

FOURTEEN
BEEFCAKE, BABY!

The dream came as I knew it would, but I didn't realize at first that I was dreaming. Before climbing into bed a few hours after Seawright and I returned to the safety of my home, I stood at the window, gazing out into the night, my forehead pressed against the cold glass as I tried to pick apart my tangle of emotions.

I understood why I wanted to see Bastian again—loneliness and the lack of sexual relationships beyond a few fleeting days scattered throughout the years left me particularly vulnerable to a sexy man—and I even understood my feeling of guilt regarding hiding information about Sandy.

But what I didn't understand was why I felt a bond with him. He'd told me several times he wouldn't help me, and yet, I was still drawn to him. He circled my thoughts, tantalizingly just on the edge of my awareness, even though he was more than thirty miles away. It was as if he had become a part of me, sinking into my being.

"There's a phrase for this," I told the indigo shadow of trees moving restlessly in the rain against a black sky, spreading my fingers on the glass as if I could reach out and touch the storm. "Fated mates."

"Mates, certainly. But fated?"

I spun around at the voice, not the one I was expecting.

Bastian stood in the doorway, leaning against it, his arms across his chest, his lips pursed a little as he thought. "It is my inclination to say that I don't believe in fate, but my own past offers evidence to the contrary. Although I do not believe daimons dictate in that manner."

"Daimons?" I asked before I could stop myself. It was then that I glanced around, realizing that although I was in my bedroom, I must be in a dream. There was no other way Bastian could have entered the house—let alone my room—without alarms sounding.

"Daimons are what mortals think of as fates. I have met one. He is a friend of the green wyvern's mate. He is helpful, yes, but I have not known him to make decisions for the person he serves. You permit?" He spread his hands wide as he finished, obviously asking my permission to enter the room.

I nodded, reminding myself that this was a dream, and he was not Xavier. Where the latter tormented me via the wanderings of my mind, Bastian had been nothing but gentle, sexy, and fascinating.

Except when he was telling me he couldn't help me.

"Since you're here, I suppose you might as well," I said, and sat on the edge of my bed before boldly patting the spot next to me. "Although I thought you said you weren't going to dream walk in my brain anymore."

He smiled and strolled into the room with the air of a panther stalking prey, all coiled power and sinuous movements. I shivered in anticipation at the look in his eyes. "I have questions that I must have answered. Besides, I find myself unable to drive you from my thoughts. Whether or not you are a wyvern's mate—my mate—you have information that I seek, and thus I have spent a great deal of effort to be here. In addition to which, we have had excellent sexual interactions. Your body gives me much pleasure to look at, and more to touch, and I assume by the way your eyes are dilating that you are not averse to my human form. Do you wish to have sexual congress?"

"Yes," I said without realizing it, then stifled a rueful smile. "Sorry, I said that without thinking. Not that I don't want to show you just how much I like your human form, but there's more to you than just your body."

"Ah, yes," he agreed, and sat next to me on the bed, not touching me, but making me very aware of his nearness. My libido woke up, took one look at Bastian, and immediately went into full party-planning mode. "I, too, have discovered that sexual congress without some interest in the lover in question does not make for more than surface gratification. I had a lover once—this was two hundred years ago, in case you are inclined toward jealousy—and although our sexual congress was satisfying, I shared little interests with him, and the relationship did not last much beyond a few weeks. I learned from that experience that one must have other things to do than just congress."

I blinked at him. "You're gay?"

"Me?" He looked surprised. "No, I enjoy sexual relations with women."

"But you said 'he.' As in your past lover, of whom, by the way, I'm not jealous. Not that we have a relationship, but even if we did, what's in the past is in the past, and has nothing to do with now."

"I am in agreement with that sentiment. You need not look so suspicious, however. I have had male lovers in the past, yes, just as I have had female lovers." He gave a little shrug. "I find there is much to be admired in both male and female forms. Does that upset you?"

"No," I said slowly. "On the contrary, I find it kind of sexy. I read a book once that featured the love story of two men. It was very ... titillating. Not that I am interested in women sexually. But I did enjoy the book, so no, it doesn't upset me that you're bisexual."

"That is good. Shall we have sex now?" he asked, his eyes glittering in the dim lights of my room.

"I'd be lying if I said I was averse to it, but there's a matter of a few things I want to know, first."

He sighed a Guinness World Records Sigher sort of sigh. "We're back to negotiating? Very well. I will answer one of your questions for every five of mine you answer."

I shook my head at him, laughing even as I put my hand on his thigh, reveling in the heat that came from the touch. "Dude. Do you really think I'm going to let you get away with that?"

"I thought it was worth a try. Very well, although it goes against every bit of my dragon self, it shall be as you like. You ask a question first."

"Thank you." I thought for half a minute, then decided to appease my curiosity. "Why do you keep telling me you can't save me in my dreams? What exactly is a dream warrior?"

"That's two questions," he said, his brows drawing together. "You must allow me two, as well."

"I will," I said, and flexed my fingers on his thigh. He covered my hand with his, his thumb gently rubbing on my knuckles.

"What I tell you, only two others know," he said after a short pause. "You are familiar with dream walkers."

"Yes. My ex is one."

Bastian's frown deepened. "This Xavier you mentioned? You said he was with my daughter. Who is he? A mage? Another diviner?"

"No." The fear that always gripped me when thinking about Xavier made my stomach turn over. "He's a dragon. Or rather, he was once a dragon. I don't know what he is now other than evil. And yes, he is also a dream walker."

Bastian was silent for a few minutes before giving a quick shake of his head. "I do not understand how one can no longer be a dragon any more than I know how he can dream walk. That ability is beyond dragons."

"It's not beyond you," I pointed out gently, my hand stroking his leg, the feel of the thick muscles of his thigh stirring all my female parts into dragging out their party supplies.

"The First Dragon bestowed upon me the gift of dream walking," he answered. I felt him withdraw from me, despite the fact that his body didn't move. It was as if his soul curled up on itself. "He also named me dream warrior, savior of mortals and immortals alike. He charged me with protecting those too weak to fight the dream walkers who would use them."

"I'm not sure who this dragon is you mentioned, but that sounds like a big honor."

He made an abrupt gesture. "The First Dragon is the demigod who created the dragonkin."

"You what?" I gawked at him, outright gawked at him. "You were bopped on the head by a god? An actual god? One powerful enough to create races of beings? I'm considering sexy times with a man who knows a bona fide god?"

"You're yelling," Bastian pointed out.

I waved my hands around. "Of course I'm yelling! You didn't tell me you were picked out by a god, a real god. And here I was thinking that you were just another bossy dragon, but you're god-touched!"

Bastian laughed, a reluctant sort of laugh, to be true, but it was still a laugh, and for some reason, that warmed my heart. "Yes, the First Dragon is a god. Demigod. But that does not mean you need to look both horrified and excited."

"I *am* horrified and excited," I told him. "I'm also extremely aroused. I kissed a guy who knows a god. I touched a god's friend's chest. I've entertained the dick of a man who is personally acquainted with a card-carrying god." I took a deep, deep breath and tried to keep my brain from exploding with the heady cocktail of lust, amazement, and flabbergasticity.

"Flabbergasticity" isn't an actual word—the pedantic part of my mind started to say, but the girls in my underwear, who were even now resurrecting the WELCOME BASTIAN banner, shouted it down and started the party going.

To my confusion, Bastian frowned at the floor for half a minute. "I feel obligated to explain to you why the honor that you believe to be so great is anything but. As my mate, you are due that consideration."

Fear gripped my belly with an iron hand. "You don't have to tell me anything you don't want to," I said, uncomfortably aware that I wasn't being honest with him.

"No. You are my mate, even if I can't claim you until after I find Alessandra, and determine what role Deus and his tribe have to play with your former lover." He seemed to be bracing himself, then told me about how a hundred years before, he'd lost control and destroyed an innocent mortal in addition to the dream walker who had been abusing him.

"I'm so sorry," I said, putting both arms around him, wanting to take away his pain, but not knowing how. "But really, you can't blame yourself. It was your first time, and if no one told you the ground rules, you're certainly not to blame for what happened. It's sad that it cost a man his life, but if you arranged for his family to not suffer from his loss ..."

"It was the least I could do." His gaze met mine, the blue in them dim with remembered pain and guilt. "You understand now, yes? You see why I can't be the warrior that you need against this man who pursues you?"

"If you think I might die if you were to go into warrior mode—"

"There is no way to banish a dream walker," he interrupted, his hands fisted on his thighs, the knuckles white. "He must be destroyed. And to do that would destroy you, as well. If there was another way ... but I am too unlearned in the ways of dream warriors. And I would not put you at risk trying to find an alternate solution."

I put my hand on his, my soul crying out in what seemed like the blackest of nights. If I had harbored even a sliver of hope that Bastian might be able to protect me against Xavier, that hope was now gone. "I understand, Bastian. Don't beat yourself up over it. If it's something that isn't meant to be, then it's not meant to be. That's all."

He was silent for a minute before he said, "I can't be the

warrior you need in your dreamscape, but I can—and will—keep your ex-lover from harassing you in the mortal plane."

"I don't need—" I started to protest.

"You do," he said, cutting short my protest.

I looked at him, this man who had borne so much pain and tried so hard to be everything to everyone, and knew that what I felt for him was more than a little brain lust. I was falling in love with him, with his lovely body, but more, with the soul that shone with such brightness I was amazed everyone didn't recognize him for what he was.

A protector.

"All right," I said without realizing my mouth was speaking. "Although I don't know what Seawright is going to have to say about it. But we'll deal with that later."

He raised my hand to his mouth, his breath hot on my fingers. "Now that you know the worst about me, am I allowed to ask you two questions?"

I wanted to hug him, kiss him silly, and ride him like a carnival ride, all at the same time. "Yes, you are, but if it's about Alessandra, then you don't have to waste your turn on it. I said she had gone off on her own accord, and I meant it." I explained briefly how Seawright and I had found her, and how I'd assumed Xavier meant to use her to force my hand.

His brows drew together as I spoke. "Force you to do what?"

I looked at nothing in particular, my fingers tracing wards on his leg. "That's kind of a complicated subject, one that I really don't want to go into just yet. Would you mind if we held that discussion until later?"

"If that is what you would like," he said, surprising me. I glanced at him, but his face showed no expression other than interest.

"OK, then. What's your question, since I gave you Alessandra's actions for free?"

He thought for a moment. "Who is this Xavier who used to be your lover, and with whom my daughter is evidently now working?"

"I don't know," I said slowly, giving his leg a pat when he stirred. "I mean that literally, by the way. I don't really know who he is. I know he had a tie to the Blood Tribe. He said he used to be a dragon, but he wasn't one anymore, and he certainly never was able to breathe fire like you can. And I don't know why Sandy has thrown in her lot with him. Xavier was very domineering and abusive, and Sandy helped me escape him. She was nothing but kind and supportive, knowing exactly what I'd been through with him. Which is why it makes no sense that she'd team up with him now."

"I need to speak with her," he said, still looking thoughtful. "But at least you have reassured me that she was making her own choices, and not being constrained."

"Definitely not. I'm sorry, Bastian. I'm really sorry. All I can think of is that for some reason, she fell for Xavier just like I did all those years ago. I hope you're not angry with her."

"I am, but only because she would betray a friend. As for her involvement with the Chaos and Blood Tribes ..." He took a deep breath, then released it. I had a feeling he was letting go of some frustration and worry with the action. "She will explain it to me."

"Spoken like a dad," I couldn't help but say with a little smile.

He made a face. "I was confined for much of her formative years, which is no doubt why she feels I have little interest in her life. I will have to prove to her that she is mistaken. But what of you?"

"Oh, I have a few things to say to her, too, although I think your conversation is going to be a whole lot less profanity-laden than mine."

"I meant, what do you desire me to do?" Bastian leaned close, his mouth teasing mine, his eyes blazing with a blue so hot it could steam cauliflower. "Tell you more about the First Dragon, or make love to you?"

"Can I have both?" I asked, deciding that since we were in a dream, I might as well be greedy.

"You may, although I don't know how coherently I can speak on the subject while we are engaged in sexual congress," he said gravely, but the corners of his mouth were curled up in the tiniest of smiles.

"Sexy times first, then pillow talk later," I said, hesitating for a moment before adding. "I have a few things to tell you, too."

"And I will enjoy hearing them. But first, let us commence."

I kept the thought to myself that he wouldn't like the truth about who I was, but pushed that away. Why ruin a perfectly good smutty dream?

"All right. How do you want to ... er ... I mean, we're both fully dressed. Should we take off our clothes and jump into bed? That seems a bit ... well, clinical, doesn't it?"

He gave a little nod. "You wish to be wooed. Of late, Rey has reminded me of this. Male lovers do not require so much wooing, but the females, yes, this I recall. I will now woo you."

I couldn't help myself. I giggled again. "OK. No one's ever wooed me before, so this should be interesting."

He stood up, and hesitated a few seconds. "What form would you like the wooing to take? Would you like me to sing to you? Or to talk? Rey says women of today find frank discussions arousing. Or perhaps you would like an erotic massage?"

"You'd really sing to me?" I asked, more than a little amazed. None of the other men I'd (briefly) been with had ever offered to sing for me.

"Yes. I'm told I have a nice voice, although I don't particularly enjoy the act. I will do so for you, however, if you desire."

I sighed. "Isn't that always the way? I love to sing, but have a voice like a crow with a pronounced smoker's cough, and there's you all golden-throated and not appreciating that fact. We'll skip the singing."

"Then I will talk to you and arouse you that way," he said in a very businesslike tone.

I felt another giggle rising, and decided I needed to take matters in hand.

So to speak.

"How about you let me undress you, and then you can undress me, and by that point, I think we'll both pretty much be wooed."

"You wish to tease me?" he asked, his eyes lighting with a glint that I was coming to recognize.

"If you like to call it that," I said, and slid off the bed to approach him, drawing one hand across his chest. He wore a dark blue suit with a pale cream shirt open at the neck, revealing a hint of golden-brown chest hair that I badly wanted to investigate. He froze when I slid my hands down his arms, taking the suit jacket with them, reveling in the thick swoops of muscles along his biceps and triceps. My breath hitched at the sensation of his heat. "I've never been one for overly muscled men, but you have just the right amount of beefcake to make me feel very feminine."

"Beefcake," he repeated, obviously turning the word over in his mind. "I have been called many things, but I do not recall this word. If I took my clothes off, it would be faster."

This was in response to the fact that I carefully draped his jacket over the back of a chair before moving to his front, and slowly moving down the line of buttons on his shirt. "I'm sure it would, but that wouldn't be wooing. That would be hot and steamy sexy times."

"That sounds perfectly agreeable to me," he commented, hope filling his eyes.

I laughed aloud. "It does to me, too, but this is my dream, and we're going to do it my way."

"Ah, yes, the dream. Very well, proceed."

"It's like unwrapping a particularly delicious present." I reached the end of the line of buttons and tugged his shirt out of his pants before turning my attention to the two cuff links.

Another one of those unreadable expressions passed over his face, but that faded when I finished with his sleeves and tugged his shirt off, pausing for a moment to enjoy the glory that was Bastian's bare chest.

"Now, that is pure wow," I said, studying it. He had lovely golden-brown curls that did nothing to hide the swoops and bulges of a man who had an obvious six-pack.

"You've seen my chest before, *cara*," he said, but his eyes shimmered with heat.

"I know, but it's still very impressive. I want to touch and taste everything I see here. I really like your nipples. They're small. I like small nipples on a man, since they aren't really working models."

He looked down at himself. "I'm glad you find them so. I will admit to not being bothered by them as such, but I appreciate your point about them being decorative. Yours, however …" He stopped speaking, his eyes wide as he gazed at my chest.

And instantly, my breasts demanded out of the confines of my clothing.

"Mine are covered," I pointed out. "Would you like me to—"

"Yes," he said. "But let me help."

Before I could so much as pull my shirt off, he had me stripped down to just my undies.

"As you can see, mine are working models, so my nipples are in no way tiny," I said. My breasts badly wanted me to place them in Bastian's hands, so I leaned forward until they brushed his chest.

He moaned softly, swallowing hard.

"Breast man, are you?" I asked, unable to keep from stroking a hand down his sides.

He shuddered. "If you mean by that one who is obsessed with breasts, then no, I have not been in the past. But I just had a mental image of you round with child, and now I can think of nothing more than claiming you."

I stared at him for half a minute, gripped with a profound sense of sadness that dampened all the joy going on in my pants. I stepped back, unable to speak because my throat ached.

"Phyllida?" He reached a hand for me, dropping it when I moved back another step. "What have I said to cause you pain?"

I fought down the need to cry, reminding myself that this was a dream, and I didn't need to bring the cares of the world into it. "You did nothing but remind me that you represent everything I can't have—a partner, a family. Children. Security. I would give anything to have those things, but—" I stopped, damning myself for ruining what was turning out to be a highly erotic dream.

"You cannot bear children?" Bastian asked, his eyes clouded with concern.

"No, no, it's not that. I don't have any reason to believe I couldn't have kids, but … oh, it's really too long to explain. Not that I want to. This is my fun-time dream, and dammit, I'm not going to let the realities of my life ruin it. If this is all the sexy-time fun I'm going to have with you, then by the goddesses, we're going to have it."

He said nothing when I reached for his belt, unbuckling it and yanking the zipper down on his pants. He'd kicked his shoes off already, so his pants and underwear came off quickly, leaving me with a stark naked, highly buffed, and incredibly aroused dragon.

"Yeah, that's still really impressive," I said, considering his erection. "We're talking kind of epic, to be honest. I mean, yes, women's bodies are meant to accommodate all sizes, and my experience with you has proved that I can fit you in, but still, holy cow, Bastian. Holy freakin' cow."

Once again Bastian looked down at himself, this time with an attempt at modesty. "I have had no complaints from female lovers. Males are a different matter, but since you told me that you do not care for—"

"No," I interrupted quickly. "I'm still very strictly traditional where that's concerned."

He gave me a little bow. "We are in perfect accord."

"So, boundaries reaffirmed, I guess we're good to go." I

was still considering the general length and girth of his penis. "If you don't mind, I'd like to touch you. All over."

"I would enjoy that," he said with a gravity that once again had the giggle rising in me, but I ignored my sillier side and allowed my fingers to dance across the thick muscles of his chest and belly. "There is nothing here I don't like," I said, tracing a line down his bicep. His skin was hot under my fingertips, hot and silky, and so enticing. I wanted to do nothing more than lick the sleek expanses of flesh, but figured there would be time for that later, before I woke up.

A little voice niggled in the back of my head, wondering why Xavier hadn't tracked me down in my dream. I decided that if Xavier had wanted me to escape—for some reason that was beyond my understanding—then he probably wouldn't torment me while I slept.

That reasoning made about as much sense as Xavier did, but I was determined to let the party going on in my downstairs have its fun. I might not be able to get together with Bastian in real life, but I sure as shooting wasn't going to miss the opportunity to indulge in a very erotic dream.

"I love how you feel," I said, moving around behind him, dragging my fingernails gently down his spine. He sucked in his breath, fire breaking out at his feet. I dragged my gaze off his behind—which wasn't easy, given how glorious it was—and cast a speculative gaze at the rug underfoot. "I'm so glad this is a dream, because I really like that rug, and it's an antique. You have a nice behind."

"Thank you," he said, his voice sounding choked and a little hoarse as he stamped out the fire. "I would like to offer you the same compliment. Since you have both hands on my ass and appear to be kneading my ass cheeks, I hope I am allowed to say that without it being considered inappropriate."

"Sorry. I couldn't resist the temptation," I said, reluctantly releasing my two handfuls of butt cheeks, and moving around to face him again. "And I'm not offended, although I don't think it's accurate."

There was a rush of wind, a blur, and the next thing I knew, I was facedown on the bed minus underwear, with a warmth behind me that I took to be Bastian.

"You underestimate your ass," he said above me, his voice now husky with desire. His hands were all over me, touching me, teasing me, making me squirm with a need to do the same to him. His fingers felt as if they were trailing fire along my skin, making me shiver with desire. "It is superb. If I was the type of dragon to write poetry, I would write sonnets about it. Alas that I am not."

"Alas," I said, giving in to a giggle as I pushed myself up, rolling onto my side while reaching for him. He lay half-draped over me, one hand cupping a very needy breast, while his mouth nuzzled a path from my shoulder up to my ear, making me shiver again.

"You are so smooth," he murmured, shifting slightly so that his other hand could get in on the breast action. My body, so long deprived of sexual stimulation, damn near set off fireworks to celebrate the arrival of Bastian, even if he was just in dream form. "So delicious. And you smell like orange blossoms."

"I like flowers," I said, my toes curling into the soft linen of my bed when he bent and took one nipple in his mouth, lathing it with his tongue. "Oh dear goddess, that is so good. Are you breathing fire on my boob?"

"Yes," he said, looking up, his eyes a molten sky blue. "Do you like it?"

"Mrrowr!" I said in a near snarl, and arched my back while trying to wrap my legs around him. "Do the other!"

"I do not normally care to be dominated," he murmured into my other breast, rubbing the slight whiskers of his cheek on the underside. "Wyverns are ever so. But I will allow this demand in you since I can see you are enjoying the attention."

"Too many words, not enough tongue on needy-boob action," I said, pulling on his hair.

He gave in to my demand, not only making me quiver with pleasure as he gave my other breast the time of its life, but moving over until he was on top of me, allowing me to slide my legs outside his. I could feel his erection against one thigh, and wanted badly for him to stop tormenting me and just get the job done. "It is as I suspected—your breasts are pleased with my attention to them. They are, in a word, delightful. As is your belly. And hips. And legs, and woman's parts, and all other bits of you. You are certain that it is not offensive for me to say so?"

I stopped writhing with complete and utter bliss and lifted my head to glare down at where he was using his hands and mouth to torment my breasts. "I don't know who this person is who keeps telling you that you can't compliment someone, but he's dead wrong."

"Rey is a female."

"She's dead wrong. I mean, yes, there are time-and-place situations, but lying in bed naked with someone is most definitely one of those times when you can say as many complimentary things as you like. Also, again too much talking. And yes, I realize that I'm doing most of it, but I'm a very verbal-communication type of person, and I say what I think. Do you like oral sex? Not everyone does, but I figured you might be the type of person to find it stimulating."

"I do, but as usual, you have me so close ... no, *cara*, not that. I can take anything but your mouth. Besides, it's my turn."

"I didn't realize we were on a strict rota," I started to complain, but when he hoisted my legs onto his shoulders, he breathed fire on my party zone, turning my entire body into quivering pleasure. And then he was there, pushing into me, my heart and soul and body rejoicing. Tears pricked in the backs of my eyes, but as I matched his rhythm, I blinked them away, reminding myself that it was stupid to mourn what couldn't be.

And when the orgasm overtook me, I held on to him, praying to any deity that would listen to me that someday I'd be free of Xavier, so I could be with Bastian in person, if only in fleeting moments.

"You weep?"

He'd rolled us over after he found his own climax, leaving me draped over his heaving chest in a boneless blob of former sentient person.

I pushed down the pain at knowing that although I had finally found a man who filled my heart with joy, I couldn't ask him to rescue me.

I'd simply have to figure out a way to do that myself.

"Phyllida?" His voice was warm with concern, almost as warm as the hand that swept up my back in a gentle caress.

"I'm just a bit hormonal right now," I told him, summoning up a smile when I propped myself up on an elbow. "I have this birth control device that normally makes me immune to such things, but a couple of times a year, hormones get to me, and I end up crying at dog-food commercials, and pictures of chonky cats."

"Ah." He looked grave. "I feel the same way. I am particularly prone to the depictions of elderly dogs climbing stairs."

I gave a watery laugh, wiped the errant tears that had leaked out of my eyes. "We're two of a kind, aren't we?"

"We are. Go to sleep, *cara*."

I snuggled into him, relaxing as I breathed in his scent, wishing with all my heart that I was anyone but who I was.

FIFTEEN
THE SWORD

The moonlight woke me sometime later. I realized that I had left the curtains opened, and got up to close them, saying as I glanced out into the garden, "Life seriously sucks."

"Loath though I am to disagree with you, I find it pleasing, if not exhilarating at times." The voice rolled out from nowhere and everywhere at once.

I stiffened in terror, instantly recognizing the dark, sticky presence that seemed to suffocate me. "Goddess, no!" I said on a whimper.

A shadow moved off the bed, taking me by surprise. Bastian leaped into the middle of the room, spinning around to locate the source of the voice. I was astonished to see he held a sword in his hand, recognizing it as one that Seawright kept in the umbrella stand next to the front door.

Quickly, I snatched up the nearest bit of clothing—his shirt—and pulled it on while tossing him his pants. "I have to hide," I said softly, not even questioning why he was still in my dream. My mind raced as I tried to think of a way to keep Xavier from finding me. "I'm sorry. This has to end now. You have to leave, Bastian. It's not safe for you."

"Who is that?" Bastian was behind me, one arm around my waist as he pulled me to his side. "Who speaks but remains hidden to our view?"

"It's Xavier. I didn't think he'd try to find me, but I guess I was wrong." I wanted to scream and yell at the unfairness of it all. I wanted to rail against the forces in the universe that had created me. I wanted to destroy Xavier once and for all so he would never torment me again.

"You do not speak to me. And there is another with you. A male? You have taken a lover? How … interesting."

"Come forth and show yourself," Bastian said, stepping in front of me, brandishing the sword in a manner that bespoke a long familiarity with such weapons.

I stared at his bare back in astonishment. What was he doing? He'd just told me why he couldn't be the dream warrior I needed, and yet here he was trying to antagonize Xavier.

"Stop it," I whispered, poking him in the shoulder blade. "You need to leave now. The fun-time dream is over."

He turned his head just enough to say softly to me, "I will ignore that insult because you are new to the ways of dragons."

The urge to say "I'm not new to your world" was strong, but I bit it back, instead poking him in the shoulder blade again. "We've already discussed this. Stop being heroic. Think of your people."

"I am thinking of them. I am also thinking of you."

"As am I, Phyllida," Xavier said, his voice still rolling around the room without a specific point of origin. "But I do not wish for this interloper to be here."

"Face me, then," Bastian called, lifting the sword.

Run, my inner self screamed at me, my skin positively itching to get away from Xavier. *Run while Bastian is distracting him. Go somewhere else. Go to a forest. A big, dark, dense forest where he won't find you.*

The vision of such a place rose in my mind's eye, but I hesitated. Part of me was sick at the idea of Xavier finding me, but the guilt of putting Bastian in a position where he had to defend me was unthinkable. I wouldn't do that to him. I grabbed his arm, and yanked him after me as I threw myself into a forest dreamscape, racing down a game path while branches slapped against my face and arms.

"What is this place? How did you move us here?" Bastian asked, pulling me to a stop and spinning me so I faced him. We stood in the shadow of a giant pine, but even in the almost-solid darkness, I could see his eyes, bright with emotion. "You are not a dream walker. You should not be able to do this."

"I've learned over the years how to manipulate my dreams so that I can avoid Xavier. I really don't want him finding my house. Come on. We have to hide. He's very good at tracking me. We can't stay there, or he'll find my physical location."

"We will not run," Bastian said, holding my arm when I tried to turn and dash into the shadows cast by the tall trees.

"You don't know him," I protested, still speaking as softly as I could. "He's evil. He follows me everywhere. He's tormented me for years. And if he finds you, then he'll … you'll …"

"I'll what?" he asked, his voice low, but filled with so much anger I wanted to throttle him.

"Try to save me," I said in a harsh whisper. "And you can't, Bastian. No one can."

I tried to urge him forward, but Bastian seemed to lose his mind then.

He let go of my arm and spun around, shouting, "I am Bastian Blu, wyvern of the blue dragons. Come and face me, Xavier of the Blood Tribe."

"Are you fucking insane?" I did a dance of sheer frustration behind him, wanting to simultaneously whomp him upside the head and haul him off into the shadows with me, to a place of safety where we could hide until Xavier grew tired of hunting for me.

Bastian's shoulder twitched. "No, and despite rumors to the contrary, I have never been so. Well?" The last word was yelled into the darkness, an obvious challenge.

"You don't know who you're antagonizing," I whispered, torn between running and trying to make him see reason. "Xavier is—"

"Here." A shadow broke off from one of the tall, elegant pine trees that rustled in the wind, moving to stand before Bastian.

I ducked down for a few seconds before my inner self called me a coward and forced me to move to Bastian's side to face my tormentor. "Fine. I guess we're going to go with outright idiocy instead of self-preservation today. Hello, Xavier. As usual, it's horrific to see you."

"A dream walker," Xavier said, eyeing Bastian. I felt a mild relief that he hadn't so much as glanced at me, and at the same time, I couldn't help but notice an odd note in his voice. It was almost as if he was … disconcerted. "I have not heard of a dragon who was such."

"You are yourself a dragon," Bastian pointed out, standing with what appeared to be ease, one hand holding the sword with effortless grace, but I could feel a sense of heightened tension within him, a heat that I realized with a start was his dragon fire. "That I am such should not surprise you."

"I am no mere dragon," Xavier replied with a curl to his lip. He reached out to the side, and from nowhere, a black sword formed apparently from shadows, glistening darkly in the light of the moon. "Not any longer. I am beyond your understanding, wyvern, but that can be remedied quickly. You asked for a lessoning, and I am happy to teach you your place in my world."

"Don't listen to him," I begged Bastian, trying to turn him to face me. "Please, we can leave. I can get us away."

"You cannot," Bastian said, never taking his eyes off Xavier, his muscles tensed. He reminded me of a tawny lion about to pounce.

"She can, you know," Xavier said in a conversational tone as he strolled a few feet toward us. "She's very talented that way. Not enough so I can't find her, but she does make a good effort. Ah, but I see by the lack of comprehension evident in your face that you don't understand exactly what I mean. Can it be that you have not told this wyvern lover the truth about you, *meelaya*?"

I pushed my hands forward just as if I was shoving him away, my bile rising at what he was doing. He was going to tell Bastian who I was, and that would ruin everything, every hope I had of ever forming a real relationship. "Don't, Xavier. Just … don't. You have what you want. Leave Bastian alone. He's not a part of this."

Bastian turned his head at last, irritation making his eyes blue sapphire. "Did you just attempt to protect me?"

"Don't you dare tell me again that you're a wyvern," I told him, suddenly so enraged that I wanted to shout and scream. Didn't the man have the common sense given to an earthworm? I was trying to save his hide, dammit! "And don't deny you were going to, because I know you were."

"I was, because I am. I protect you, not the other way around."

"Oh, we are not having this conversation now," I told him, wondering if I had something heavy with which to hit him over the head and knock him senseless. That was the only way I could think to get him out of the dream.

"What truth do you think to use against Phyllida?" Bastian asked Xavier.

"Gah!" I screamed, and stomped away from both men, intending to wash my hands of them. If Bastian was too stubborn to leave with me, then I'd just let him duke it out with Xavier.

Without him being able to use his dream warrior abilities? my pesky mind asked me.

I spun around to face them.

"She's a hellerune," Xavier said, strolling toward me, twining a finger around one of my curls. I slapped his hand away and took a couple of steps back, my heart sobbing with what was about to happen. "And the renaissance will begin in a matter of minutes, at which point she will become the most valuable person in the mortal realm, the desire of anyone who wishes to have an almost endless supply of dark power. And lucky, lucky me, she is also my mate."

Bastian's gaze found me, the pain in it so stark, it almost dropped me. "Is this true?" he asked, his voice as hard as granite.

"Which part?" I asked, my shoulders sagging under the knowledge that I would never again be with him. Xavier had killed my love as surely as he had doomed me. I shook my head, answering my own question. "They're both true. I am a hellerune. The renaissance means that the interdiction that keeps me from being kidnapped by every asshole in the mortal and immortal realms is about to dissolve into nothing. And I agreed to be Xavier's mate because I thought he was going to force Sandy into that position. I thought I was saving her. I wasn't."

Tears were streaming down my face now, but I refused to acknowledge them, or the pain that was just about enough to bring me to my knees.

"I see," Bastian said, then, turning, strode out of the clearing, disappearing into the shadows.

I stared after him, taking one stumbling step before stopping, unable to believe what I was seeing. He left me? He just walked out and left me with Xavier?

Of course he did. You told him to leave. He explained that he can't save you, my inner self pointed out.

I wanted to curl up into a ball and scream at the world, but instead I straightened my shoulders, turning slowly to face Xavier.

Nothing had changed. I had found a man, fallen in love, and dreamed of a life filled with light and love. But that vision was false. I was left with no one but myself.

And a lifetime of emptiness.

"Happy?" I asked Xavier with enough acid to choke a scorpion.

"Not yet, but soon, very soon," he said, and started toward me, but at that moment, a miracle happened.

Light filled the clearing, a brilliant gold-white light that came from seemingly everywhere, stripping the breath from my lungs with its beauty.

And out of that light strode the figure of a man with eyes that burned with crystal clear blue.

"Bastian?" I ran toward him, my heart suddenly singing. "What—"

"I had to call my men. I couldn't do that in your dreamscape," he said softly, then pulled me behind him, and faced Xavier. "You will not torment Phyllida any longer, Xavier of the Blood Tribe."

"Do you think to stop me, wyvern?" Xavier asked, laughter rich in his voice.

"You don't have to do this," I whispered, placing my hand on Bastian's bare back.

"I can do this without using the light sword," he answered. "Although a mortal weapon is not strong enough to do anything but ensure he leaves you alone."

I bit back the warning that Xavier was beyond powerful and no mere dream walker would be able to stop him, unsure of what I should do. I couldn't let Bastian sacrifice himself, but at the same time, if there was a real chance that he was strong enough to scare off Xavier, then I would be stupid to not let him try.

I'd just have to make sure he didn't do anything that would put himself in jeopardy.

SIXTEEN
THE CHALLENGE

"You will not use Phyllida, nor will you sell her to the highest bidder," Bastian said, moving forward, his gaze pinpointing his prey. The fact that this being, this former dragon, thought he could use the woman who held Bastian's heart was beyond his understanding. "She is not an object to be so abused."

"It has been some time since I had the pleasure of breaking a dream walker." Xavier lunged before he finished speaking, but Bastian was ready for him and had his sword up to block the attack even as Phyllida's scream echoed in his ears.

"You can't seriously think that can do anything but annoy me," Xavier said, taking a step back, his hand drawing symbols in the air.

To Bastian's horror, the symbols evaporated into a dust that clung to his borrowed sword, strange runes growing up the length of the blade. It became unbearably cold, and Bastian flung it aside just as the creeping blackness touched his fingers.

The sword shattered upon impact, leaving an oily black residue on the forest floor.

"That's much better. Now I—" Xavier's words came to an abrupt stop when Bastian allowed his dragon fire to rage within him, pulling from his pocket the blue crystal that seemed to thrum with energy.

His mind screamed warnings, but he told himself that this time he was in control. He would not kill the tormentor Xavier, simply banish him from Phyllida's dreams.

"Now you will leave," Bastian told him, allowing the white-blue arcane sword to pulse into being. He was momentarily surprised to see that the blade was licked with fire, his fire, but forced himself to focus on holding back the power that wanted to flow through him.

That power was his doom. He would not give in to it. Phyllida's life depended on him keeping it leashed.

Xavier's eyes narrowed on the sword. "What is this? A dream walker wielding arcane magic? You are not one of the Firstborn."

"Nor are you, dragon," Bastian countered. Although the kin were difficult to kill in their own right, Firstborn children were more so.

"Dragon hunter, not dragon," Xavier said on a snarl, sheathing his weapon in order to pull a gray-black sword from a scabbard on his back. "Although I am soon to be so much more."

Bastian checked for a moment, studying his opponent. It was true the man was not a dragon, although he had a feel of dragonkin to him, but a dragon hunter? Mentally, he shook his head. The monster could not be allowed to threaten Phyllida. "It matters not what you are, so long as you leave my mate alone."

"*Your* mate?" Xavier laughed. "You think to take her from me? You'll have to beat me first."

Before Bastian could respond, Xavier leaped forward, his blade slashing through the light, slicing deep into his left arm.

"No!" Phyllida screamed, trying to run forward to get to her tormentor, her face filled with fury and anguish.

Bastian caught her as she passed him, spinning her around so that she was headed in the opposite direction before flinging himself forward, his blade dancing on the fading light, finding only the dull black of Xavier's sword.

"It has been too many months since I spilled the blood of the dragonkin. Killing you will be a pleasure," Xavier taunted, kicking out at Bastian's knee.

But Bastian had been expecting the move, and shifted his weight, catching only the edge of the kick. He slashed as Xavier regained his balance, and was more than a little satisfied when his blade sank deep into the monster's thigh.

Xavier roared in fury, slamming his fist forward at the same time he swung for Bastian's head, coming a fraction of an inch from decapitating him.

Behind him, Bastian could hear Phyllida chanting a prayer in Italian, her words catching on sobs. His heart ached with the knowledge of the hell she'd bravely shouldered her entire life, and it filled him with determination to be the savior she so desperately needed.

He just had to do that without his losing control to the power of the dream warrior. So far, his dragon fire harnessed it, keeping it bound tightly within him. If he could drive Xavier from Phyllida's dream, he could draw on the defenses of his sept to keep her physically safe. As for her dreams … well, he'd just have to show Xavier that he would tolerate no further abuse.

"This ends now," Xavier spat out, trying to gut him, but Bastian had been trained by one of the finest swordsmen in Italy, and he parried the thrust only to use his momentum to swing the sword around behind Xavier, smashing him on the back, and throwing him off-balance.

And that's the moment that Bastian realized that Xavier was far cleverer than he'd given credit, for rather than turning on Bastian to fight, he leaped forward toward Phyllida, swinging his sword upward, clearly in preparation for cleaving her in two.

"No!" Bastian yanked hard on the power that lay coiled inside him, the light filling his mind even as he threw his sword at Xavier, catching him in the arm that was beginning its downswing. At the same time, Bastian allowed the power to erupt from him, fighting desperately to keep it focused on Xavier's arm, the need to just let it flow out of him overwhelming his mind.

Xavier screamed as the golden light slammed into his arm, sending his sword skittering along the forest floor.

Bastian stalked forward, his mind filled with vengeance. He fully intended to blast another stream of power into the monster who threatened them, secure in the knowledge that at last, he was fulfilling the blessing placed upon him.

Xavier got to his feet, listing heavily on one side. He said nothing, just curled a lip back while his black eyes spat hatred at Bastian, then backed into the shadows, retreating from the dreamscape.

Bastian's spirit soared with the power that flowed around him. He would be a weapon of the First Dragon, deployed to make the world a better place. He would be everything to everyone—

A noise caught his attention, a gasping sob that cut through the golden light that poured through his being. Slowly, he turned his head to locate the source of the noise.

A woman stood before him, her hands clasped together as if in entreaty, her cheeks wet with tears.

No, not a woman, Phyllida. His Phyllida, his mate.

Nothing would take her away from him. Not even the First Dragon. He doubled over, fighting the flow of power through him, fearing he was lost to it, lost to everything and everyone he loved. He would truly go mad this time, and Phyllida—who would save her from the madman Xavier?

"Never," he snarled, the mental image of her stirring his dragon fire to an inferno, pushing down the golden light in his head. "Not again. *Never* again."

"Bastian?" Phyllida's voice was stark with mingled fear and horror. She moved toward him, and he felt the warmth of her hand gently touching his arm. "Are you all right? Your eyes—your eyes turned gold, just like the light that surrounded you."

He remained doubled over for a few more seconds, the pain of quelling the First Dragon's power so great, it stripped him of speech. At last his fire caged the dream warrior self, and he straightened, his breath coming short and hard as if he'd run a great distance.

"Oh, thank the goddesses, they're back to pretty blue topaz," Phyllida said on a hiccuped half sob, throwing herself on him, kissing his neck and face. "I didn't know that you were going to—is that what happened the last time? I'm sorry, so sorry that you had to do that. But you didn't lose yourself, Bastian. You didn't kill him when you could. You held on to your dream warrior and drove him away, and for that, I'll be eternally grateful. Even if you never want to see me again, I'll owe you the moon and stars for driving him away."

He allowed her to kiss him with random, fleeting touches of her mouth, wrapping his arms around her and just holding her, taking comfort in both the feel of her against him and the knowledge that he could best his dream warrior self. "Do not praise me too much, *cara*. It was a close thing. I almost killed you in my desire to see him destroyed."

"But you didn't. You stopped in time. You controlled your power." Phyllida took his face in her hands, her eyes laughing despite the silver tracks of tears on her cheeks. "You really are amazing, do you know that? I mean, I knew you were, but what you did—it was the most amazing thing I've ever witnessed."

Gently, he put her from him, his joy in knowing he had not lost himself fading with the realization of what faced them.

"I can't wait to tell Seawright about it. ... Why ... you're not celebrating?" Her expression dimmed as she studied his face. "Why aren't you happy? You beat Xavier."

"I drove him from your dream, that's all. Come. We must leave your dreamscape. There is work to be done."

"Work? What work?" she asked as he led her from the woods, trusting that she would return them to her bedroom.

The darkness of the forest lightened until the shapes of square furniture could be seen in the moonlight that streamed in her open drapes.

"Bastian, I don't want to wake up if it means you won't tell me what's going on," she said.

He clicked on a standing lamp, and turned to face her, watching her eyes grow round as her gaze flickered at various points in her bedroom. "Wait … we are asleep, aren't we?"

"Not now. We've left the dreamscape." He took her by the arms, looking deep into those beautiful eyes, seeing confusion and concern in them. He wished he could give her back the joy she had a few minutes ago, but he couldn't. Not yet. Not until he found a way to get what he wanted from Xavier. "*Cara*, do you have another location, a place you have never been? Somewhere you can be safe from Xavier?"

"I have my house," she said, a little frown pulling her brows together. "I'm safe here. It's warded everywhere. Wait just one second. If we're not dreaming, if you're really here, then did we—" She glanced toward the bed.

"Yes." One side of his mouth quirked at the memory of their lovemaking. She'd obviously convinced herself it was a dream, and thus lowered her inhibitions. "I have a friend who is a Guardian. She put me touch with one of her kind here in Oregon. She got me through your wards."

"But my security system—"

"Another friend, another expert," he admitted, wanting badly to take her back to bed so he could reassure himself that she was still his. His woman. His mate. "She turned it back on once I was inside," he added, lest she thought he took her security for granted.

"Then we have nothing to worry about," she told him, heaving a sigh of relief that he didn't in any way share. "This house is safe from beings of a dark nature, and although Xavier can wield dark magic, he can't wield dark power, and thus he can't get through the wards and banes protecting the house. Not to mention that he doesn't know where I live. The Committee is very good about hiding my whereabouts. Not even if Xavier paid the best hacker in the world could he dig out my address."

"He doesn't have to," Bastian told her, not wanting to bring her pain, but needing to keep her safe. "He's already here."

She stared at him, fear chasing despair, her eyes losing some of their brilliance. "Here in Oregon?" she finally asked.

"Outside your house. *Cara*, he's a dream walker. Just as I could find you via your dreams, so could he. The minute he found you in your dreamscape, all he had to do was withdraw from it to the shadow world, and he would find himself in your location. The protections on your house have kept him out of it, but it's only a matter of time before he breaches it."

"He can't," she protested, shaking her head. "The wards and banes that Lin and Jordan draw each week—"

"Can be broken. Come." He took her hand and led her from her bedroom to a window that overlooked the front of the house. The small garden was mostly dark, with long inky fingers reaching across the silver-tipped grass, but a slight movement below them had Phyllida gasping and backing away from the window.

"Who is that?"

"Demons," he said grimly, scanning the yard for signs of Luca and Gio. He knew it would take them a little time to get here, and even then, he'd told them not to try to fight the demons on their own. He had no idea how many dragons the monster had with him. "Xavier is using them to try to break the protections."

"Oh, goddess," she said, wrapping her arms around herself, stumbling backward a few steps.

"Phyllida." He took her firmly by the shoulders, giving her a gentle shake until she stopped staring in horror at the window and met his gaze. "I will not let anyone harm you. Do you understand? You are my mate. I am a wyvern, and I do not give up what I hold. Do you understand?"

To his relief, she stopped looking frightened and straightened up, pulling herself out of his grip, her eyes spitting green fire at him. "Of course I understand. I'm not an idiot, Bastian. I've taken care of myself for ninety-six years, after all."

He didn't point out that evidently part of that time included being in Xavier's control, instead giving her a curt nod. "You are anything but an idiot. Now, tell me what a hellerune is. I have only a vague idea that it has something to do with dark power."

"Dark magic, not power, although the two things are commonly confused. Many beings who can wield dark magic cannot handle dark power. It has to do with origins. Magic is created by individuals. Dark power comes from a direct source, like a demon lord," she said, and quickly detailed her history, how she'd been taken into custody of the Committee at an early age, and spent her life in isolation, monitored for her own safety, and that of the mortal world.

"But if you have only a minute fraction of your powers, why does the Committee guard you so closely?" he asked, pacing the length of the hallway as he thought about just how valuable Phyllida would be to anyone who understood the Otherworld.

"Two reasons: one is the renaissance, which, as Xavier said, is occurring in"—she peered over his shoulder to where a narrow grandfather clock ticked quietly in the corner—"approximately thirty-seven minutes."

"The Otherworld renaissance happens only every forty years," he said, checking his phone to see Luca's location. He was close, he had texted, and would leave their car a short distance from Phyllida's house so that they could evaluate who was outside.

"True, but an interdiction can be broken. It's not easy, and you need three archimages working in concert to do it, but it can be done." She bit her lip, drawing his attention to her mouth. Before he could stop himself, she was in his arms, and he was kissing the fear from her eyes.

"No one will harm you," he promised when he had no breath left. "I swear this on my life."

"Oh no, you don't," she said, firing up again, slapping both hands on his chest. "I'm falling in love with you, dammit. I am not going to let you sacrifice yourself now. Not when I've found you, and I want to keep you."

He smiled, a moment of happiness giving him strength. He brushed back one of her errant curls, trailing his fingers down her soft cheek. "I don't want to lose you, either, *cara*."

"You don't …" She cleared her throat, but kept her gaze locked on him. "You don't happen to be falling in love with me, too?"

"No," he said with all honesty, then wanted to laugh at her furious expression. He kissed her again, his lips savoring the Italian profanities she said into his mouth, before he gave her delightful ass a little squeeze. "I fell in love with you the first time I saw you in that flower shop."

"That was a dream," she said, but he couldn't help but notice that she turned pink with pleasure.

"It was. But that didn't stop me from knowing you were the one woman placed on this earth for me. Now, let us make some plans. We must ensure your safety while I gather forces to protect this house."

"I'll get Seawright," she said, and turned to go down the stairs.

"Must you?" he couldn't help but ask.

She made a face over her shoulder. "I know she's a bit of a pain, but she can also be helpful in a tight spot. Besides, she has a Taser, and if there's any chance on this good, green earth for me to Tase the ever-living hell out of Xavier, I want to take it."

"Show me your secret exit," he said quickly, stopping her before she could go further. "I will use it while you and your companion work up interior defenses."

She showed him a doorway cut into the back of a closet, hidden by a massive tree so that it remained unseen by anyone on the outside.

"Stay safe, mate," he told her, cracking the door to peer outside. This side of the house was evidently not considered of interest to Xavier, since there were no entrances but the hidden door. "I will be back as soon as I can. I've asked for help from the green and silver dragons, but they will not be able to be here for an hour or so."

"By then the renaissance will be upon us," she said, clinging to his shirt, which she'd given back to him after donning a pair of leggings and a hoodie. "Bastian, please, please be careful. Xavier is—"

"I know what he is, and what he means to do to you," he said, ice entering his veins despite the ever-present dragon fire. "What is unclear is exactly how he intends to use Deus and the Chaos dragons to harm the weyr and dragonkin, but have no fear. He won't succeed on either front."

She kissed him quickly, then closed the door behind him as he climbed out onto the tree, pausing to see if anyone heard the sound of the branches rustling.

He made it to the ground and, running as lightly as a fox, headed for the road, knowing Luca was nearby. Hopefully, the other dragons would arrive before Xavier's demons did much damage to the house. Bastian refused to acknowledge the possibility that he could fail.

Too much was at stake. This time, he was fighting not just for his sept, but for the woman who held his heart, and he'd be damned if he let either down.

SEVENTEEN
THE CHOICE

"Do you have the pans set up in front of the kitchen door?" Seawright—in the act of passing through the hallway with her arms loaded with the knife block from the kitchen, a small hatchet, and a long machete that I knew wasn't mine—accompanied her question with a look so pointed, it should have poked a hole in my head.

"No, because as slapstick as it would be to have Xavier try to enter though that door, stumble over a mountain of pots and pans, and slide across the kitchen floor on a non-stick skillet, reality tells me that's not going to happen. Besides, I want that door left clear so we have a way to escape, assuming his bastard demons break the protections on the front door. Where are you going with that?"

"Living room windows. Stay in the hall or upstairs until your boyfriend gets back." She paused to breathe heavily through her nose for a few seconds. while giving me another pointed look "I will, naturally, have to report to the Committee the fact that you let him into the house without first notifying me."

I looked at the clock sitting on the buffet in the dining room, where I was holed up. "The Committee is going to be in existence for approximately eighteen more minutes, so knock yourself out."

"My job doesn't stop just because of the renaissance," she said with a sour look, then took herself off to duct-tape her collection of sharp objects to the inside window frames.

I peered out into the hall, worriedly watching the front door. I could hear faint noises from beyond it, no doubt the demons who I had glimpsed from upstairs working to break the protections. Thus far, the layered protection had held, but I had seen at least three different wards flare to life before being dissolved into nothing, which told me the demons were making progress. "I just hope Bastian is safe," I said to no one.

"Did he tell you how he was locked up for almost a hundred years because he was insane?" a woman's voice spoke from behind me, making me stifle a shriek as I spun around.

Sandy stood leaning against one side of the arched doorway that led to the kitchen, a faint smile on her lips.

"What the hell?" My heart turned to lead as I stared past her, expecting to see Xavier loom up, but there was no movement in the brightly lit kitchen. "What are you doing here? Goddamn it, Sandy! How did you get in? And where's your bastard friend?"

"Which bastard friend?" she asked, tipping her head slightly. "Xavier? Outside, getting very annoyed. He is most unpleasant when he's annoyed, so I thought I would pop in and have a little chat with you about the choice you're going to have to make."

"How did you get in?" I asked, for a few seconds the crazy squirrels in my head unable to process what I was seeing.

"Kitchen door."

Angry, scared, and worried, I marched into the kitchen, not being any too gentle when I pushed past her. The door was shut, a small red light on a device above it blinking slowly, telling me the alarm was still active.

"How?"

She held up one hand, two narrow pieces of metal in her hand. "Lockpicks. I turned the alarm back on after I came in, so you don't have to make that face at me."

"I am so calling up the alarm people and telling them they're doing a crappy job, because it appears anyone who wants to can disable it and pop in without so much as a beep," I said, storming over to her, wanting to yell and make a scene, but too afraid she might call in help to do more than glare.. "You've proven your point that you can come and go at any time you like. Why don't you take yourself off."

She gave an exaggerated sigh, still leaning against the doorway, her arms crossed. "I knew you would be hurt, but really, you have to believe me that there was no other way."

"You're right that I'm hurt—betrayal by an old friend will do that to you—but there is no way in hell I'm going to believe anything else you tell me. You've proven which side you're on, Sandy, and it's not mine."

"I know it looks that way, but sometimes you have to look beyond the obvious, and trust in what you know in your heart, not what you see. That's the whole method behind diviners, you know. We look beyond things to find the truth."

"You wouldn't know the truth if it bit you on the ass," I said, fury rising in me that she had the nerve to come into my safe place and lecture me, just like she was still someone I trusted.

"I understand, I really do, but sweetie, you have to listen to me because this is important." She came toward me, which just made me back up, looking around wildly for something I could use as a weapon in case she tried to attack, but Seawright had taken anything even remotely stabby. "Listen to me, Phil. Very shortly you're going to have to make a choice. You have just one shot of getting it right, so you have to look beyond what you see. You understand? You have to trust your heart, not what your brain tells you." She reached out to touch a spot on my chest where my heart was beating wildly.

"How you have the nerve to come here and act like you have the right to give me advice after what you did to me ..." I bit back the rest of the sentence, since it was going to be nothing but profanities. "Just so you know, your father is worried sick about you."

"Is he?" Her eyebrows lifted, her pale blue eyes studying me in a way that made me profoundly uncomfortable. It was as if she could sense what I was thinking. "Could it be that you told him about what happened at Narmar?"

"Of course I did. He believed you had been kidnapped, or worse. You know, the same sort of bullshit you fed me to get me out there. Bastian is a nice man, Sandy. You may not have had a chance to know him, but he is a loving, thoughtful man, a natural-born protector, and he's put his own welfare on the line to find you and save you from what he assumed was a heinous fate."

"And you told him it was no such thing?" she asked, tipping her head to the side again. I had a horrible feeling she was laughing at me, which just made me angrier.

"Yes. I told him everything," I said, honing my glare to razor sharpness.

"Now, that you did not do," she said, and actually had the audacity to smile before patting me on the shoulder. "I'll leave, since you look like you very much want to punch me in the face. Just remember what I told you."

"I'll be sure to tell Bastian that you don't even care enough to call him," I said, aware that I was striking out in a deliberate attempt to hurt her, but unable to keep from doing so. I knew how worried Bastian had been, not to mention confused as to why his daughter had chosen this path. "You ought to be ashamed of yourself, Sandy. I can understand you betraying me because I was just a friend. But to treat your own father the way you have—it's cruel beyond anything I've seen."

She was silent a moment, the smile fading. "It's important that he remain focused right now, or I would take the time to see him and reassure him that I have things well in hand."

"Bullshit," I swore, at my limit.

"Look beyond appearances, Phil. My father has the ability to do it, and you must do the same, or everything I've worked so hard for will turn to dust. And that would be a devastation that I don't think any of us could recover from." She touched the keypad next to the door, switching off the alarm, then was through the door itself before I could do more than twist the dead bolt and turn the alarm back on.

"What the hell?" I asked the air, feeling like I was lost in a sea of confusion. "What plans? More betrayal? Why did she make it sound like she was doing something nice for me? How could binding me to Xavier be good?"

"I don't know, is it a trick question?" Seawright asked as she reentered the kitchen.

It was on the tip of my tongue to tell her about Sandy's visit, but the resulting meltdown she would have kept me silent.

Until the world seemed to blur for a second, then focus again. I took a deep breath, the sensation of freedom sending body-wide goose bumps. Seawright, who was in the process of searching through the kitchen drawers, no doubt for more knives, gasped and turned around.

"Interdiction is gone," I said, taking another deep breath.

"The renaissance has begun." She blinked a couple of times; then her tablet started pinging with messages. She pulled it out, tapping frantically. "I'll alert you just as soon as the Committee re-forms. The archimage who will reapply the interdiction is just now landing in Portland. You must go upstairs, away from the attackers."

"You don't have to tell me twice," I said, taking the stairs two at a time. I was heading for my closet when my phone pinged with a message from Bastian, telling me to open the secret door for him.

"Thank the eighty-seven goddesses you're here," I said, stepping back when he leaped into the closet from the tree, yanking the door closed behind him and hitting the lock. "Your friends aren't coming?"

"No. They remain outside with three green dragons who have arrived to help us." He pulled me into the bedroom, glancing around it as if making sure it was secure. "Phyllida, we must get you to safety."

"I'm not leaving the house," I said quickly, before he could continue. "This is the safest place for me. The wards and protections—"

"Will not last. Even now Xavier and Deus have all but one bane destroyed. It is the only thing standing between them and you." He held my upper arms, his hair mussed, a small leaf poking out of one of the curly bits behind his ear. "*Cara*, I do not ask you to do this lightly, but you must flee before Xavier gets into the house."

"You can't stop him?" I asked, feeling helpless and frustrated. "No, forget I asked that. This isn't your fight. It's my problem."

"It is my fight, and it is *our* problem," he corrected me, giving me a little shake, then pulling me to his body, his lips on mine giving me comfort when I just wanted to cry with despair. "My brave one, my love, you matter more to me than anything. I swore to keep you safe, and so I will, but I do not have enough men to stop both Deus and Xavier. We have eliminated Deus's men, but Xavier has a demonologist who is summoning demons one after another as soon as they are destroyed trying to break the bane. We can't fight all of them with only six of us. You must go into the dreamscape, where you will be safe from Xavier. I will keep his attention here until reinforcements arrive in a few hours."

"You want me to go to sleep? Now?" I asked, wanting to yell in frustration. "Even if I wanted to go to sleep, I wouldn't. My body would still be here, and all Xavier would have to do is scoop up my sleeping self—"

"You have a songline," Bastian interrupted. "Unlike most dreamers, your body does not remain when you walk the dreamscapes."

"Songline—I've heard of that. It's something to do with Australia, isn't it? My family is from there. My dad was from Western Australia, and Mom was born in Madrid—"

"Songline in this case refers to the fact that you can take your physical form with you when you dream. That is what you must do now."

"There is no way I'm going to run away and leave you to fight Xavier," I told him. "And stop giving me that stubborn look. No, Bastian. I'm many things, but I do not leave others to fight my fights. We'll face him together."

"It is too dangerous for you," he argued, his jaw set. "The renaissance has begun. It is imperative that you get to safety until enough dragons arrive to help us stop Xavier from—"

A massive blast shook the house, sending us both reeling, the ground slipping away from under me at an angle that left me staggering into a wall. Dirt and dust cascaded down on us as part of the ceiling and Sheetrock crumbled.

"What the hell—"

"Are you hurt?" Bastian asked, helping me up.

"No. Just startled. What was that?"

Bastian yanked the door open even before I finished speaking. He took two steps into the hallway and stopped, his body blocking my view when I followed.

I tried to go around him, but halted when he pulled me to his side.

The entire front part of the house was gone, a thick cloud of debris floating gently to the ground. The hallway continued for a few yards, then crumbled into nothing, hanging in midair. The sides of the house leaned drunkenly inward, their jagged edges making it look like a bomb site.

From under a blown-apart hall table, an arm holding a tablet emerged, followed by the sound of coughing, the smashed wooden planks shifting as a ghostly Seawright emerged. It took me a minute to realize she was covered in white plaster and dust, and hadn't actually turned into a spirit.

"If I asked you to go now—" Bastian stopped when I pointed past him.

"Too late."

We watched as Xavier picked his way through the debris to stand in a relatively clear spot in the hall, his hands on his hips as he looked around the room before noticing us on what remained of the upper landing. "How fortunate to find you with your dragon lover at your side. Deus is out hunting for him. It would appear that some of his tribe have gone missing."

Bastian turned to me, taking my hand in his. "Phyllida—"

"No," I told him, squeezing his fingers. "Thank you for wanting to keep me safe, but that's not the answer. He'll just follow."

Bastian thought about that for a moment, then nodded. "Do not do anything rash. There are blue and green dragons outside, but not enough to protect us. Not until the reinforcements arrive."

I said nothing as Bastian swung himself down, leaping onto the floor below before holding his arms up for me. Ignoring Xavier as he stood watching with what for him passed as a tolerant expression, I dangled for a few seconds in midair until Bastian caught my legs and eased me down to the ground.

"Now," he said, dusting me off before turning to face Xavier. "I suppose you are here to demand that Phyllida go with you. I cannot allow that. I cannot allow you to—"

"Actually, I don't want her," Xavier said, brushing off a bit of dust that had drifted down onto his shoulder.

I stared at him for a few seconds, then turned to Bastian. "I think the blast knocked my squirrels over."

"Your what?" he asked, giving me a look that spoke volumes, and none of it made any claims about the quality of my sanity.

"The squirrels in your head. You know—when your thoughts go tumbling around and chasing each other. It's just like you have a couple of squirrels running around in your mind."

"You are an odd woman," Bastian told me, entirely serious.

"But you like that, yes?" I asked, ignoring the fact that Seawright, who had staggered to a chair when Bastian was helping me down, made an annoyed click of her tongue, and dusted off her tablet before making notes.

"Flirtation," she muttered to no one. "Again."

"I like it, yes," Bastian agreed, then turned back to Xavier. "Would you explain your statement?"

"Ah, remembered I was here, did you?" He made a grandiose gesture toward me. "I thought it was sufficiently clear. I don't want her."

"But ... the renaissance has started," I said, feeling stupid for saying it, but at the same time being fully aware that he must have known that very fact. Seawright squawked in protest. I ignored her and continued. "I'm the queen of magic breaking right now. Why aren't you forcing me to your unholy whims?"

"I am so reporting this conversation just as soon as the Committee completes its re-formation," Seawright informed me.

Xavier waved a hand at my question. "I don't want any magic unmade."

"It makes dark power," I argued, taking a step forward, but was instantly pulled back to Bastian's side. "Of course you want it."

"By all the gods and goddesses and little tiny sprites, the woman is trying to unmake the world," Seawright moaned, clutching the tablet to herself.

"I can't use it," Xavier told me. "Not yet. Later ... later we will be having an entirely different discussion. But for now, I do not seek to use your unique, if somewhat archaic, talents."

"Then why did you claim her?" Bastian demanded to know. He felt very hot to me, and I realized with a start that it was his dragon fire I could feel, spinning around inside him, ready to burst out the moment he allowed it to do so. "Why did you turn my daughter so that she would betray Phyllida?"

"She came to me, as a matter of fact," Xavier said, looking mildly bored. "She told me that her divinations pointed to me. I am not one to refuse a useful tool when it is offered to me, and it saved me some trouble to have her bring Phyllida to heel."

"Is it wrong that I feel insulted?" I asked Bastian.

"Yes," Seawright answered, shooting a potent look my way before resuming filling out yet another tattling report.

"I would very much like to know why a man who doesn't want you would go to such extent to get to you," Bastian said, his gaze never leaving that of Xavier.

I had one hand on his bicep. It felt as tense and tight as steel.

To my extreme discomfort, Xavier smiled. "It's quite simple, wyvern. Phyllida is part of an exchange, a very important part. One could say a vital part, since without her, the exchange cannot be made."

"With whom?" Bastian asked, his voice dripping with suspicion.

"You." Xavier sauntered toward us, stepping over broken bits of wood, plaster, Sheetrock, and furniture that had been blasted when the front of the house was destroyed. He stopped a yard in front of us, his smirk fully in place. "You want her, don't you? Very well. I will retract my claim upon her, and allow you to claim her as your mate."

"Why?" I asked.

Xavier ignored me, his mocking gaze on Bastian.

Bastian's fire was so high, it manifested itself at my feet. Mindful of what remained of my nice parquet floor, I tamped it out with my foot. "And in return, you want what?" he asked.

"Your relic."

I swear that Bastian turned to stone next to me. I glanced at him, my fingers tightening on his arm when he appeared to have stopped breathing. "Bastian?" I gave his arm a little joggle. "What relic is he talking about?"

Deus appeared in the doorway. He was battered and covered in blood, and one arm hung from his elbow at an angle that indicated a compound fracture, but his face was black with fury. "Your demonologist ran off, taking his demons with him. Half my tribe are gone. Missing. We can't even find their bodies. Did you get it? I want to leave before I lose any more tribe members to these devils."

A flash of fury appeared in Xavier's eyes before he spun around, thrusting his hands out before him. Deus was flung backward several yards, slamming into an apple tree that stood at the end of my pathway. "Do not speak to me in that tone," Xavier snarled.

I'll say one thing for Deus: as beat up as he was, he managed to get to his feet. He limped forward, his voice scratchy with anger. "You treat me like a lackey, a slave here to do only your bidding, and not a master of a tribe—"

"A tribe I gave you. I can take it away if I so desire," Xavier snapped, beginning to turn back toward us, obviously done with his henchman.

"Father—" Deus started to say, but went flying again, this time crashing through my tiny garden into a brick wall. He slid down it to the ground, and didn't move.

"Father?" I said softly.

Seawright sucked in her breath.

"That explains much," Bastian said just as softly.

Xavier lowered his hands and spun around to face us, giving Bastian a look that warned he was at the end of his not very evident patience. "What say you, wyvern? Will you exchange your piece of the dragon heart for your mate?"

Three men appeared in the doorway, coming to a staggering halt at his words. One of the three was Bastian's buddy Luca, while the other two were dark-haired strangers, most likely some of the green dragons who had been called in to help.

Luca looked stricken at Xavier's words.

"What's a dragon heart?" I asked, my stomach turning sour and feeling as if I was going to vomit right there and then.

"What you ask is impossible," Bastian told Xavier. I could feel him gathering his fire, obviously about to attack. "That relic binds the sept to the weyr. Without it, the blue dragons would cease to be a part of the weyr."

Luca, his head swiveling between Xavier and Bastian as he sidled around the edge of the room, continued to look as if a mule had just kicked him in the gut.

"The weyr, the weyr," Xavier mocked Bastian before adding, "The weyr is nothing. Dragons are nothing. Soon enough, you will all be remade in my image. Until then, either you take the woman, or I will. And I can guarantee that she will not survive the taking."

My eyes widened as I realized at last what Xavier had done.

Luca reached Bastian's side, his gaze searching, but Bastian did nothing but give him a short nod of acknowledgment.

I was too busy coping with the facts that my deranged mind squirrels rolled into place, each piece clicking into the next. "He set me up," I said, goose bumps of pure horror pricking my arms and legs. "He set this whole thing up—chasing me in my dreams, involving Sandy so that you would be drawn to the area, and we'd meet and fall in love. He lined us all up, and watched as we fell just as he knew we would."

"Alessandra is a very good diviner," Xavier said, his gaze flickering over me for a moment. "She has been of much use to me. Well, wyvern? Make up your mind. You can have either your sept or your mate, but not both."

Luca made a word of protest.

"Don't be stupid," I told Xavier, knowing I'd pay the price for being so flip to him, but uncaring at that moment. The realization that it wasn't me all along who had been his target, but Bastian, put me into a fury unlike anything I had experienced. "No wyvern would give up his sept. Even I know that."

"I accept your offer," Bastian said, his voice so full of pain that it seemed to belong to a stranger. I spun around to grab him when he started forward, moving quickly to block him, my hands on his chest. Luca stared at him as if he couldn't believe what he was hearing.

"No," I told Bastian, slapping my hands on him when he refused to meet my eyes. "Dammit, you are not doing this. You are their wyvern. You can't leave them—they depend on you. You have to lead them, Bastian. It's what you were born to do. We can find a way to deal with Xavier without you sacrificing everything you love."

"Not everything," he said, his gaze at last touching mine, his eyes so full of love that I wanted to weep with the wonder of it all. "I was born to protect, yes, but it appears that the sept does not need me any longer."

He pulled from his neck the gold chain with the little crystal that I'd seen before.

"Bastian—" Luca choked to a stop when Bastian shot him a look.

"You must tell Rey what happened here," was all he said before pulling me to his side as he strode forward to Xavier, offering the chain and crystal. "Release my mate."

Xavier smiled. I swear if I'd been mortal, it would have taken a few years off my life. He lifted a hand and said simply, "I refuse your fealty. You are no longer named a member of the Blood Tribe. I refute any honors given you as my mate, and release you from your ties to me and my kin."

I staggered to the side a step as he unmade the bond between us. It was almost as good as the feeling of the interdiction lifting ... *the interdiction.*

"I have kept my part of the deal," Xavier said, and suddenly, the world seemed to slip into slow motion. It was as if each second were now stretching to five. Xavier's hand started to reach for the crystal that Bastian held, and as he did so, the word kept echoing in my head.

Interdiction. The interdiction was off me. Which meant I was a fully functioning hellerune, a breaker of magic, one who could transform magic into a form that offered tremendous power.

My gaze slid to the crystal. If I broke it, if I unmade the magic that was contained in the relic, I would have an immense amount of power at my control. I could do anything with the sort of power that resulted from a dragon relic. I could wield it for good, forcing the dark power into creating … My gaze shifted to Xavier's satisfied face.

Or I could use it to destroy.

The crystal was in my hand before both Xavier and Bastian realized, although I heard another squawk from Seawright that warned she had guessed what I was thinking.

"I think I'll take that," I said, my gaze on it as it lay in my hand.

"Phyllida?" Bastian frowned as I took a couple of steps away from him. Luca made a move like he was going to jump me, but Bastian put out a hand to stop him. "What are you doing? I have agreed to the price to release you."

"Yes, but I didn't," I said, holding the crystal to my chest as I backed up a few more feet, the people in front of me frozen like a tableau. "This relic, this dragon heart—it's important, isn't it?"

Bastian's jaw worked even as his fingers flexed. Luca was almost dancing with impatience and kept glancing earnestly at Bastian, but didn't move toward me, clearly abiding by his wyvern's dictates. "It is. It is one of five pieces that together make up the dragon heart. It is a gift from the First Dragon."

I looked past him to Xavier and caught the instant that he realized what I was intending on doing. For a second, his facade slipped, and his face was twisted with a rage that sent little black tendrils of power crackling from him. "In other words, its destruction would return a tremendous amount of dark power, would it not?"

"You would destroy our shard?" Luca asked, starting toward me.

Bastian grabbed him before he got a foot, jerking him back and saying, "No. Do not touch her."

"She has our shard," Luca said, almost pleading to Bastian. "She will destroy us."

"On the contrary," I said, almost dancing with joy. "I'm going to make everything right. I'm going to blast Xavier to kingdom come. He won't be able to do anything to anyone."

"At the cost of the blue dragons," Luca said, venom dripping from his words.

"Do not do this, *cara*," Bastian said, holding out a hand for me.

"If I don't destroy him, he'll just continue to torment me in my dreams," I whispered to Bastian.

"I will be at your side if he tries."

"You can't—" I started to protest.

"I can." His voice was filled with confidence that made me feel that all would be well with the world. "You showed me that I can be what I was meant to be. I can be a dream warrior, but only if I have you in my life."

I hesitated, unsure what was the right path.

"Come, Phyllida," he said, waggling the hand that was waiting for me. "I have made an agreement, and I will stand by it."

"At least if it is given to that one, we can get it back." Luca looked very much like he wanted to pounce on me and snatch the crystal away, but managed to keep himself in check.

"I'm sorry about the crystal," I told Bastian, "But this really is the perfect solution. It solves all the problems, and maybe if we go to your First Dragon and explain the circumstance, he'll give you another one. There's no downside."

Luca sank to his knees with a groan, his head in his hands.

"Except your life." Seawright, who had been obviously transcribing what was going down, now stepped forward. "The Committee is quite clear on what happens to hellerunes who use their powers. They are sent to the Akasha, there to remain for eternity."

"The Committee is not in existence," I pointed out.

She held up the tablet. Displayed on the screen was a notice of the re-forming of the Committee, effective three minutes ago.

"Well ... my contract ..." I stopped, knowing full well that the contract that had bound me to their rules continued to exist during times of renaissance, even if it wasn't enforceable during that time. Any act I performed during the short period of time before the Committee had remade itself might be argued to be unpunishable, but now that they were back in business, I was once again bound by their rules.

"You will end up in the Akasha," Seawright told me, her expression tight with what very much looked like concern. I was touched that she appeared to be so worried about me.

Look beyond appearances, my brain whispered, repeating Sandy's warning. *Listen to your heart, not your head.*

The crystal, chased with silver, dug into the flesh of my hand while I thought about that. What did my head want?

That was easy. I wanted to see Xavier destroyed.

But my heart, oh, my heart wanted Bastian.

And he wanted me. Enough to give up everything that mattered to him. His sept, his people, his future. It took him seconds to decide to give that up because I was more important to him than anything else.

Tears burned my eyes as I took his hand, searching his face. "Are you sure you want to do this? Your sept—"

"The blue dragons are strong. They will not only survive the loss of the shard—they will triumph over their enemies." His eyes blazed with a light that warmed me to my toenails. "Likewise, we will survive and grow stronger because we are together, unbreakable and complete."

"You may not think you're a poet, but damn me if you didn't make me love you more than I did a minute ago." I gave him back the crystal. Without even looking at it, he handed it to Xavier, who shot me a dirty look that promised retribution.

Behind us, Luca gave a choked sob.

"What do we do now?" I asked as Xavier, without saying a word, spun on his heel and left the ruined front of my house.

"Now we begin," Bastian answered, and gently kissed me.

EIGHTEEN
THE BEGINNING

"If we are all present, we will start this first *sárkány* of the new weyr." Drake Vireo stood and cast a glance around at all the wyverns and their mates distributed around the big oval table.

Bastian sat with Phyllida, his heart filled with sadness, but at the same time, he had never been so contented. Drake met his gaze.

"Am I late? Dammit, I am! I really have to tell the First Dragon that his delivery-service people are perpetually tardy," Charity said as she burst in the door. "Sorry if I'm interrupting. Hello, everyone." She gave Phyllida a curious look, but when Bastian rose and pulled a chair for her on the other side of Phyllida, she happily sat.

Bastian made the introductions before retaking his own seat, adding quietly in Phyllida's ear, "Charity is the mate of the First Dragon."

Her eyes grew huge as she said without moving her lips, "The demigod has a wife? Is she also a god?"

"No. But she is nice. You will like her."

"As I was saying, I believe we can get started." Drake gave Bastian a long look. "Before we get to the several requests we have for membership into the weyr, Bastian has something he wishes to say."

Bastian hesitated a second, pained by what he had to do, but after three days of arguing with Luca, Rey, and other senior members of his sept, he had come to a decision. Phyllida gave his leg a sympathetic squeeze before he rose and took a moment to meet each person's eyes. "As you know, my mate is a very special person. Due to her nature, and the situation that resulted in the exchange of the blue shard for her life, I have chosen to step down as wyvern of the blue sept."

The wyverns looked startled, all but Drake, with whom Bastian had consulted an hour before.

"What is this?" Kostya demanded to know. "Why would you leave your sept just because your mate is a hellerune? Aisling said the interdiction had been put back on her, making her useless."

"Gee, thanks," Phyllida said, giving him a look that made Bastian want to kiss her.

Then again, he always wanted to kiss her.

Charity choked back a laugh, and bent over her notebook.

"I do not make the decision lightly," Bastian told Kostya, feeling Phyllida slide her fingers between his. He rubbed his thumb across the tops of her knuckles. "Naturally, I informed my heir, Rey, that she was now wyvern. However ..." He stopped, momentarily unable to get the words out.

"We decided not to remain in the sept," Luca said from where he stood behind Bastian.

It took another three minutes before everyone assembled stopped their exclamations, demands for explanations, and, in the case of Aisling's demon, Jim, a request for a lunch break because it was on the verge of expiring due to starvation.

"—and I told you to eat your diet kibble, so don't blame me if you're hungry because you said your breakfast tasted like ass," Aisling could be heard telling it when Bastian raised his hand for silence. "If I have to sit through your vet telling me again just how chonky you are—oh. Uh. Sorry. Go on, Bastian."

"The members of the blue sept decided, *en masse*, that since we no longer possessed a relic needed to join the weyr, then we would withdraw from it," Bastian said, catching Luca's eye for a second. His old friend gave him a nod.

"You know, you could just borrow Baltic's Firstborn talisman," Ysolde offered, causing Baltic to flare his nostrils at her. "Oh, don't waggle your nostrils at me. You let Constantine borrow it to form the silver dragons hundreds of years ago, so you could do the same for Bastian and his people."

"It's not a toy to be passed around to anyone," Baltic protested. "Besides, Constantine has his own relic now that the First Dragon recognized his part in banishing Bael."

Constantine grimaced, but his hand went to the chain around his neck.

Bastian's gaze met Drake's for a few seconds. "I don't believe Drake will mind if I reveal what we talked about earlier. Given the demand by three different ouroboros tribes who have applied to join the weyr—"

"Four. Another application was submitted a half hour ago," Drake corrected.

"—it behooves the weyr to maintain the rule that all members must provide an artifact with appropriate provenance proving it has been owned by the sept—or tribe—for an appropriate length of time. Borrowing Baltic's talisman, alas, would not meet those terms."

"But ... there has to be something we can do," Aisling said, looking troubled.

"There is another consideration," Bastian said, his dragon fire rousing at the thought of what faced them. "If I am outside the weyr, there can be no repercussions for any actions I make against other tribes."

"Other tribes? You mean you—" May looked stunned.

"Yes." He took a deep breath; then with a flash of a smile at Phyllida, who damn near beamed with pride, he told the others, "As of this moment, the blue sept will go into dormancy. We will be reborn as the Song Tribe. And as ouroboros dragons, we will be outside the weyr's protection ... and laws."

Charity smiled, and Bastian couldn't help but notice that she did not make any notes. He had a feeling that the First Dragon knew that something had happened to the dragon heart shard.

"I can't be the only one who doesn't understand," Aisling complained. "Why would you want to be outside the laws?"

"Because we're going after Xavier," Phyllida answered, getting to her feet and leaning into him. "For one thing, I don't intend to let him have Bastian's pretty crystal. And for another, Xavier's got a whole lot of payback coming to him."

"For tormenting you in your dreams?" May asked, the mates and wyverns having been given a summary of the happenings during the last few days.

"For what he intends to do to dragonkin," Bastian said. He looked at Drake, who made a gesture at one of his guards. The redheaded István slipped out of the room. "And because he does not expect the tribes to work together. So that's what we're going to do."

"What tribes? The one belonging to that annoying Deus that we kicked out?" Aisling asked. "Or this evil Xavier?"

Bastian was about to reply when the door opened, and three people stepped in, two men and a woman.

"If you would allow, I present to the weyr the master of the Storm Tribe, Archer Andras; his mate, Thaisa; and Hunter Vehar, master of the Shadow Tribe."

The wyverns all rose, all but Bastian and Drake surprised by the newcomers.

"As you can see, Archer and Hunter are twins ... and dragon hunters."

"Oh, we heard about you," Ysolde said, craning her neck to see behind her. "Back when Jian died. Are you guys going to help get Bastian's shard back?"

"No," Archer told her, his arm around his mate. Bastian, feeling Phyllida press into his side, did the same, relishing the warmth of her. "We're going to help Bastian destroy our father, Xavier."

Hunter smiled at them all, cracking his knuckles.

"There's nothing like the thought of a little patricide to stir the blood, eh?"

The *sárkány* descended into chaos after that, with everyone on their feet, swarming the newcomers with questions and demands for explanations.

Except for Charity.

"Would it be presumptuous of me to suggest that the First Dragon knew what I was going to do before I decided?" Bastian asked her.

"Before?" She scrunched up her nose for a few seconds. "Maybe. Maybe it was after you'd made the decision."

"He's not … er … angry with us, is he?" Phyllida asked, obviously worried that she'd be seen as at fault for the loss of the dragon shard, even though Bastian had sworn that no one would hold her to blame for the actions of Xavier.

"Not at all. In fact …" Bastian could see a twinkle of amusement in Charity's eyes. "He's pleased that you finally decided to accept his gift."

Bastian caught himself before he made the face that he couldn't seem to stop when it came to thinking about the dream warrior side of his psyche.

Charity laughed despite his best effort. "He did say it might take you a bit of time before you realized that it was a gift, and not a burden, but he's confident that you'll get there in the end."

Bastian kept his opinion to himself as to the likelihood of that day being in the very distant future, and instead murmured a thanks and bowed to Charity before she moved off to join the others.

Luca leaned in to Bastian, and said, "Rey sent me a text. She is busy with her new son, but said if you change your mind and insist on the sept staying with the weyr, and making her wyvern, she'll geld you slowly, with a dull spoon."

"Hey! You can just tell her to keep her hands off Bastian's balls," Phyllida said, looking adorably indignant. "They're mine. If anyone is going to geld him, it's going to be me."

Bastian laughed and, despite the roomful of wyverns, wrapped his arms around her, his heart full, his soul singing a song of happiness. "*Cara*, you are the only woman I know who is willing to fight for the right to geld me."

She wiggled against him in a way that was not at all the way a proper mate behaved at a dragon gathering, causing Luca to grin at him before he moved off to gossip with the other wyverns' guards. Phyllida wiggled again, instantly making Bastian hard. "Tell me again how much you love me, my nonpoetic dragon master."

"I love you to the moon and stars, and back. I love you to the depths of the earth. I love you the length of your songline, and all the centuries that will make up our lives. I love you because to me you are life."

She sighed happily. "You know, I feel a bit of a nap coming on. What say we slip away and go back to your hotel room, and maybe find a beach dreamscape where we can lay naked in the sand, and let the waves lap at our feet. Oooh! What if we went to Iceland and the blue lagoon? Or! Better yet, an Amazon rain forest, where it's all steamy and we can get really sweaty—"

Bastian laughed again, happy, aroused, and so in love he thought he might burst into song.

EPILOGUE
THE UNION

"So." I sat looking at the other four ladies, and tried not to feel like the odd man out.

"So," Aisling agreed, smiling. She seemed friendly enough, but Bastian had told me that she was a Guardian, and had her own personal demon. I had a hard time resolving what he swore was a friendly demon to the large black Newfoundland dog that greeted me with a snuffle and, "Hiya, name's Jim," when we entered the home of the green dragons, but I was learning to go with the flow on many aspects of my new life.

"So, indeed." Ysolde was glaring at her phone as she texted someone, her fingers flying over the screen. "Seriously, I told Brom he had to be home by midnight, and he's in Saint Petersburg. Saint Petersburg!" She looked up at me. "Is he deranged?"

"I don't know," I said, wondering if she was asking a rhetorical question, or if I missed something.

"Brom's her son," Aisling interrupted herself in midsentence to May, mate of the silver wyvern. "He's eighteen."

"And is having his first ever date. The dating part is important, especially when Baltic keeps encouraging him to sow his wild oats. Have you ever heard anything so ridiculous? I don't want my son oat-sowing. We all know how that's going to end up—the light dragons will have a new member, and I am so not ready to be a grandmother. Sorry, I'm monopolizing the conversation. Shall we get to business?"

"I'm not sure what business you want me here for," I said, glancing at the fifth member of the group.

"Me either," Thaisa said.

"Oh, didn't we tell you? We're holding an impromptu Mates Union meeting. The others had to return to their respective homes, but since the men are holed up in Drake's study making plans to tackle that asshat Xavier—sorry, Thaisa. I forgot he was your father-in-law."

"Don't mind me," she replied with a wave of her hand. "He is a huge asshat. No one likes him, least of all his sons."

I thought of the way Xavier had slammed Deus around, and said nothing.

"We're here to formally induct you both into the Mates Union," May said, tapping a tablet of paper. "Normally Bee is our recording secretary, but she's in the throes of morning sickness and wanted to get home so she could barf in peace, so I'm doing the job."

"Mates Union?" Thaisa asked.

"Yes, it's our way to keep sane around all the dragons. We get together once a month or so, or have a Zoom meeting if we can't be in person. We induct all the new mates as they join the weyr."

"But—" I glanced at Thaisa, who looked as bewildered as I felt. "But we're in tribes, not the weyr."

"Eh," Ysolde said, waving away that point. "We decided that mates to wyverns or wyvern substitutes would be admissible. Besides, we have questions."

"So many questions," May said, nodding.

"And dragons never answer questions," Aisling said.

All the ladies nodded.

"Questions about what?" I asked.

May tapped her pencil on the tablet of paper. "What happened to your little friend?"

"How did Bastian kick Xavier out of your dreams?" Aisling asked.

"Why, exactly, did he want Bastian's piece of the dragon heart?" Ysolde added to the list.

I looked at Thaisa.

"Oh, I'm good," she said with a smile. "Although I do want to know more about this dragon named Deus. Archer had no idea he had a brother, but he said it must be a half brother, because their mom died when he and Hunter were babies."

"And most important of all," Aisling added, "what are you going to do?"

I held up a hand to tick off the answers. "Seawright is still my scribe. She agreed to stay at the hotel only if I agreed to wear a transmitter, so she could overhear everything I say." I pulled a small square box from my pocket and held it up. "Say hi to Seawright, everyone."

The ladies all murmured a greeting.

"Number two, Bastian …" I hesitated. We had decided to keep his dream warrior status quiet until he had more time to learn about it. The fact that he was a dream walker was enough of an oddity that it kept everyone amazed. "Bastian took Seawright's sword with him into my dreamscape. When Xavier realized I wasn't alone and defenseless, he bailed."

"But you said he tried to kill Bastian in your dream." Aisling looked puzzled. "Why would he do that if he wanted to trade you for the dragon heart shard?"

"All part of the window dressing that he used to drive Bastian to the point where he'd do anything to get me back. And unfortunately, it worked," I answered with a grim twist of my lips.

"Which brings us to why he wanted the dragon heart," Ysolde pointed out, and looked expectantly at me.

"That I can't answer. He hinted at some grandiose plan, but what it is exactly, we don't know." I turned to Thaisa. "Do Archer and Hunter know?"

"Beyond destroying dragons? No. Not really."

"I suspect we'll find out sooner rather than later," I said, feeling glum despite my happiness at my new life with Bastian. "And to answer your question, Thaisa—I also don't know much about Deus. He seems angry most of the time, and clearly was working with Xavier, but he wasn't around ten years ago when I was being held prisoner."

"So many unanswered questions," May said, circling several items on her paper. "So much confusion. I have a bad feeling about Xavier, though."

"Archer was saying the same thing about the sudden preponderance of tribes," Thaisa added, looking solemn. "They're popping up left, right, and center, and he says they're mostly gangs of rogue dragons bent on trouble—present company excepted, Phyllida."

I gave her a wan smile. "So what are we going to do?"

"We the mates, or we the dragonkin?" Aisling asked.

"Both," I said, looking at each woman in turn, hoping to see an answer to the grim feeling in the pit of my gut.

Xavier was out there planning. Plotting. Arranging for something so horrible, he needed a dragon relic to pull it off.

"We abide," Ysolde said, picking up her phone again when it pinged at her. "Oh dear, Gabriel has set off Baltic. I'd better go fetch him before things deteriorate to a level where they're beating each other up again. Thaisa, Phyllida—welcome to the Mates Union. We'll send you the official T-shirt and Dragons Do It Better mug in the next few days."

Aisling and May followed Ysolde out the door, evidently off to soothe their respective dragons' rumpled feathers.

I looked at Thaisa.

She looked at me.

"Want to be new-kid-in-the-union buddies?" I asked her.

She held out her hand, which I shook. "Tribes rule, others drool."

I laughed, and rose, going with her to the room at the end of a big hall, my heart lightening as I glimpsed Bastian clearly trying not to laugh at the sight of Baltic storming off with Ysolde in tow.

He raised an eyebrow when I moved next to him, welcoming the arm around me that kept me safe from the world … and surrounded by love.

I wasn't sure what Xavier had planned for us, or the rest of the dragons, but with Bastian in my life, I knew all things were possible.

NOTE TO READERS

My lovely one! I hope you enjoyed reading this book, which I handcrafted from the finest artisanal words just for you. If you are one of the folks who likes to review books, I'd love it if you posted a review for it on your favorite book spot (be sure to tell me if you do, so that I can lavish praise all over you).

If you're looking for some fun behind-the-scenes tidbits and exclusive material—including the PERILS OF EFFRI-JIM short story, which is available free just for you via Book-funnel—hie thee over to my website at katiemacalister.com and sign up for the newsletter.

And finally, if you enjoyed the Bastian's story, but haven't read the all the dragon books, here's the list of the complete series, in chronological order:

Aisling Grey Novels
YOU SLAY ME
FIRE ME UP
LIGHT MY FIRE
HOLY SMOKES
THE PERILS OF EFFRIJIM (short story)

Silver Dragon Novels
PLAYING WITH FIRE

UP IN SMOKE
ME AND MY SHADOW

Light Dragon Novels
LOVE IN THE TIME OF DRAGONS
THE UNBEARABLE LIGHTNESS OF
DRAGONS
SPARKS FLY

Intermediate Dragon Catch-up Novel
DRAGONBLIGHT

Dragon Fall Novels
DRAGON FALL
DRAGON STORM
DRAGON SOUL
DRAGON UNBOUND

Dragon Hunter Novels
MEMOIRS OF A DRAGON HUNTER
DAY OF THE DRAGON
A CONFEDERACY OF DRAGONS
YOU SLEIGH ME (October 2022)

ABOUT THE AUTHOR

For as long as she can remember, Katie MacAlister has loved reading. Growing up in a family where a weekly visit to the library was a given, Katie spent much of her time with her nose buried in a book.

Two years after she started writing novels, Katie sold her first romance, *Noble Intentions*. More than seventy books later, her novels have been translated into numerous languages, been recorded as audiobooks, received several awards, and have been regulars on the *New York Times, USA Today, Publishers Weekly*, and *Wall Street Journal* bestseller lists. Katie lives in the Pacific Northwest with two dogs, and can often be found lurking around online.

You are welcome to join Katie's official discussion group on Facebook, as well as connect with her via TikTok and Instagram. For more information, visit her website at www.katiemacalister.com

www.ingramcontent.com/pod-product-compliance
Lightning Source LLC
Chambersburg PA
CBHW050843190726
48286CB00007B/2202

9781952737626